DEADLY JUSTICE

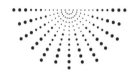

D. S. BUTLER

❀ Created with Vellum

DEADLY JUSTICE is the fourth book in the DS Jack Mackinnon Crime Series.

Time to run. Time to hide. Time to die...

A late summer heatwave seems to have triggered an unusually high number of suicides.

As the dead bodies pile up, DS Jack Mackinnon and the rest of MIT realise things aren't as straightforward as they seem, and when similar letters are found at the scene of each 'suicide,' Mackinnon is convinced they are dealing with a serial killer. A killer who is determined to deliver his own deadly justice.

DEADLY JUSTICE is a British police procedural, perfect for fans of Peter James and his Roy Grace series.

CHAPTER ONE

1976

"YOU ARE A LIAR." The woman leaned forward and snarled at Mr. Johnson.

Her lips curved back over her small pointed teeth.

Mr. Johnson shifted back in his chair and placed his hands on the solid oak desk that separated them. He wished it was a little wider. In his thirty-year teaching career, the headmaster of White House primary school had never encountered a parent quite as aggressive as this young woman.

Strands of her light brown hair had fallen loose from the tight bun at the base of her neck. Her skin, usually so pale, was now red and blotchy.

Her hand shook as she jabbed a finger in his direction. "You are a disgrace. You're not fit to be in charge of innocent little children."

He had needed to discuss disciplinary issues with parents and guardians in the past, and no one liked to be told that their child was not perfect, but he had never come across a parent so determined to ignore the truth.

She shook her head vigorously, freeing more wispy strands of hair. "Junior would never do such a thing. I can't believe you could even suggest it."

Mr. Johnson took a breath and waited. He hoped she would run out of steam soon. Since she had stormed into his office five minutes ago, she hadn't paused for breath.

He glanced down at the small boy sitting by her side, the child they were discussing. His large grey eyes regarded the headmaster steadily. He didn't seem surprised or at all worried by his mother's outburst.

Finally, the woman seemed to gather herself, gripping the neck of her blouse with one hand and smoothing her skirt over her thin thighs with the other. She raised her chin. "I hope this is an end to the matter. I don't want to hear any more of this nonsense."

Mr. Johnson shook his head and said as gently as he could, "Another child saw him do it."

The woman gripped the side of her chair. "Then the other child is lying. Junior would never hurt an animal. He loves them."

"The hamster was..." Mr. Johnson hesitated over his word choice, but there really wasn't a pleasant way to put it. "The hamster had been cut... several times, and Junior was seen by the cage..."

"Oh, so Junior was seen by the cage, well that proves everything, doesn't it?" The woman snorted, then turned as if addressing an imagined audience. "Why don't you lock him up and throw away the key? He's a little boy, for goodness sake. He would never do anything like that."

The woman tugged the arm of the six-year-old boy sitting next to her. His face was blank, seemingly the picture of innocence.

"You'd never do such a terrible thing would you, Junior?"

"No, Mother," the little boy said, his big grey eyes wide and serious.

This wasn't the first time the little boy had been in trouble. Since Junior had been admitted into the reception class, he had been known as a biter and pincher, and he was sly with it. The teacher would never actually catch him in the act. They only saw the results: a sobbing child with bruises or teeth marks buried in their flesh. But Mr. Johnson found it hard to believe anyone, even Junior, could do such a terrible thing to the school pet.

The children had spent the school year taking care of the animal, feeding it, watching it play and taking turns to stroke its soft fur. To think that someone could do that to the defence-less creature, something so inherently evil, let alone a child... Well, it was unthinkable.

The boy stared back at him, unblinking, with those huge, round grey eyes.

Could he be telling the truth?

"Junior doesn't lie. Do you, Junior?"

"No, Mother."

"You see. He's a good boy. It's the other children. They bully him. You need to talk to the other parents, not me." She smoothed the little boy's hair and reached over to straighten his school tie.

"Which child told you Junior had hurt the hamster?" she asked, in a deliberately light tone.

Not hurt, Mr. Johnson thought, but killed, sadistically.

He shook his head. "It won't do any good to bring them into this debate."

She pursed her lips together for a moment then said, "I see. So you're more than willing to spread these malicious lies about my son, but you won't give me a chance to defend him.

How can I confront these lies if I don't know who is behind them?"

Mr. Johnson shook his head again. There was no way he would let this awful woman, or Junior, know which child had come forward so they could take their revenge.

"Why would you trust one child's word over another?" she demanded, leaning forward and clasping her handbag with white-knuckled fingers.

Mr. Johnson regarded her steadily. Because it isn't the first time, he thought. Because this little boy has serious problems.

"Have you ever considered taking Junior to a doctor to discuss his behavioural issues?"

She shot up from her chair and slapped her hands flat against the oak surface as she leaned over the headmaster's desk. "He doesn't have any issues. You're the one with the problem. He's a good boy." She looked over her shoulder back at Junior. "He's good with his reading. Good with his numbers and his adding up, aren't you, Junior?"

"Yes, Mother."

She turned back to face Mr. Johnson, triumphant. "See."

"It isn't a matter of intelligence. Junior is ahead of his peers in many subjects, but he doesn't make friends easily and has a tendency to be violent towards the other children."

She folded her arms and began to pace the office. "I knew it," she said, forced a high-pitched laugh and shook her head.

The little boy watched his mother. His eyes followed her across the room.

"I knew you'd bring that up again, even though I already explained this to you. Junior is the one who gets bullied. They call him names; nasty, cruel names, and when he stands up for himself, he gets into trouble."

She stopped pacing and turned to face Mr. Johnson with her hands on her hips.

"He hasn't done anything wrong. I told him to fight back.

It's the only way to deal with bullies." She nodded, pleased with herself. "You lot don't do anything about it, so he has to deal with it himself."

"I can't condone that type of behaviour in my school. If Junior is bullied, then he must tell me or his teacher, Mrs. Adams."

"Mrs. Adams? Don't make me laugh." The woman folded her arms over her bony chest. "She's useless. She hates Junior. She won't do anything to help him. She has favourites."

"Mrs. Adams is an excellent teacher. I regard her very highly. I'm sure she'll do everything in her power to make sure Junior is well looked after and feels comfortable and secure during class."

The woman made a tutting sound then sat back down next to Junior. "She isn't a good teacher. Junior tells me everything, you know?" She leaned forward and lowered her voice to a whisper. "And Mrs. Adams doesn't like that."

Mr. Johnson wanted to bury his head in his hands. This wasn't working. There was no way he could get through to this woman.

He turned his attention to Junior.

"Would you like to say anything, Junior? If you know what happened to the hamster, you could tell me now. You won't be punished, but it is very important to tell the truth."

The small boy stared up at the headmaster with solemn eyes. He swung his little legs back and forth and tilted his head to the side. His big, grey eyes narrowed a little.

Mr. Johnson suppressed a shudder. Something in the way the child studied him sent a prickly chill over his skin.

He is only six-years-old, Mr. Johnson told himself, an innocent. A little boy who needs help. But he couldn't shake the overwhelming desire to shove both the little boy and his mother out of the office.

As if he read the headmaster's thoughts, the little boy smiled. Then he opened his mouth, "I..."

His mother yanked him by the arm. "You don't have to say anything, Junior. We've told the truth. We can't say more than that."

"Yes, Mother."

The little boy turned back to the headmaster with the trace of a smirk on his lips.

Mr. Johnson could almost believe the boy was laughing at him. He stared down at the papers on his desk, trying to collect his thoughts. He was clearly being ridiculous, and these fanciful notions weren't doing anyone any good. The boy needed help. Was it really a surprise the boy was struggling with a mother like that?

After a moment, he looked up to see Junior and his mother staring at him. The headmaster took a deep breath and tapped his pen against the pile of papers on his desk.

"I'll have to include it in my report."

"What? And have it on Junior's school record? How will that look?"

"It will look ... better than expulsion." He couldn't turn his back on the boy. He had to give him another chance. Perhaps if Mrs. Adams could give the boy a little more one-on-one time...

"Expulsion!" The woman reared back as if he had hit her. "You can keep your poxy reports. There's no way my Junior is coming back to this school." She sprang up like a jack-in-the-box and grabbed Junior's hand. "I'll put him in another school - something I should have done a long time ago."

"Of course, you must do what you think is best for Junior," Mr. Johnson said, feeling a surge of relief and hating himself for it.

"If there is any justice in this world, that little tattletale will get what's coming to him." The woman spun on her heel and stalked out of the office pulling Junior behind her.

For a few moments after Junior's mother had slammed the office door, Mr. Johnson didn't move. He set his pen down on his desk with a shaky hand and exhaled heavily.

The encounter had really shaken him. At fifty-two years old, he was no longer wet behind the ears. On a previous occasion, he'd had the misfortune to be grabbed around the throat by an irate father during a heated discussion at a parents' evening, and he'd even dealt with a ten-year-old boy trying to sell his mother's anti-depressant tablets in the school playground. After almost thirty years of teaching, he'd thought he had seen it all, but there was something about that little boy and his mother that chilled him to the core.

He took a deep breath and stood up, leaning heavily on his desk. Standing by the window, he looked out on a view of the playground and the school gates. The woman was striding across the playground to the exit, tugging at the boy's arm to make him walk faster.

Suddenly, Mr. Johnson felt incredibly sad.

"That poor boy," he muttered to himself. "That poor, poor boy..."

CHAPTER TWO

PRESENT DAY

VINNIE PEARSON STARED across at the skinny Pakistani newsagent. He leaned in close then said, "I ain't paying a hundred quid. I'll give you twenty-five."

Syed Hammad puffed out his chest and straightened behind the counter. "On your bike, son."

Hearing that expression from Syed was so unexpected, Vinnie wanted to laugh. But he didn't. This was business, and Vinnie took business seriously. The newsagent had something Vinnie wanted.

Vinnie moved closer and peered over the counter at the cardboard box, resting by Syed's feet. "How many have you got down there?"

Syed kicked the box under the counter, out of sight, but not before Vinnie caught a glimpse of the shiny, black smartphones. "None of your business," Syed said. "Keep your sticky beak out." He tapped the side of his nose.

Vinnie gritted his teeth. He sensed a movement behind him, someone else had entered the shop.

"All right," Vinnie said. "I'll stretch to fifty, but it's daylight robbery."

Syed folded his arms across his chest. His sparse moustache stretched thin as he smiled. "You can take your money somewhere else. I don't want it."

Vinnie flushed. How dare the little bastard talk to him like that? If there hadn't been someone else in the shop, Vinnie would have taught him a lesson right then and there. Vinnie glanced back over his shoulder. The customer was a man of around forty, dressed in jeans and a dark jacket. No one Vinnie recognised. Still, Vinnie didn't want word to get out that he had been disrespected by Syed Hammad of all people.

"What's wrong with my money, Syed?" Vinnie's voice was low and dangerous.

"It's dirty," Syed said and screwed up his nose. "You and your lowlife friends robbing, stealing from hard working people like me. Don't think I don't know who trashed my shop and the others in this street last summer."

Vinnie kept his smile fixed in place. "You don't have any proof."

"I don't need proof. I know what you did, and I want you out of my shop now." Syed raised his voice, causing the customer to pause by the magazine rack and turn to look at them.

Vinnie could feel his cheeks glowing, and his mouth grew dry. No one spoke to him like that and got away with it.

"Watch your mouth, Syed."

"No. No, I won't. You can't push me around. I'll call the police. I pay my taxes, work hard and you..."

"You what?" Vinnie gulped down air as he tried to control his temper. "What do you reckon the police would have to say about them?" Vinnie jabbed a finger in the direction of the smartphones. "They're nicked, you bloody hypocrite. I'm sure the police would love to have a look at them."

Syed shrugged. "No. No. They aren't stolen. They are from my friend's sister's boyfriend's father. Perfectly legitimate."

"Bollocks. They are nicked. Stolen goods. You're no better than a thief!"

"How dare you. Get out!" Syed screamed. He was bouncing up and down on his toes. "Get out of my shop now. I'm calling the police. I have a witness," Syed pointed to the man still standing by the magazines.

"A witness to what?" Vinnie shook his head. "You're a bloody nutcase."

"Out! Get out!" Syed Hammad picked up one of the smartphones and made a big show of pretending to dial 999.

"I'm going," Vinnie said. As he turned to leave he kicked out at a pyramid made of carefully stacked packets of biscuits, sending them tumbling to the floor.

Afterwards, Vinnie stood outside the hairdressers and smoked a cigarette as he tried to calm down. That little bastard. Who the hell did he think he was?

The blonde woman who owned the salon kept shooting him nervous looks. Normally, Vinnie would feel gratified. He liked people being afraid of him. It showed respect.

He'd get back at Syed, but not now. Not when he was so worked up. He needed to make a plan. A plan that made sure the bastard would never disrespect Vinnie again.

As Vinnie walked back down the street, he kept his head low as he passed the newsagent's. The cafe next door was full to bursting, which was crazy considering the awful food it served. Even if he hadn't been banned from the premises after the riots last summer, Vinnie wouldn't have eaten there.

Mitch Horrocks, the cafe owner, stared out at Vinnie. He'd run the place for years. Mad Mitch, the local school kids called him. Vinnie and some mates had trashed the cafe last summer, and Vinnie had taken great pleasure in wrecking the joint. If anyone deserved it, it was Mitch. Vinnie smiled and waved and got a two-fingered salute from Mad Mitch in return.

Ahead of him, Vinnie saw a man dressed in jeans and a grey hoodie standing at the bus stop. He didn't recognise the man at first, but as he drew closer he realised it was the man who had walked into the newsagent's. The bloke who'd been hanging around the magazines. He'd pulled up the hood on his sweatshirt, but Vinnie was sure it was him.

The man slouched back against the glass panel of the bus shelter, but as Vinnie approached him, the man straightened up and turned to face Vinnie.

Vinnie recognised a threat when he saw one. The bloke had obviously witnessed his argument with Syed and pegged Vinnie as an easy mark. There was no way Vinnie would back down. He couldn't, not if he wanted to keep his reputation.

Vinnie jutted out his chin and gave him the look. The look that said if this bloke was looking for trouble, Vinnie had plenty to supply.

The hoodie stepped forward blocking Vinnie's path.

This was a direct confrontation. Vinnie couldn't back down. If he wanted to get past, he would have to step into the road or shove his way past.

Vinnie shoved his hands in his pockets and felt the reassuring cool, smooth metal of the knife. If there was going to be trouble, Vinnie was ready for it.

The hoodie surprised Vinnie by smiling. The hood of his sweatshirt kept most of the bloke's face in shadow, but Vinnie could see the lower half of his face and he was definitely grinning.

Vinnie glanced across the road. Maybe he should cross the road and avoid the stand-off. That was the sensible thing to do. Vinnie wasn't a hot-headed kid any more. He didn't like to take on fights unless he was sure he could win, and this bloke looked a bit of a dodgy character. Besides, the police were just waiting for him to slip up again.

"What do you want?" Vinnie asked.

The hoodie looked up and down the street, his eyes shifty. "I've got a proposition for you."

"Oh, yeah?" Vinnie said. "Well, I'm not interested. I don't do business with people I don't know."

"You'll be interested in this," the hoodie said.

Vinnie scoffed. "I don't think so, mate."

Now he was closer, Vinnie could see the bloke was older than he first thought. He had at least ten years on Vinnie. That should have made Vinnie more confident. Vinnie was ten years younger and fitter, but for some reason it made him nervous.

Vinnie tried to sidestep the man but felt the hoodie's fingers dig into his shoulder.

Vinnie stared down at the man's hand. "What the hell do you think you're doing? Get your hands off me, unless you want me to break your fingers."

The man laughed but removed his hand. "No need to act like that, mate. If you're not interested..." He shrugged. "I'm sure someone else will be. Maybe the Brewerton brothers?"

Vinnie scowled. The Brewertons were his closest rivals. They wouldn't be happy until they had driven Vinnie out of the area.

"All right. What's this proposition? I'll give you two minutes."

"Money. An easy job. I saw you earlier, trying to get a phone off that newsagent." The bloke nodded down the street in the direction of Syed's shop.

Vinnie folded his arms across his chest. He hated the idea anyone else had witnessed his embarrassment. Who was this guy anyway? Some kind of spy for the Brewertons? Vinnie stared at him, determined not to show any reaction. He wouldn't give him the satisfaction.

The hoodie smiled slowly, as if he understood. "You were right. He was trying to cheat you. I wouldn't mind one of those fancy new phones myself, but there's no way I'm paying one hundred quid for it."

Vinnie shrugged. "They are nicked anyway. The dodgy bastard. It's a rip-off."

"So why don't we just take them?" The hoodie grinned. "It's hardly stealing if they were already stolen once."

Vinnie licked his lips. "Are you suggesting we rob poor old Syed?"

Vinnie tried to stifle his grin. He would enjoy teaching that stupid bastard, Syed, a lesson.

"Few of your mates, few of mine. We could do it like last summer. A smash and grab. In and out before he knows what's hit him."

Vinnie grinned. He liked that idea. But he wasn't about to let this bloke think he was a pushover. He shrugged. "I'm not sure it's worth my time for a couple of poxy phones."

The man looked around again nervously, as if he expected somebody to be watching them. "Your loss. But if you change your mind, we do it at six o'clock tomorrow night."

"Why are you telling me? Why not just do it yourself?"

"Strength in numbers," the hoodie said. "If there's a lot of us, the owner will back down. We can split the phones fifty-fifty. I bet some of your mates would do this sort of thing for a chocolate bar."

"Maybe," Vinnie said and side-stepped the man. He was probably right. Most of the kids he hung around with didn't take things seriously. They didn't see it as a career, more as a way to have fun. That was their problem. It didn't stop Vinnie using them for backup now and again. And the man was right. There was strength in numbers.

"Yeah, well, I might make it if I haven't got anything better to do."

"Your choice," the hoodie said. "But there's a whole box of phones, and he's selling them for a ton apiece."

"Like I said, I'll see."

Vinnie carried on walking and didn't look back. He didn't notice that the man was still watching him. He was too busy planning who to contact for tomorrow night.

There were lots of eager kids he could call on, but he didn't want to involve too many. The more people in on the action, the more they would have to divide the profits. And Vinnie didn't like to share. He pulled out his old Nokia and opened the Facebook app. It took ages to load, which was exactly why he wanted a new phone in the first place.

He decided to invite four others. Four others he could trust, and more importantly, four others who would be happy with just a few cigarettes for their trouble.

He typed their names into the search bar and sent each of them a message. Then he shoved the phone back in his pocket and smiled. Only one more day before he could dump that plastic piece of crap. Yeah, he would look a lot better with a brand-new, fancy smartphone clamped to his ear.

As Vinnie swaggered up the road, full of plans for tomorrow, he had no idea the man watching him had plans of his own.

CHAPTER THREE

THE FOLLOWING EVENING, VINNIE PEARSON grinned at the little old lady who quickly moved out of his way. She dashed across the road, dragging her shopping trolley behind her.

She found Vinnie and his mates intimidating. The gang swaggered down the road, laughing and joking, with their hoods pulled up to hide their faces. Nervous energy crackled around them. Vinnie could feel the tension, and the promise of things to come.

After he'd spoken to the bloke at the bus stop, Vinnie hadn't wasted any time in sending out messages on Facebook. He had only invited people he trusted. He didn't want a large group descending on Syed's shop, getting out of control. That would only attract more attention.

Really, Vinnie was just interested in getting his hands on the phones. The rest of the stuff in the shop was just gravy. He'd leave that for the others.

He'd invited enough people to intimidate that bastard, Syed. That was the key, knowing how many people he needed to get the job done. Vinnie wasn't just a looter. He had a plan – a business plan.

It was Syed's own fault. He had this coming. How could he expect to get a hundred quid for a phone that was nicked anyway? What a bloody rip-off.

Vinnie smiled at the only girl in the group, Joanne James. He'd gone out with her for a couple of months last year. She was one of those girls whose daddy paid for everything, but she liked a bit of rough and used Vinnie to add some excitement to her boring life.

She grinned back at him, showing too many teeth. Vinnie wasn't interested in re-visiting the past, but he needed to keep her sweet for tonight.

Craig Foster, a great big fat lump of a bloke, lumbered along next to Joanne. Craig wasn't intelligent enough to put one over on Vinnie, and he did what he was told, which was exactly what Vinnie needed.

Vinnie had also invited Tyrell Patterson, who was the closest thing Vinnie had to a best friend. They did most things together. Although they hadn't spent much time together lately because Tyrell had knocked up his girlfriend. Vinnie shook his head. He couldn't believe that in less than a month Tyrell would be a father. Vinnie held back a snort of laughter as he imagined Tyrell up to his elbows in dirty nappies.

Vinnie smirked at Tyrell. Bloody fool, getting himself trapped like that.

The only person in the group who Vinnie worried about was little Robbie Baxter. He was so eager, wanting to be in with the older kids. Vinnie watched Robbie swagger along beside Craig with a cheeky grin on his face. Next to Craig, Robbie looked even smaller. He kept his hands in the pockets of his baggy jeans, and his trainers, clearly several sizes too big for him, slid across the floor as he walked. The shoes probably belonged to one of his older brothers. Not that either of his brothers would notice. Both of Robbie's brothers had been sent down for armed robbery last year.

Robbie was all right really. As long as he kept his mouth shut and did what he was told, Vinnie couldn't see the harm in him hanging around.

Vinnie liked the fact he had a small, select group with him. He didn't need many people to intimidate the newsagent. Most likely Syed would wet himself as soon as he got a glimpse of big, fat Craig barrelling into the newsagent's.

When they were level with the old post office, Vinnie paused and looked at his watch. Six p.m. exactly. It wouldn't be dark for hours. The smell of fried onions drifted down the street from the cafe. Two girls, wearing short skirts and cropped t-shirts, showing off their muffin tops and scoffing Magnum ice-creams, walked towards them. The dark-haired girl shot Vinnie a flirtatious look, and Vinnie felt Joanne bristle and move closer to him.

Vinnie ignored them. He had more important things on his mind.

There was still no sign of the hoodie and his gang. He chewed on his thumbnail. Should he wait? The others were getting restless, messing about, pushing and shoving each other. Drawing attention to themselves.

Sod it. It wasn't Vinnie's fault they weren't on time. He beckoned the others to follow him.

As they drew closer to the shop, Vinnie crossed the road, and the others trailed behind him. They huddled together just short of the newsagent's in a loose circle, ignoring the glare from mad Mitch in the cafe. Vinnie didn't say anything but gestured with his hands so they lined up behind him. He didn't want to give Syed a chance to spot them and call the police.

Vinnie raised his hand, holding up three fingers ready to count.

"What are you doing?" Craig said, breathing heavily in Vinnie's ear. "Let's just get on with it. I've got other stuff to do today."

Vinnie rolled his eyes. As if... Craig Foster was unemployed with no girlfriend or family to speak of. Any money he earned came through Vinnie. For Craig, other stuff probably involved getting McDonald's for dinner.

But there wasn't much point in counting down now. Not after Craig had given the game away, with his large booming voice just outside the shop.

He needed to act now.

Vinnie jogged the last couple of steps to the newsagent's, but when he got to the front of the shop, he frowned.

The door was shut.

Syed never shut this early. Had he seen them coming? Had the hoodie and his gang already done the place over?

Vinnie stared at the closed sign on the door, then peered through the glass panel. There was no sign of a disturbance, so why was the shop closed? Vinnie had never known Syed to shut the shop before nine p.m.

Vinnie gave the door a little push and exhaled with a low whistle when it opened. Their luck was in. In his panic, Syed obviously hadn't bothered to bolt the door.

Vinnie felt the group's bubbling energy behind him as they pushed forward, eager to get inside and create a bit of chaos. Vinnie turned around and caught a brief glimpse of Robbie Baxter's eyes gleaming with anticipation.

Vinnie pushed the door open wider and heard the sound of breaking glass and a muffled splash.

He looked around the shop, but he couldn't work out what had made the noise.

Maybe one of the others had broken a window, but he couldn't see it if they had. Everything looked intact. There was a mop and a couple of buckets propped up against the wall by the door, and more importantly, there was no sign of the owner. Had Syed been cleaning the shop when he spotted them? Was he hiding out the back?

Everything looked fine. There was no sign that the hoodie and his gang had been there yet. Although the sign above the shop said "Newsagent's" Syed's shop stocked groceries and alcohol as well as papers. Syed had re-stacked the packets of biscuits Vinnie had knocked over yesterday into another neat pyramid.

Vinnie stepped forward cautiously, but the rest of the gang pushed around him, desperate to get inside.

Craig Foster went straight for the magazines on the top rack. Pulling down handfuls of girlie mags. Predictable. Vinnie shook his head.

Little Robbie Baxter made a beeline for the chocolate bars and began shoving handfuls of them into his pockets.

Vinnie hadn't told the others about the phones. He wanted those all for himself. Vinnie took a quick look around the shop. Where would the cunning bastard have hidden them? He moved behind the counter, kicking a bucket out of his way.

Vinnie paused for a moment. There was a funny smell in the air, like rotting eggs. No wonder Syed had been in the middle of cleaning. The place needed it.

Vinnie edged past Joanne James, who was helping herself to packets of cigarettes. She gave him a little smile as he went past. In her eyes, this little outing probably meant they were back together. Silly cow. Vinnie only invited her because he knew she wouldn't be interested in the phones. She had enough money to buy her own phone, or at least her old man did.

Vinnie wrinkled his nose. Jesus, the smell was getting worse. He covered his mouth and nose with the sleeve of his sweatshirt, but the smell faded quickly. He rubbed his forehead. He was getting a headache. Where the hell were the phones?

Underneath the counter, by the till, Vinnie discovered a battered old cardboard box, just where it had been yesterday. Vinnie smiled. Syed hadn't even tried to move them.

Vinnie pulled out the box, so he could take a good look. There was a pile of old newspapers stacked on top. Vinnie lifted them up and grinned when he got a glimpse of the black phones underneath. Vinnie reached for one, admiring the sleek, black finish. Too late, he realised that little Robbie Baxter had been watching him.

Robbie crouched beside him on the floor. "Whatcha got there, Vin?"

Vinnie scowled. The kid was too sharp by half.

Robbie made a grab for one of the phones in the box and whistled as he turned it over in his hands. "Nice one," he said.

Vinnie tried to shove the box back under the counter before anyone else saw the phones, but it was too late. The rest of the gang's interest had been spiked by Robbie's squeaky admiration. Joanne and Craig wandered over.

Craig peered over the top of the Big Jugs magazine he'd been leafing through. Then Tyrell leaned across and pulled the cardboard box out of Vinnie's hands. In the next moment, it was like a pack of dogs fighting over a chicken carcass.

Vinnie watched as they each helped themselves to a phone, then he made a grab for the cardboard box.

It was empty.

That didn't make sense. Why were there only five phones? He'd been sure Syed had a whole box full. He guessed Syed had been doing a roaring trade today and sold most of them already. Bloody typical.

Vinnie stood up and put his hand on the counter to steady himself. His headache was getting worse. Hanging around with this lot wasn't helping. He was pissed off. All this effort for five poxy phones.

He pinched the bridge of his nose with his thumb and forefinger. He needed to concentrate.

He'd been banking on getting his hands on those phones. He could have turned a tidy little profit. He turned back and his eyes flickered briefly over the till, but there was no point in taking that. It was too heavy, too obvious.

But it gave him an idea. If Syed had already sold the phones, the cash must be around here somewhere. What would Syed have done with the money? He wouldn't have put it through the till. He must have stashed it somewhere, and Vinnie was going to find it.

There was a door at the back of the shop leading to what Vinnie assumed were the living quarters. Syed seemed like the type to keep money stuffed in his mattress.

As he walked towards the door, Vinnie blinked. His eyes felt funny. They wouldn't quite focus.

That was why he'd almost stepped on the body before he saw it.

Shit.

Vinnie staggered backwards and then grabbed the doorframe to support himself.

There, lying at the foot of the stairs, was Syed Hammad, the skinny, Pakistani owner of the newsagent's.

Vinnie's breath quickened as he edged forwards. He didn't dare get too close, but he reached out and nudged him with the toe of his shoe.

Syed Hammad didn't move.

Vinnie struggled to draw in a breath. He needed to get out of here. The police couldn't find him here with Syed's body. He'd get the blame.

Where the hell was the hoodie who had organised this? It

had been all his idea. He'd been so keen for Vinnie and his friends to be part of it. Vinnie ran a hand over his face.

How could he have been so stupid? Why had he trusted him? The hoodie had probably been in here before they arrived, nicked most of the phones and topped Syed, happy in the knowledge that Vinnie and his gang would soon arrive and take the blame.

Right now, the bastard was probably laughing at home, imagining Vinnie getting arrested for murder.

As a million thoughts crowded into Vinnie's brain, he found it harder to get enough air in his lungs.

Vinnie clutched his stomach. He felt dizzy and sick, and he was pretty sure it wasn't just the sight of Syed's dead body on the floor in front of him making him feel so bad.

There was something wrong in here, something really wrong.

This had to be the Brewertons' doing. Those brothers had always wanted Vinnie out of the way. This would be perfect for them. They'd have Vinnie banged up and a load of smart-phones to make a profit on. Two birds, one stone.

He needed to leave now.

Vinnie staggered back to the front of the shop.

When he got there, he couldn't believe his eyes. Craig Foster was sprawled on the floor all over the magazines. Vomit covered the shiny pages. What was going on?

"We need to get out," Vinnie said. His voice came out croaky and weak.

He couldn't explain any more, he didn't feel he could string the words together.

To Vinnie's right, Robbie Baxter was on the floor shaking violently. His eyes rolled back to reveal the whites. He was having some sort of fit.

Joanne was rattling the door handle, trying to get out. "It won't open," she screamed. "I can't get it open."

She dropped to her knees as she turned to Vinnie. "Help me... Heee mmaaa" The rest of her words were too slurred for Vinnie to understand.

Vinnie staggered towards the door. It felt as if he was wading through treacle. He reached out his own shaking hand to pull the door as hard as he could, but she was right. The door wouldn't open.

They'd been locked in.

Beside him, Joanne leaned forward on her hands and knees and began to retch.

This was some kind of trap, and he'd walked right into it. How could he have been such a fool?

It was only then that Vinnie noticed the man standing on the pavement outside. He stared in at them. His vast bushy eyebrows met in the middle as he wiped his hands on the white apron tied around his waist.

Vinnie recognised him...

It was the owner of the cafe next door. Mad Mitch. The one who had given them the evil eye as they approached.

Vinnie rapped on the glass door, trying to get Mitch's attention. "Help! We can't get out."

Mitch stared back at him. His face blank, completely unconcerned.

The pain in Vinnie's head was getting worse. Mitch wasn't going to help.

Vinnie slumped to his knees. His legs felt too heavy. They couldn't support his weight anymore.

The palm of Vinnie's hand squeaked against the glass as he slid down to the floor.

He heard a smash and it took all his energy to turn his head. His eyelids flickered as he saw that Craig had heaved himself up and thrown a stool at the huge, glass window fronting the newsagent's.

Vinnie felt the rush of cool, fresh air. But it was too late. He couldn't move.

The last thing Vinnie felt was a sharp pain in his ribs as one of his friends stepped on his back in their scramble to escape the shop.

CHAPTER FOUR

ON THE OTHER SIDE OF London, DS Jack Mackinnon stood staring up at a three-storey townhouse. Despite the fact it was early evening, the air was warm and still. Behind him, a car stereo blasted out a few bars of the song In the Summertime by Mungo Jerry. The clink of glasses, sound of laughter and the smell of a barbecue wafted over from the house across the street.

Guilt churned in Mackinnon's stomach. He remembered the last time he had visited this house to talk to DI Bruce Evans. Now Bruce was gone, leaving behind a wife and two children.

In the months since Bruce's funeral, Mackinnon had made it this far on three previous occasions, only to turn around and leave without knocking on the door.

This time he was going to see it through.

He walked up the stone steps, and held up a hand to rap on the door, but paused when he heard a noise coming from inside.

The sound was muffled, but Mackinnon was sure someone

was crying. He immediately pictured Bruce's wife, Fiona, sobbing. Jesus. What the hell was he doing here? Did he really think he could help?

Mackinnon stood on the steps, his hand still raised, ready to knock, hesitating. It might make him feel worse, it might be the last thing in the world he wanted to do now, but he couldn't just leave.

He needed to make sure Bruce's family were all right. He owed them that. If there was something he could do, anything, he would.

Before he could change his mind, he pressed the doorbell. The cheerful chimes ringing from inside seemed ridiculously unsuitable right now.

Fiona Evans opened the door, and Mackinnon saw straight away she hadn't been the one crying. She carried a little girl on her hip.

The child buried her head in her mother's neck, but after a moment, curiosity got the better of her, and she turned her head to get a look at the visitor. Her tear-streaked cheeks confirmed it was her cries Mackinnon had heard.

Confusion flickered over Fiona Evans' face as she stared up at Mackinnon. She bit her lower lip and narrowed her eyes as if she recognised him from somewhere but couldn't quite place him.

Mackinnon put her out of her misery. "It's Jack Mackinnon," he said. "I worked with your husband."

Fiona pushed her hair back from her face and smiled. "Of course, I remember you. You were working on the same case as Bruce just before ..."

She stepped back into the hallway opening the door wide. "Please, come in," she said. "Sorry, I'm not quite with it at the moment. We've just lost Luke's carer. He decided to take a year out in America." She shook her head. "I'm having a horrendous time trying to find a replacement."

Mackinnon followed her down the hallway towards the kitchen. It was a lovely house, open-plan, spacious and got plenty of natural light. Mackinnon remembered wondering how Bruce could afford a house like this on a Detective Inspector's salary.

"Would you like a cup of tea? I was just about to make one," Fiona said. She lowered the little girl to the floor. "Why don't you play with your dolls, sweetheart."

The little girl stared up at Mackinnon through wet eyelashes, then picked up a plastic doll with an oversized head and began to wrap the dolls blonde hair around her fingers. Mackinnon smiled at her but received a stony look in return.

Mackinnon tried not to let it show, but he was shocked by the state of the kitchen. There were dirty plates and cups scattered on every kitchen counter and piles of unopened mail on the kitchen table. The contrast to the appearance of the kitchen the last time he'd been here couldn't have been greater. But that was to be expected. Fiona was having to bring up two kids, one of them severely disabled, without Bruce.

"Tea would be great," Mackinnon said. "I thought I'd pop by and see how you're doing. I meant to come earlier but…"

"That's very kind of you," Fiona said as she searched the cupboard for some clean cups. She quickly gave up on that and began to wash up. "We've been getting along okay. Obviously it's been hard, but we've been coping. Until Luke's carer left, I was managing to keep things under control."

Mackinnon wished he had an answer. He wished he knew the right words to say. Some people were great at it, offering the perfect words of condolence. Mackinnon wanted to help, but how? He wished he hadn't come empty-handed. Maybe he could have bought a bottle of wine and some sweets for the little girl.

"If there's anything I can do…"

Fiona turned to face him with the kettle in her hand. She

smiled. "I appreciate that. Everyone is afraid of saying the wrong thing. They seem to think I will collapse if they even mention Bruce's name."

"Does it help to talk about him?"

"Sometimes." Fiona switched on the kettle. "And sometimes the only way I can get through the day is by not talking about him and not thinking about him." She sighed. "I think it's harder on the children, though."

Mackinnon's eyes flickered towards the ceiling.

"I know what you're thinking. Luke can't express himself, but I know he misses his father."

"My daddy was a policeman," the little girl said. She sat on the floor staring down at her doll. She pulled off a plastic arm, then reattached it.

"I know he was," Mackinnon said. "I worked with your daddy. I'm a policeman, too."

The little girl stared at him then got to her feet and held out the plastic doll. "This is Rosie."

Mackinnon took the doll and turned it over in his hands. "She's very pretty," he said.

Satisfied, the little girl took the doll back and pulled out a chair to sit down at the table. She was so small her chin was level with the tabletop.

Fiona removed a few toys from the other chairs and motioned for Mackinnon to sit down. She set the mugs of tea on the table and sat down beside him.

"Are you planning to stay in the area?" Mackinnon asked.

She nodded. "My parents bought us this house when Bruce and I got married, so that's one less thing to worry about."

Mackinnon picked up his mug and took a sip of the steaming hot tea, scalding his mouth. He'd believed that Bruce had been paying for this huge house with bribes. Clearly he'd been wrong. Perhaps Bruce hadn't been quite as corrupt as he'd seemed.

"Is there anything I can do?" Mackinnon asked. "I'd like to help, but honestly, I have no idea how."

"That's really kind of you, Jack. I know Bruce would have appreciated it. He thought highly of you."

Mackinnon swallowed more tea, ignoring the sting of the hot liquid as it hit his tongue. He'd only known Bruce for a little while and most of that time he'd suspected that Bruce was bent. The fact that Mackinnon had guessed correctly didn't make him feel any better now. Bruce had been on the payroll of a notorious drug dealer, and the night before he committed suicide, he asked Mackinnon to keep it secret.

Mackinnon refused, and now at night when he couldn't sleep, he lay there wondering whether Bruce would still be alive if he had handled things differently.

"I only worked with Bruce for a short time," Mackinnon said. "But I felt like I got to know him well." That wasn't a lie. Mackinnon knew things about Bruce that no one else did, not even his wife.

Fiona glanced at her wristwatch.

"Sorry," Mackinnon said and reached for his jacket. "I know you must have a million and one things to do. I don't want to get in the way."

"No, don't go. I need to go and check on Luke, but I'll only be a few minutes. Perhaps you could keep an eye on Anna for me?"

Mackinnon looked down at the little girl, still playing happily with her dolls at the table.

"My daddy's growing sweetcorn."

"I'm sorry?"

"Big ones in the garden. Do you want to see?"

Mackinnon looked at Fiona. "Is that okay?"

Fiona grinned. "Sure."

"Can we water them, Mum?" Anna asked.

After Fiona nodded and left the kitchen to attend to Luke,

Anna slid down from the chair and held her hand out to Mackinnon. "Come on."

Mackinnon did what he was told. He felt Anna curl her tiny hand in his and let her lead him through the kitchen door into the garden. The garden was about twenty-foot square and mostly laid to grass, but a small patch at the end of the garden had been made into a vegetable garden.

The garden looked well-tended, despite dry patches on the lawn. As Anna called him closer to the vegetable garden, Mackinnon saw that the runner beans and sweetcorn plants were crying out for water. At least, this was something he could do. Something useful.

"Here they are," Anna said. "They're getting big."

The plants were attached to bamboo canes. There were six in total and each one came as high as his hip.

Mackinnon peeled back the light green sheath covering one of the immature cobs. The corn was very pale yellow, and the plant itself looked dry. The green leaves felt almost like tissue paper beneath his fingers.

"These plants look like they could do with some water, what do you think, Anna?"

Anna nodded. "Daddy used to water them every night."

At the other end of the garden, Mackinnon unravelled the green garden hose, turned on the brass tap and filled the old watering can. Anna insisted she fill up her own little blue watering can so she could help. Together, they gave the sweetcorn and runner beans a thorough drenching.

Anna took off her shoes and socks and squelched the mud between her toes, giggling. This was obviously something she used to do with Bruce. The thought felt like a heavy pressure on his chest.

Mackinnon carried the watering can back towards the house and pretended to look horrified at the mud covering

Anna's toes. "Look at the state of your feet! You better get cleaned up before your mum sees you."

Anna squirmed and giggled as she held out her feet, one at a time, to be rinsed clean by the water from the garden hose.

"That's better," Mackinnon said as Anna struggled to pull socks onto her wet feet.

The sound of an excited Olympics' broadcaster, building up to a crescendo, spilled out through the downstairs windows of the house next door. Fiona's neighbour had opened every window at the back of their house in an attempt to catch a cool breeze on this warm night.

Anna smiled, showing off the dimples in her plump cheeks as she slipped on her shoes, so Mackinnon wasn't expecting what she said next, "It's a shame my Daddy's gone to heaven, isn't it?"

Those simple words caught him unawares, and as his mobile phone began to ring and the screen flashed with the name DI Tyler, Mackinnon swallowed the lump in his throat then nodded. "Yes, Anna, it is."

CHAPTER FIVE

WHEN MACKINNON ARRIVED AT THE newsagent's on East Street, the place was already crawling with emergency services. Two specialist fire trucks blocked the crossroads where East Street met St Michael's way, and four police cars were parked up near the old post office.

The street was still closed to motorists, but residents and business owners were being herded under the police tape, back to their properties. Mackinnon waved to one of the uniformed PCs, who took his name, then lifted the blue and white tape, allowing Mackinnon to approach the scene.

A few steps later, the smell hit him. It was a foul odour, like bad drains mixed with rotten eggs, a heavy sulphurous smell.

The newsagent's was in the centre of a small parade of shops, flanked by a cafe on one side and a hairdressing salon on the other. Further along the street two uniformed officers stood outside a mobile phone shop, peering in the window. They could have been looking for evidence or checking out the latest Blackberry.

On the opposite side of the road, low rise residential buildings signalled the start of the Towers Estate.

As Mackinnon approached the newsagent's he could see the huge window at the front of the shop had been smashed. Through the splintered glass, he spotted the familiar figure of DI Tyler. DC Charlotte Brown stood next to Tyler, her forehead creased in concentration. They were talking to the crime scene manager, David Oakley, and a SOCO Mackinnon didn't recognise.

Mackinnon stopped at the door. "Is it all right to come in?"

DI Tyler nodded. "Watch out for the broken glass."

"What have we got?" Mackinnon asked.

"One victim," DI Tyler said. "Syed Hammad, forty-two, suspected suicide, and a couple of kids have been taken to hospital after inhaling the gas. David here was just telling us what he thinks happened. Carry on, David. We're all ears."

As Mackinnon stepped inside, the crime scene manager pointed to the floor where three plastic buckets were lined up under the broken window at the front of the shop.

"At first glance, it looks like we have three buckets and a whole load of broken glass. But if you look closely you can see this broken glass isn't from the window. Take a look."

Mackinnon leaned forward with Tyler and Charlotte to study the glass, but it all looked pretty much the same to him.

From the puzzled look on Tyler's face, Mackinnon knew he wasn't alone.

"This glass is thinner, and in smaller pieces," the crime scene manager insisted. "Now look at the set-up here." He pointed to the top of the window frame.

It looked like a metallic curtain rail ran the length of the window, but instead of curtain hooks, small metal clamps were attached to the rail above each of the buckets. Each clamp gripped fragments of broken glass.

"Fascinating. Are you getting to the bit where this has

something to do with the poisonous gas that killed a man and made us evacuate over a hundred people?"

The crime scene manager seemed oblivious to Tyler's sarcasm. "Yes. This is the ingenious bit. Each of these clamps held a glass vial, containing a liquid chemical. When the shop door opened, it triggered the glass to smash and the contents to fall into the buckets below."

Mackinnon stepped forward to look into the buckets. They were empty.

The crime-scene manager frowned at the interruption. "Well, there's nothing in them now, of course. The place has been decontaminated. But there would have been a chemical in the bucket and a different chemical in the glass vials. Both substances on their own aren't dangerous, you could find them under the sink in quite a few households in the UK, but when they are mixed, they are deadly."

"They produce hydrogen sulphide," Tyler said.

"That's right," David screwed up his nose. "Nasty stuff."

"So opening the door caused the chemicals to mix and release the gas?" Charlotte asked.

"Yes. Opening the door caused the metal rod to shoot across and break the glass vials."

"Hydrogen sulphide is the suicide gas," Tyler said and turned to Mackinnon. "We've been briefed about these. Only a few cases in this country, though."

Mackinnon nodded. Death by hydrogen sulphide became a hugely popular method of suicide in Japan a couple of years ago and to a lesser extent the USA, and it was feared that the UK might follow their lead.

"What about the kids?" Mackinnon asked.

"Wrong place, wrong time. Two boys, Vincent Pearson and Robert Baxter. They're known locally as troublemakers. They probably saw the shop unoccupied, thought they'd take the opportunity to rob the place and got more than they bargained for."

"I don't understand why he did it here," Charlotte said. "Why do it here in such a large area. If Syed Hammad wanted to kill himself, why not do it in a bathroom or a car, somewhere smaller, somewhere other people were less likely to get hurt."

Tyler frowned. "People who take their own lives often aren't thinking straight."

"And why the elaborate set-up?" Mackinnon nodded at the buckets. "I mean, why not just mix the stuff himself."

Tyler shrugged. "Could be religious reasons. Maybe suicide is forbidden. This way maybe he felt he wasn't actually taking his own life."

Mackinnon mulled it over for a moment, then said, "Syed Hammad died from inhaling the hydrogen sulphide?"

The crime scene manager stared down at the buckets. "I can't say for sure, but it does look that way."

"He was declared dead at the scene," Tyler said. "But he wasn't examined here. They have to take special precautions with this one because of the toxic gas."

"What about the kids, Pearson and Baxter? Does it look like they'll make it?" Mackinnon asked.

"They've been taken to St. Barts," Charlotte said. "We haven't had a status update on them yet. But the others disappeared into thin air."

"The others?"

"Witnesses have told us at least two, maybe three, other youths were seen running from the shop before emergency services arrived."

Mackinnon pointed at the security camera above the counter. "Tell me that was working."

"It was working. But don't get too excited. We can't get it to playback." Tyler ran a hand over his face. "It needs a bloody password. We're taking it back to the station. We'll get our guys to look at it."

Mackinnon looked around the shop, taking in the mess. Newspapers and magazines lay scattered on the floor, splashed with vomit. Squashed chocolate bars lay on the floor where they had been trampled underfoot. He tried to imagine the panic the kids felt as the gas levels rose and it became hard to breathe.

Tyler's theory was feasible, the kids noticed the shop was abandoned and decided to break in. Most thefts were opportunistic, after all. But what if it was something else?

"All right, Mackinnon, out with it."

"Sorry?"

"You've got that look."

"What look?"

"That pained look, that tells me that underworked brain of yours just had an idea. So spit it out."

"Seeing as you asked so nicely," Mackinnon said. "I was wondering if this was some kind of trap."

"Trap?" Tyler frowned. "I can't see it."

"What if the kids were the target?" Mackinnon suggested, then shrugged. In recent years, there had been examples of people taking the law into their own hands. Mackinnon remembered a case where a man who'd had his car stolen three times in a year, wired up his BMW to give the thief an electric shock.

Mackinnon continued, "Maybe Syed Hammad wanted to scare them and underestimated how powerful the gas would be."

Tyler gave Mackinnon a withering look. "Yes, because that is so much more likely than a straightforward suicide."

Charlotte was a little more open-minded. "I suppose he could have been using the gas as a deterrent. The shops along here were wrecked in the riots last summer."

"A harsh bloody deterrent," Tyler said.

Mackinnon nodded. "True, but the stuff stinks. Maybe he thought the smell would be enough to get rid of a few kids. Maybe he screwed up his calculations."

Mackinnon paused, then turned to David, the crime scene manager. "That's something else that doesn't make sense. I mean, it smells bad enough now and that's at safe levels. So why didn't the kids leave as soon as they smelt it? It must have been horrific."

"Actually," David said, "At high enough concentrations, hydrogen sulphide can paralyse the olfactory nerves. You can smell it at low concentrations, but when the gas is very concentrated, you can't actually smell it anymore. That's why it's such an incredibly dangerous gas. And another thing..." David took a step to his left, so he was level with the door. "Opening the door caused the metal rod to smash the glass vials, but when the door closed, the rod slipped back across the door, effectively bolting it shut."

Charlotte shivered. "They were locked inside?"

"That's my best guess," David pointed at the window. "It's probably why they broke the window to get out."

"All right we'll let you get back to it, David," Tyler said, then turned to Mackinnon and Charlotte. "I want you two to go and speak to the other shop owners. Reassure them that it's safe now. Then find out what you can. See if Syed Hammad has been going around like weeping Willy recently."

Charlotte rolled her eyes.

"And make sure you talk to that cafe owner, Mitch Horrocks. He was the one who called it in." Tyler frowned. "He's a funny bloke. See what you make of him."

Mackinnon nodded. He might not always agree with Tyler's strategy, but the detective inspector did have a good nose for dodgy characters.

CHAPTER SIX

CHARLOTTE AND MACKINNON DECIDED TO talk to the cafe owner first. From the outside, as the sun began to sink behind the rooftops, the cafe seemed less than inviting. A faded sign hung above the entrance, and stickers covering the window, advertising an all-day breakfast for three pounds, had begun to peel away.

As soon as they pushed open the door, despite the fact the sign hanging on the cafe door had been turned to open, a vastly overweight man, dressed in a white T-shirt smeared with grease stains and an apron tied beneath his prominent belly, snapped, "We're closed."

The man wiped his meaty hands on his dirty apron and squirted the tables with a bottle of cleaning fluid. Its lemony scent mixed with the smell of fat and fried onions.

Charlotte showed him her warrant card. "We would like to ask you a few questions, sir," she said. "It won't take long."

He banged the bottle of cleaner down on the tabletop. "I told you lot already, I don't know anything. I just called 999 when I saw those kids collapse." He scowled at them. "I wouldn't have bothered if I'd known I would get such hassle for being a Good Samaritan."

"Are you Mitch Horrocks, the owner of this cafe?" Charlotte asked, then introduced herself and Mackinnon.

The man gave a surly nod.

Charlotte hooked her thumbs in the loops of her belt. "We appreciate you making the call, sir. Could you tell me what made you realise something was wrong?"

"What made me realise?"

Mitch Horrocks' fierce expression dropped from his face and was replaced by a confused frown. "They were making a bloody racket. I saw the little bastards walking down the road, and I knew they were up to something. It doesn't take a genius to work that out."

"How many of them were there?" Mackinnon asked.

"I saw five of the little buggers."

"Did you get a good look at any of them? Recognise anyone?"

"I recognised that bloody Vinnie what's-his-name," he snapped. "But I didn't get a good look at the rest of his little gang. I was too busy locking up. I wanted to get the place secure before they decided to wreck it."

Mitch Horrocks rubbed vigorously at a dried ketchup stain on the table. "I'm sure it was the same gang that trashed my place last summer. Not that you lot..." He pointed a hairy finger at Mackinnon. "...did anything about it."

Charlotte made a note. She looked around the cafe, taking in the yellowing walls and scratched linoleum floor. The equipment in the kitchen and behind the counter hadn't been updated for a few years. It wasn't the type of cafe to have a fancy coffee machine, but she expected perhaps a few more mod-cons if it had been done up since last summer.

"Were you insured?" she asked. "Did you have to get the place done up afterwards?"

"Of course I was insured," Mitch said. His bushy eyebrows met in the middle as he frowned. He scratched his belly with a chubby finger. "That didn't make it any easier to clean up, though. And my old mum's nerves were wrecked for weeks."

"Your mum? Does she live upstairs with you? Perhaps we could talk..."

The confused frown slid from Mitch Horrocks' face. He started to undo his apron strings. "You leave my mum out of it. Look, are we done here? Only I've got stuff to do."

He looked towards the back door and chewed on his fleshy lower lip.

"You both live upstairs?" Charlotte asked again.

"Yeah, but she didn't see anything," he said and slapped his apron down on the counter.

They were interrupted by a crash sounding from upstairs, followed by a high-pitched screech.

"What was that?" Mackinnon said and moved forwards.

Mitch trotted after Mackinnon. But before either of them reached the door, it slammed open.

A slim man rocketed through the entrance. He raked a hand through his floppy, brown hair, catching it in wet tangles. The front of his blue shirt was splattered with some type of brown liquid.

He ignored Mackinnon, shoving past him to storm up to Mitch Horrocks. "That is it! That is the last straw. You can find someone else to look after your mother. I've had enough."

Mitch Horrocks' cheeks flushed. "Don't be soft. She's only an old lady."

"She's a vindictive old cow. And she..." He trailed off as he seemed to notice Mackinnon and Charlotte for the first time. "She's just awful." He picked up a cloth from the counter and tried ineffectively to wipe away the mess on his shirt.

Mitch Horrocks crossed his arms over his chest. "It's your

job. How difficult can it be to look after a little old lady in a wheelchair? You're getting paid enough for it."

"You're not paying enough for me to put up with that… that kind of thing. She just chucked her dinner over me because the beef in the stew was too tough."

Mackinnon decided it was time that he introduced himself and Charlotte. After Mackinnon explained why they were there, the man's eyes widened, and he dropped the cloth he'd been holding.

"You told me it was a minor gas leak," he said to Mitch.

"I didn't want to distract you. You find it hard enough to do your job properly as it is."

"What's your name please, sir?" Mackinnon asked.

"Tim Coleman." He held out a hand to shake Mackinnon's. "I'm a carer. I look after Mrs. Horrocks in the evenings, but not for much longer." He shot a dark look at Mitch.

Tim Coleman tried to run a hand through his hair again but as his fingers came into contact with the gloopy, gravy-splattered strands he gave up, letting his hands fall down by his sides. "I did think it smelled funny earlier. At first, I thought it was the drains."

"Bloody idiot," Mitch mumbled under his breath.

Tim Coleman picked up the gravy-covered cloth he'd dropped on the floor and threw it at Mitch Horrocks. "That's it. I'm off. You can find some other poor sap to look after your mother."

"Wait a minute, please," Mackinnon said before Tim Coleman reached the door. "I'd like to ask you a few more questions."

Mitch Horrocks hung his apron on a hook behind the counter. "Well, if you can't be arsed to do your job, Tim, then I suppose I better go and check on her. Leaving a poor old woman up there to care for herself, you ought to be ashamed of yourself."

Mitch Horrocks looked down his nose at the three of them. "Close the door on your way out, Tim," he said and disappeared through the doorway. His heavy footfalls carried down the stairs.

Tim Coleman shook his head. "Bastard. We were at school together. You know, I only took this job because I felt sorry for him. I should have known better, though. He was an unlikeable sod then as well. People don't change."

"How long have you worked here?" Mackinnon asked.

"Longer than I should have. I guess it's been almost six months. Feels a hell of a lot longer. It's only for a couple of hours in the evenings, to give Mrs. Horrocks her dinner and help her with anything else she needs."

"Did you know Syed Hammad?"

"Syed who?"

"Syed Hammad from the newsagent's next door."

"Oh, right. Well, I've popped in the shop now and again, but I haven't seen him recently. I didn't even know his name. Is he all right? Was he the man who died?"

Mackinnon nodded.

"Because of the gas leak? God, how awful."

"It wasn't a gas leak," Mackinnon said. "We believe the gas was generated inside the shop intentionally."

"Jesus. I had no idea what had happened. Bloody Mitch bloody Horrocks. He told me there had been a minor gas leak. Was anybody else hurt?"

"A couple of kids were taken to hospital suffering from gas inhalation. Did you see anything, or hear anything? We think it is likely a gang of youths broke into the newsagent's."

"Again?" Tim Coleman shook his head. "The little gits. But I didn't get here until eight o'clock tonight. Mrs. Horrocks doesn't sleep well, and she prefers to eat late. I doubt she heard anything either. She always has her radio blaring out all day."

After they'd finished the routine questioning, Mackinnon turned back to Tim Coleman as they walked to the door. "Do you only look after the elderly?"

Charlotte shot him a puzzled look, clearly not following.

"I just go where the agency sends me. Usually it's someone elderly, but sometimes I'm employed to help disabled people who can't get about on their own."

"Bruce Evans' lad, Luke." Mackinnon said, answering Charlotte's unspoken question. "Fiona told me his carer left, and she's struggling to find a replacement."

Tim Coleman shrugged. "I'll give you the agency's card. They do take on NHS work sometimes. Tell Fiona to give them a ring."

"Thanks." Mackinnon took the card and slid it into the breast pocket of his jacket.

All three of them stepped out into the warm summer evening. The sulphurous smell had dissipated and even the traffic-choked air on East Street smelled fresh compared to the heavy odour of old fried food in the cafe.

"That's all right," Tim Coleman said. "I'm off home to wash this bloody gravy out of my hair. Honestly, it's the worst job I've ever had." He pulled out a set of keys from the pocket of his trousers and locked the door of the cafe.

"I take it Mrs. Horrocks is a little difficult," Charlotte said with an amused smile.

"She's evil. Just plain nasty," Tim said and shoved the keys through the letter box. "And you saw how Mitch is, rude, arrogant, throwing his weight around. But he's absolutely terrified of his mother. He turns into a nervous wreck whenever she's around. It's weird."

CHAPTER SEVEN

AFTER CHARLOTTE AND MACKINNON LEFT Tim Coleman, they spotted a small, blonde woman standing outside the hairdressing salon on the other side of the newsagent's. She held a cigarette in her hand and tilted her head to one side, looking at them curiously.

She flicked the ash from her cigarette onto the floor and walked towards them. "You're the police, aren't you?"

Charlotte and Mackinnon introduced themselves, and the woman told them her name was Kathy Walker.

"I've been a nervous wreck tonight," she said. "I can't believe this has happened. Syed was such a nice man, really polite." She shook her head. "Is it true what people have been saying? You think he killed himself?"

"We can't say anything for sure at the moment." Mackinnon knew that wasn't very reassuring. Kathy Walker raised a shaky hand to her cheek. She seemed beside herself with nerves.

"Is this your shop here?" Mackinnon asked nodding towards the salon.

The woman nodded. "Yes. Usually I work late tonight. But when we were evacuated, I had to cancel all my appointments. Good job really." She held out a trembling hand. "Look at that. I'm shaking. I couldn't go near anybody with a pair of scissors in this state."

"We don't have any reason to believe that there is any danger to you or the other residents in the street," Mackinnon said. "The gas has been contained."

"I'm sure I can still smell it," she said. "It's awful. It smells like bad eggs."

Mackinnon nodded. "The smell will linger for a while, but the gas is no longer at harmful levels. We've had specialist crews out here and they've measured the level of gas."

She looked sceptical. "That's what they said when they came to check out my place, but I don't know what they were looking for."

"Just routine," Mackinnon said.

She blinked and pressed a hand to her chest. Appealing to Charlotte, she said, "This sort of thing doesn't usually happen around here. Are you really sure it is safe?"

"We can come in and take another look if that would make you feel better."

Kathy Walker smiled. "Oh, yes please. I'd appreciate that." She led the way back to the entrance of her salon. She dropped the cigarette on the floor and stamped it out with her heel before picking up the cigarette end and carrying it inside.

Opening the door wide, she gestured for Mackinnon and Charlotte to follow. A slight sulphurous smell tinged the usual salon smells of hairspray and shampoo. There were four hair-dressing stations, two on each side of the room, each with large mirrors, adjustable chairs and a selection of brushes and combs scattered in front of them.

Kathy Walker bolted the door behind them, walked across to the reception counter and put her packet of cigarettes down next to the till and then led them out the back into a small kitchenette.

Kathy switched the kettle on. "Can I get you some tea? Coffee?"

Both Mackinnon and Charlotte declined.

"How well did you know Mr. Hammad?" Charlotte asked.

"Syed? I saw him most days. He would save me a copy of the Daily Mail. I like to do the crossword in the evenings. We'd have a quick chat, nothing very profound, just talk about the weather and things."

"Had he been depressed recently?"

Kathy shook her head. "Not that I noticed. So you do think… you think he killed himself?"

Mackinnon let her question hang in the air.

Kathy looked down at the floor and chewed on her thumbnail. "I wouldn't have thought he was the type. I suppose you never know, do you?"

"We don't have all the answers yet," Charlotte said. "We're still gathering information, talking to people like you, and trying to work out what happened."

Mackinnon watched Kathy dunk a tea bag into a pink mug. "Did you see any of the gang hanging around the newsagent's?"

"I saw two of them taken away by ambulance, but I didn't get a good look at them, to be honest. I know Syed had some problems with kids from the Towers Estate. He put a notice up on the shop door, saying schoolchildren were only allowed in the shop one at a time."

"Do you know the names of any of the kids he had trouble with?"

"They didn't bother me much." She gestured around the salon. "There's nothing to nick here."

A heavy banging sounded at the front of the shop.

Someone was pounding on the door and rattling the door handle. Kathy's eyes widened. She really did look terrified.

Mackinnon put a hand on her shoulder. "It's all right. I'll go and see who it is."

She swallowed hard and nodded.

As Mackinnon walked out of the kitchen area and into the salon, he sensed Kathy behind him. It was dark now and hard to see, even though the front of the shop was mainly glass. He could just about make out the dark outline of a male figure. He unbolted the door and reached for the door handle.

As soon as Mackinnon pulled the door open, the man burst inside. His face was screwed up in a mask of aggression.

"Who the hell are you?" His nostrils flared as he grunted out the words. He wore a black leather jacket, over a white vest top. His arms were crooked at the elbow, ready for a jab.

"I'm Detective Sergeant Mackinnon, City of London police. Who are you?"

The anger seemed to drain away from him, and his shoulders slumped.

"It's Stuart." Kathy rushed up to them. "It's all right, he's my brother."

Stuart Walker rubbed his forehead. He seemed full of pent up anger, rage bubbling beneath the surface. He was tall, only an inch or so shorter than Mackinnon, and he looked like he took care of himself. Probably a regular at the gym, judging from the width of his neck.

"What the hell is going on, Kathy? I just checked my phone, and there's a hysterical message from you going on about poisonous gas. I came round as soon as I got the message."

"There was gas. Hydrogen something or other. We were evacuated. Syed's dead, Stuart." Kathy's eyes brimmed with tears.

Her brother put an arm around her shoulders and pulled her to him. "Christ." He looked up at Mackinnon. "Sorry I reacted like that. But I was worried. I didn't know you were police. I just saw a big bloke I don't know opening my sister's door. I didn't know what to think." He took a breath. "Was anyone else hurt? Is Mitch okay?"

Kathy sniffed. "A couple of kids were taken to hospital, but Mitch is fine."

"Mitch Horrocks?" Mackinnon said, exchanging a look with Charlotte.

"Yeah." Stuart smiled at his sister. "If you're all right, I'll go and see how he's doing."

After the door closed behind Stuart, Mackinnon turned to Kathy.

"Are you and your brother close to Mitch Horrocks?" Mackinnon asked, wondering if they'd encountered Mitch's bad side earlier. Perhaps he could be friendly under different circumstances.

Kathy's eyes narrowed. "I'm not. I can't stand him."

They left the hairdressing salon and waited as Kathy bolted the door behind them. Turning to head back to report to DI Tyler, Mackinnon saw DC Collins, pen and notepad in hand, heading towards them.

"Any luck at the mobile phone shop, Nick?" Mackinnon asked.

Collins shook his head and stuffed his notebook into his pocket. "It's closed. The manager, Pete Morton, lives out Walthamstow way apparently. I haven't been able to track him down yet. How about you? Found anything useful?"

"Not yet. No one seems to know the victim very well."

Collins exhaled. "Webb is tracking down the family. The parents are dead, but there's a brother back in Pakistan." He leaned a little closer to Charlotte and Mackinnon. "Do you really think he did this himself?"

Mackinnon shrugged. "I don't know. Funny way to do it. Why not do it somewhere more … private?"

"Yeah," Collins said. "It doesn't feel right."

Mackinnon knew what he meant. It didn't feel right at all.

CHAPTER EIGHT

1976

WHEN JUNIOR'S MOTHER DRAGGED him along the street towards their house, Junior knew something bad was going to happen.

She yanked him up the steps to their front door, pausing only to glare down at him as she fumbled in her bag for her keys.

Junior knew what was coming, and it was going to hurt.

Across the road, old Mrs. Gladstone leaned heavily on her walking stick and raised one hand to wave at them. Junior raised his hand to wave, but his mother quickly snatched it back down and dragged him inside, slamming the door behind them.

"Take off your coat, Junior," his mother said.

He removed his coat slowly, easing off the sleeves one at a time. He stood on tip toes to hang his coat on the stand by the door. If he took a long time, maybe his mother would forget why she was angry. It was worth a try. Sometimes she forgot. In a few moments, she could swing from wanting to scratch his eyes out to showering him with kisses.

From the way his mother watched him through narrowed eyes, he knew he wouldn't be lucky this time.

"Go in the kitchen, Junior."

"Yes, Mother."

He straightened his school tie and made sure his shirt was tucked in. Mother didn't like him to be untidy, and he didn't want to give her another reason to be angry.

He stood in the kitchen, waiting.

His mother put down her handbag on the kitchen table and began to wipe the kitchen counters down with bleach, even though the kitchen was spotless. The smell of the chlorine stung Junior's nose.

He wiped his sweaty palms on his school shorts. The anticipation was the worst part.

"You know I don't like to do this, don't you, Junior?"

"Yes, Mother."

He stared at the wet kitchen counters that glistened with bleach. He swayed from side to side.

His mother pursed her lips and took a deep breath. "Come over to the drawer, Junior," she said. She opened the cutlery drawer wide, rearranging the knives and forks, making sure everything was perfect.

Junior could feel his heart beating. It felt like a panicked sparrow was fluttering in his chest.

"Put your hand in the drawer, Junior."

His hand felt heavy as he tried to lift it, but he managed to place it over the drawer, barely touching the wood.

She curled his little fingers, one by one, over the front of the drawer.

Junior's breath came in shaky little gasps. He knew what would happen next.

"He that spareth the rod hateth the child." His mother slammed the door shut, trapping his fingers in one quick movement.

Junior inhaled, but he didn't make a sound.

His fingers remained wedged between the two pieces of wood.

His lower lip wobbled, but he didn't cry. Crying made it worse. He tried to think about something else. He pictured his teacher's head clamped in the drawer.

His mother pulled back the drawer, inch by inch, then shoved it closed. Harder this time.

A small whimper escaped Junior, though he did his best to subdue it. The pain of the wood smashing into Junior's already bruised fingers rocketed up his arm.

He didn't cry any more. He taught himself to keep it inside.

But at the back of his mind, Junior was screaming.

His mother let out a strangled sob and staggered over to the kitchen table. Falling into the hard-backed chair, she put her head in her hands and began to cry.

"Oh, Junior, why do you make me do this to you? Do you think I like it?"

"N... No, Mother."

Junior remained where he was. He didn't think his fingers were broken this time, but it took some moments before he gathered the courage to look down at his wounded fingers.

His knuckles were streaked with blood. He cradled his hand, looking down with fascination at the red gashes on his white skin.

His mother raised her head. "Does it hurt very much, Junior?"

"It's okay, Mother."

"Junior why'd you make me do this to you?"

Junior didn't know. He thought there might be something

inside him, something very bad, but it was best not to mention that. "I don't know, Mother."

"Are you sorry?"

"Yes."

He reached out to touch her arm, but she withdrew quickly.

"Junior, your fingers." She reached out and cradled his hand gently in hers, as if she were surprised.

Junior blinked up at her.

"We'd better get this cleaned up," she said and moved towards the cupboard under the kitchen sink. She routed through the contents, looking for her first-aid kit.

His mother held up the bottle of brown fluid. "Now, this is what we need after you've been clumsy. Aren't you a clumsy boy, Junior?"

Junior's toes curled, imagining the sting of the disinfectant fluid touching the cuts on his raw skin. He grabbed onto the back of the chair, bracing himself as his mother poured neat disinfectant onto a ball of cotton wool.

"Yes, Mother."

CHAPTER NINE

PRESENT DAY

AFTER THE LATE briefing, Mackinnon headed back to Derek's place. Mackinnon would have the flat to himself tonight as Derek was staying with Liz, his new girlfriend. He seemed to be staying there quite a bit these days; perhaps it was getting serious – that would be a first for Derek.

Mackinnon opened the front door and Molly, Derek's border collie, bounded towards him, her tail wagging furiously. Mackinnon reached down and scratched her behind the ears.

"Hello, sweetheart," he said. Molly rolled over, loving the attention. "Not much of a guard dog, are you?"

She might not have been much of a guard dog, but what she lacked in killer instinct, she made up with enthusiasm. She definitely knew how to make someone feel wanted. She was the kind of dog that made Mackinnon wish he had one of his own.

Inside the flat on the kitchen counter, Mackinnon found a note from Derek, asking him to remember to feed Molly and take her for a walk. Mackinnon rolled his eyes. He didn't really feel like taking a walk at this time of night, but when he looked down into Molly's big brown eyes, he shrugged.

"All right you win," he said.

The Indian takeaway was open until midnight. If he went the long way round that would give them both a bit of exercise. And a curry at the end of it would make it worthwhile.

"Come on then, sweetheart. Let's get you some exercise."

Mackinnon picked up Molly's lead from the coat stand by the front door and hooked it onto Molly's collar. They headed out together into the warm summer night.

Molly trotted along happily beside him as they turned right outside Derek's apartment building. As they walked, Mackinnon thought about Syed Hammad. He had never worked on a case involving a toxic suicide before.

He definitely wasn't convinced with Tyler's working theory that this was a straightforward suicide. There were so many unanswered questions. Annoying niggles that didn't quite add up.

Why would a man intent on suicide use his shop where anyone could walk in? The potential for contaminating innocent bystanders was huge. Why would anyone take that risk? Maybe the crime analyst and the rest of the team could come up with some answers before tomorrow morning's briefing.

He breathed in the smell of warm beer as he passed a pub. It was closing time, and a group of people enjoying the balmy evening had spilled out onto the pavement in front of the pub. If it had been any earlier, Mackinnon would have been tempted to join them. At that moment, nothing seemed more attractive than enjoying a pint on this warm summer's evening. Like the rest of Britain, Mackinnon always felt he should make the most of nights like this. They didn't get enough of them.

It only took them ten minutes, even though they walked the long way round, to get to the Indian. It was Derek's favourite restaurant and Mackinnon had popped in quite a few times over the past couple of months.

Mackinnon secured Molly's lead to the bicycle rack next to the restaurant and headed inside.

The smell of spices wafted over him as soon as he entered the small waiting area. The distinctive sound of Indian music dominated by the sitar played out in the background. A young couple sat close together on one of the red velvet sofas. A bowl of poppadoms sat on the small coffee table in front of them.

Mackinnon's stomach rumbled in anticipation.

The pretty Indian girl behind the counter looked up and smiled at him. "Hello, good to see you back again."

Mackinnon had been in here last week, around this time. But surely once a week wasn't too often to have an Indian takeaway, was it?

He pulled out his wallet from his back pocket. "I can't stay away. I'll have…"

"Rogan Josh? Extra spicy?"

Mackinnon smiled. If she remembered his order, perhaps he was coming here a little too often. When New Year came around, they would probably send him a calendar.

He thanked her and ordered a plain naan with his curry, then took a step back and looked outside to check on Molly. She looked happy enough, sitting patiently, waiting for him.

The woman behind the counter ripped off Mackinnon's order. "Five minutes," she said. "Take a seat and help yourself to the poppadoms. Can I get you a drink?"

Usually, Mackinnon would have taken a seat and had a beer while enjoying the smell of the food, but he felt bad leaving Molly sitting outside.

He turned down the offer of a drink and headed back to Molly to keep her company.

A single-decker, red bus rumbled past, the passenger's blank faces staring out.

A couple of young men spilled out of the pub a few doors along. Mackinnon noticed Molly tense beside him. He leaned down and patted her flank. "It's all right, sweetheart."

The two male voices got louder and angrier. There was definitely a problem between them.

Although the most common form of murder in the UK was domestic, usually a husband or boyfriend killing their partner, the most common form of murder between two unrelated individuals occurred like this. Confrontation killings between two unknown males.

Mackinnon stared at the two young men and considered whether he would need to intervene.

Molly let out a low growl.

You never knew these days who might be carrying a knife. They might look completely respectable, like someone you could share a beer with, yet get a few drinks inside them and they could transform.

He didn't think these two would be much of a problem. It was more posturing, neither one wanting to back down and lose face.

Another tense minute passed before the taller of the two men staggered away.

Mackinnon let out the breath he didn't realise he'd been holding and headed inside to collect his Rogan Josh.

They took the quick way home. Mackinnon was all for exercise but not when he was hungry.

"Sorry, Molly," he muttered. "You only get a short walk tonight."

Mackinnon didn't think Molly looked too bothered.

Inside Derek's flat, before he served up his own curry, he

opened a tin of gourmet dog food. No Pedigree Chum for Molly. Sometimes Mackinnon thought Derek spent more money on food for the dog than himself.

Mackinnon forked the contents of the tin into Molly's blue ceramic bowl and set it on the ground next to her water. It didn't look very appetising, but Molly seemed to love it. She impatiently pushed his hands away with her nose, eager to bite into the lumps of meat and jelly.

Mackinnon washed his hands, then plated up his own dinner and carried it and a Kingfisher lager over to the sofa. He switched on the TV, settling back with the plate on his lap. He didn't get a chance to do this kind of thing very often these days. Chloe preferred to eat dinner as a family at the dining table.

It had taken a while, but Chloe's girls had slowly accepted him into their family. They didn't seem to resent his presence quite so much.

He drank some of the Kingfisher and made a mental note to buy Derek some more tomorrow. Derek had only been with Liz for a matter of weeks, but he'd hardly been home since he met her, preferring to spend all his time at her place. Talk about moving quickly. But then Derek didn't ever do anything slowly.

Mackinnon turned down the volume on the news. It was a depressing run of stories on violence in the Middle East.

After he'd finished his curry, Mackinnon fired up his laptop and yawned while it booted up. If he could keep his eyes open long enough, he planned to have a look at some of the hydrogen sulphide cases around the world.

He typed: 'hydrogen sulphide suicide' into Google, and the first few results listed were the cases from Japan. It seemed that the chemicals involved had been very easy to get hold of there, and Japan was known for its unusually high suicide rate. There had also been a few cases in the US where the victims took their own lives, usually in a car, or a similarly small enclosed space.

And that was exactly why Syed Hammad's suicide was odd. Why would he choose to do it downstairs in his shop? Of all the places he could have used, like his car or his bathroom, he chose the shop floor – a large open-plan space, which would require a great deal of the gas to get the job done.

Anyone coming into the shop would have been put at risk. But he supposed Tyler was right when he said people contemplating ending their lives weren't thinking clearly.

Maybe it didn't even cross Syed's mind that he might be risking other people's lives. Mackinnon leaned back and took another sip of Kingfisher beer. What made somebody decide that they'd had enough?

The team would know more soon. They would dig up every last detail of Syed's background. Maybe he had been jilted? Or his business was doing badly? Or maybe he had been diagnosed with an incurable disease? Whatever it was, they would find out.

CHAPTER TEN

THE FOLLOWING MORNING, MACKINNON GOT to work just in time for the early briefing. Even at this time of the morning it was still warm, and the cloudless blue sky promised another hot day.

With a couple of minutes free before the meeting, Mackinnon grabbed himself a coffee before heading down the corridor towards the incident room which had been allocated to the investigation.

In the incident room, jackets already lay discarded over the backs of chairs. The mechanical drone of the air conditioning sounded in the background, but somebody had opened the windows.

There was a constant argument in the station between those who preferred open windows and fresh air and those who preferred the air-conditioning, who argued that fresh air was all well and good but it wasn't particularly cool at the moment.

There were more tourists on the streets this summer, attracted to London by the Olympics. On his way to work,

Mackinnon had seen a Chinese family on the tube, waving little flags, and a group of school children with the Olympic circles painted on their cheeks.

As Mackinnon laid his jacket over the back of his chair, he heard DC Webb complaining that he was sure the recent rise in prices at his local were because of all the tourists.

Tyler was heading up this investigation. His first major case. Although a suicide wouldn't normally be considered an important case, the presence of the toxic gas had far-reaching consequences. It was potentially a politically delicate case, and Mackinnon had heard gossip around the station that Tyler might not be the best man for the job. But the DCI had made his decision, and the more Mackinnon got to know Tyler, the more he realised they didn't disagree on absolutely everything. Most things, but not everything.

DI Tyler was already in the room, standing at the front between a whiteboard and the blue felt board. The boards were covered with notes about the operation. Tyler looked very pleased with himself.

The head and shoulder shot of Syed Hammad, sporting a wispy moustache, was posted on the right hand side of the blue felt board. It looked like a blown-up passport photograph. Syed stared out of it, his eyes wide with a look of surprise.

The familiar faces of DC Collins, DC Charlotte Brown and DC Webb were gathered near the front of the room.

Charlotte was nursing a cup of coffee. She looked like she'd had a late night. There were other people in the room that Mackinnon didn't know quite so well. A new indexer was working the case, and there were a few other members of support staff that Mackinnon had seen around but hadn't actually worked with before.

Collins slumped in his chair, looking half asleep. His

eyelids fluttered, and his linked hands rested on his stomach. His legs stretched out in front of him.

As Mackinnon sat down, Tyler looked up from the front of the room. He nodded at Mackinnon.

"All right," DI Tyler said. "Let's make a start. DCI Brookbank won't be attending, so I'll be leading the briefing this morning."

He nodded then looked down at his logbook.

Mackinnon didn't envy Tyler the responsibility of this case. Although they'd barely scratched the surface, Mackinnon had a bad feeling about this investigation.

Over the next few days, they would get to know everything about Syed Hammad. They would find out things even his closest family wouldn't know. They would unravel his secrets, his financial records and his love life... Anything that could give them an indication as to why he would have killed himself.

If it was suicide.

After Tyler had made some preliminary remarks, he set up the laptop so it projected on the screen behind him. In silence, they watched the short video recording of the scene.

Syed Hammad had been found at the foot of the stairs, apparently overcome by the gas. Tyler looked around at everyone in the room.

Mackinnon sat forward in his chair, studying the position of Syed Hammad's crumpled body.

Tyler said, "We were first alerted to the situation by a Mr. Mitch Horrocks, who owns the cafe next door to Syed Hammad's property. He told the attending officers he came to investigate after seeing a group of teenagers acting suspiciously by the newsagent's. According to Mr. Horrocks, this particular gang of youths has caused trouble along this shopping parade in the past."

As Tyler summarised a few of the witness statements,

Mackinnon's mind wandered. Had this whole thing been some kind of elaborate setup to punish this gang of kids? A punishment gone wrong? The team found the newsagent's had been broken into twice last year, and Syed Hammad had complained on multiple occasions about shoplifters. Could Syed have miscalculated and been overcome by the gas?

Tyler's voice broke through Mackinnon's thoughts. "The suicide note…" Tyler nodded at the screen behind him, which displayed a blown up image of a printed note on a piece of generic A4 paper. It said:

I'm sorry. I can't go on with this on my conscience.

Mackinnon frowned. "Where was the note found?" Mackinnon asked. He hadn't heard any mention of the note yesterday. From the start, Tyler said it looked like a suicide. Maybe he was right.

"It was in the inside pocket of his jacket," Tyler said. "He wasn't examined properly until late last night as we had to be careful of the body releasing gases and so on."

"Strange place to keep it," Mackinnon said. "I would have expected him to leave the note where someone could see it, not hidden away in his pocket."

Tyler nodded. "We'll get to that in a minute; first things first."

Tyler took his time, asking everyone individually to give their reports. He picked on people randomly, trying to make sure people were paying attention.

From the team's feedback, it seemed people in the area hadn't seen very much at all, or if they had, they weren't prepared to share the information with the police.

When Charlotte's turn came around she had slightly better news. "Vincent Pearson and Robert Baxter were admitted to St. Bart's. Their symptoms match those expected after inhaling hydrogen sulphide gas, but they are recovering well. The hospital thinks they'll both survive, but the doctors say they aren't up to questioning yet."

"There's a surprise," Tyler muttered.

"Robbie Baxter is only fourteen, so we will need a parent or guardian present when we question him," Charlotte said. "But Vinnie Pearson is twenty-two, and I'm hoping to speak to him later today."

Tyler's mouth set in a firm line. "Good. We can go over potential interview questions after the briefing. I think DCI Brookbank will want to be involved.

"As for the other houses, businesses and residents..." He zeroed in on Mackinnon. "How did you find Mitch Horrocks?"

Mackinnon filled the team in on Mitch Horrocks' odd behaviour, then said, "I think he had some trouble in the riots last summer and he blames it on Vinnie Pearson and his gang, although no one was ever charged."

After other members of the team gave feedback from various witnesses, Tyler sighed, and perched on the table. "Wasn't he close to anyone? No one noticed he was suicidal. How depressing."

Mackinnon wasn't sure if Tyler was referring to the state of their investigation or the fact that Syed Hammad had no one to turn to.

"Kathy Walker, who owns the hairdressing salon, said she didn't think Syed was the type. They weren't exactly close, but she did see him most days."

"Hardly bosom pals then. Let's move on to family," Tyler said.

Part of the victimology involved establishing a family tree for Syed Hammad. A family liaison officer had been assigned, and so far they'd found out his parents were deceased and he had a brother living in Pakistan.

Collins looked down at his notebook and reeled off some

new information. "Syed Hammad was engaged to a woman living in Pakistan. Her name is Fatima Abdullah. She's been informed of his death and is obviously distraught."

"Right," Tyler said. "Will we need a translator because I'll need to plan resources accordingly?"

Collins shook his head. "She speaks English."

Tyler nodded and picked up his briefing notes. He pulled at his tie, loosening it a little and opened the top button of his shirt. It was hot in here already and it wasn't even half past eight yet.

He turned to the analyst, Evie Charlesworth, who was generating a timeline of events and looking at whether there were any similar cases recently. "Anything to add, Evie?"

Evie reported on a few cases of toxic suicide in the last three years, but nothing recent. "I'm looking into similarities or potential links. But so far it looks like a stand-alone."

Tyler nodded. "Good, the last thing we want is cases like this springing up all over the country."

Towards the end of the briefing, Tyler paused to gulp down coffee, and then assigned actions to the team. He asked Charlotte to visit the hospital and talk to Vinnie Pearson if he was well enough for questioning, and he gave Mackinnon the task of chasing up CCTV footage from the incident. He wanted Collins to go back to East Street and speak to the only shop owner who hadn't yet been questioned: Pete Morton, the manager of the mobile phone shop.

"And I'll be having a chat with Syed Hammad's fiancée this morning," Tyler said.

While talking to the relatives of the recently deceased wasn't a task anyone relished, it was important to talk to them as soon as possible after the death when details were still fresh in their minds. If anyone could give them a good indication of Syed Hammad's frame of mind, it should be his fiancée.

Once he'd finished getting updates from everyone in the

room, Tyler raised his hands to indicate an open-floor. They tended to do this at the end of the briefings, particularly when the case was as perplexing as this. Taking a few minutes to brainstorm and come up with theories or new questions could take the investigation in a new direction and generate fresh leads.

DC Webb said what everybody else was thinking, "Why go to all that trouble for a suicide? Why not just take some pills and drink a bottle of whiskey? Or even if he had his heart set on that stinking gas, why didn't he do it in the bathroom? Why put other people at risk?"

Tyler said, "I did suggest yesterday there could be religious reasons behind the method. In many religions suicide is a sin. Maybe by using that elaborate setup and not actually mixing the chemicals himself meant, from his point of view, he didn't kill himself..."

DC Webb snorted.

Charlotte spoke up, "We can't rule out the possibility that this was some kind of vigilante effort by Syed Hammad. We've got records of him complaining about harassment from a group of youths. It's a huge coincidence that they are in the shop at the exact moment he tries to kill himself. Maybe this was an attempt to deter the gang that went wrong."

Tyler nodded. "That's a fair point, but we do have a suicide note."

Mackinnon ran a hand through his hair. There was something about the note that struck an odd note. A suicide note was pretty clear evidence Syed Hammad had intended to take his own life and yet ... there was something off.

"The note was printed on a generic printer," Mackinnon said.

Tyler nodded. "We should have confirmation of the likely type of printer used by the end of today."

"But he didn't have a printer in the shop, or in his flat upstairs?"

Tyler paused, pursed his lips, then said, "No, he didn't, and we need to find out where it was printed. At a friend's perhaps, or the local library. He did have a computer, an old model and that's gone to the high-tech crime unit for analysis."

As there were no more comments forthcoming, Tyler began to gather his briefing notes. "I shouldn't have to say this, but I will anyway. None of this gets out to the press. There'll be a lot of interest in this case, but everything released to the media will go through official channels." He looked around the room, making sure he had made his point.

There were murmurs and nods from the team, and Tyler drew the meeting to a close. "You all know what you have to do. Do it well," he said with a wink. "Make me look good."

After the briefing, Mackinnon took a moment to call Fiona to let her know he had contact details for a potential carer for Luke.

Fiona Evans sounded on edge when she answered his call. But Mackinnon liked to think her tone warmed a little when she knew it was him.

"I can bring the card round after work, if you like?" Mackinnon offered.

He could have given her the agency number over the phone, but he felt like he should go in person. He wanted to see how they were doing.

CHAPTER ELEVEN

COLLINS TURNED HIS CAR INTO East Street. The street looked very different today, with people bustling along, going about their day-to-day business. The only sign that anything unusual happened yesterday was the police tape across the front of the newsagent's.

He slowed the car to a crawl and pulled over in front of the parade of shops, managing to squeeze into a parking bay just ahead of the bus stop.

He killed the engine, climbed out and walked towards the mobile phone store. The glass frontage was plastered with banners advertising special offers and deals for different networks.

A bell rang as Collins pushed open the door. There was only one member of staff behind the counter, and a female customer stood in front of him, leaning over and studying a mobile phone.

The man serving her was around five foot eight. Mid-thirties, Collins guessed. He had far too much gel in his hair, which stood up in little tufts. A gold earring glinted from one ear, and his skin, despite the fact it was still early in the morning, had a greasy sheen to it. The smile on his face was stretched too wide to be genuine.

The man caught Collins' eye, smiled, gave him a nod and said, "I'll be with you in a minute."

Collins used the time to look around the shop, looking at the new, fancy models of mobile phones. It seemed to him, only a couple of years ago the trend had been towards smaller and smaller phones. The smaller the better. Now they seemed to be getting bigger. The phones most prominently displayed had large screens and were more like computers than phones.

He stared at one particularly bulky phone. How was that supposed to fit in your pocket? He thought the whole point of these things was the fact they were supposed to be mobile.

Unfortunately the female customer was rather taken with the mobile phone she'd been looking at and decided to buy it. The man behind the counter was grinning and almost bowing as he pulled out forms for her to fill in.

Some ten minutes later, the woman, with her new mobile phone in a bright-blue carrier bag, strolled out of the shop, smiling.

The man turned his attention to Collins. "I'm sorry to keep you waiting. How can I help? Are you looking for an upgrade?"

Collins held up his police warrant card. "DC Collins, City of London police."

The smile slid from the man's face. "Oh, I thought I was due a visit. You'll be wanting to ask me about the stuff that went on at Syed's place."

Collins nodded.

"I don't really know anything. Not much I can tell you."

Collins tried for a friendly tone. "What's your name, sir?"

"Oh, sorry. It's Pete Morton. I'm the manager here."

"What time did you shut up shop yesterday?"

"We close at five-thirty, and I went straight home," Pete Morton said and nodded furiously, almost as if he was trying to convince himself. "So I can't help you because I wasn't here when it happened."

"And where's home?"

"Walthamstow." Pete Morton recited his address, and Collins wrote it down.

"You weren't here during the incident ... but you know what time it occurred?"

Pete Morton's eyes widened slowly. He swallowed hard. "Well, yes, but only because everyone around here has been talking about it today."

Collins noted the flush in Pete Morton's cheeks. Some people were better at concealing the truth than others.

Pete Morton was hiding something.

"Did you notice anything unusual yesterday? Anyone hanging about?"

Pete Morton frowned. "Hanging about? I thought Syed killed himself."

Collins nodded, but stayed silent, using Mackinnon's trick of letting the person he was questioning stew for a bit.

"I mean," Pete Morton continued. "That's what I heard. He made some kind of chemical gas and topped himself, didn't he?"

Collins took a breath. "There was hydrogen sulphide gas at the scene. We are trying to talk to people who knew him, people who came into contact with him every day like you."

"Why?" Pete Morton's Adam's apple bobbed up and down. "Am I at risk?"

"No. The gas has dispersed. The levels were closely monitored last night, so you don't have anything to worry about on that score, but we do want to find out as much as we can about Syed. It seems he didn't have family in the UK, so we're finding it quite hard to gather information. How well did you know him?"

Pete Morton shook his head and looked down at the floor. "Oh, well, hardly at all. I said hello now and again. You know how it is." He licked his lips.

It was hard to find the right questions. Collins knew Pete Morton was trying to conceal something. But it was hard to tell whether his secret had any relevance to Syed Hammad's death.

Collins liked to think he was a good judge of character, but sometimes it could be a problem. He might sense when someone was lying, but they might be lying about something completely irrelevant. Pete Morton might be sweating because he had a series of unpaid traffic tickets.

As Collins continued with routine questions, Pete Morton started to shuffle from foot to foot. His arms swung at his sides, then crossed his chest, only to fall back to his sides again.

Usually Collins would have just asked a few general questions, perhaps a ten minute chat, especially with someone like Pete Morton, who hadn't been anywhere near East Street during the incident, but the longer Collins spent talking to him the more likely Morton would make a mistake, and Collins could get to the bottom of whatever he was hiding.

"Phones these days," Collins said. "Quite amazing how far they've come in the last few years. You can make notes, take photos, send emails – they're like mini computers, aren't they?" Collins walked across to the display of mobile phones dotted across the wall.

Pete Morton looked a little thrown by the change in subject. "Yeah, I suppose they are."

Collins picked up one of the phones. It was a plastic model with a fake screen and was attached to the wall with a stretchy black cable. Presumably so it couldn't be stolen, although why someone would want to steal a pretend mobile phone, Collins had no idea.

"So, you said you didn't see Mr. Hammad at all yesterday. Are you sure?"

Pete Morton was now sweating profusely. Under his arms damp patches were spreading. "Erm, I can't really remember. I suppose I may have seen him in the morning. But I didn't notice anything out of the ordinary."

"Had he seemed depressed recently?"

Pete Morton blinked. "Depressed? Well, I suppose he must have been if he topped himself, mustn't he? But, like I said, I hardly knew him."

"How long had you known him?"

"A couple of years, I suppose. As long as I've worked here."

Despite the fact Pete Morton was getting more and more uptight, Collins couldn't work out what he was hiding.

Pete Morton wiped his hands on his suit trousers, and his eyes flitted around the shop, resting on the phone display, the till, then the window. Looking everywhere except at Collins.

"So you think he topped himself then? I heard that those kids had been bothering him again. They were always hassling him. Maybe he'd had enough."

Collins shrugged. "Maybe."

Pete Morton seemed very eager to distance himself from Syed Hammad. Collins might not find out why today, but he would. If there was a link between Pete Morton and Syed Hammad's death, Collins would find it.

CHAPTER TWELVE

CRAIG FOSTER GRUNTED WITH RELIEF when he opened the front door to his ground floor flat in Bexley house.

Sweat trickled down his back. The walk back from the kebab house seemed to get longer with each visit. He supposed he should think about getting a little fitter and maybe cutting down on the takeaways.

He'd start on Monday. There was no way he could start cutting out his favourite foods now, not with all the stress he was going through.

Craig pulled out his new mobile. He'd been scared to use it at first. He had some crazy idea it might lead the police to his door. He considered chucking it in the Thames, but in the end, decided as he had been through hell to get it, he may as well use it, and he'd put his old sim card in it this morning.

A quick glance at the screen told him he had no missed calls, no messages. Craig tightened his grip on the phone.

He hadn't heard anything from Vinnie since the newsagent's job went tits up. Rumours had been flying around the estate. Lowered voices, gossiping away, talking about how

Syed killed himself and tried to take the rest of East Street with him. But none of them knew what really happened. They hadn't been there.

Craig shuddered remembering the feeling of being trapped in the shop. It was bloody Vinnie's fault. There was no doubt in Craig's mind it had to do with the Brewerton brothers. Everyone knew Vinnie had pissed them off. But what annoyed Craig was the fact Vinnie must have had some idea of the danger they were walking into, but he'd said nothing. He let Craig and the others walk into a trap.

It was the last time he did any jobs with Vinnie.

He'd really thought he was a goner. God, what a horrible feeling. If he hadn't gathered the strength to lift that stool and smash it through the glass, they'd probably have all gone the way of Syed Hammad.

Craig had never really liked Syed. He always felt like the newsagent was looking down at him somehow. Judging him if he bought a copy of the Sun, or if he bought more than one chocolate bar at a time.

No. He would never work with Vinnie again, but he did want to know what was going on. The police would want to nab a suspect, and Craig didn't want it to be him. He'd have to lie low for a while and hope the police concentrated on Vinnie and the Brewertons. But as he'd heard Vinnie was still in hospital he would have to wait. There was no way he could risk a visit.

He walked down the hallway, squeezing past a bag of rubbish he hadn't taken out to the chute yet. It was getting a bit whiffy. He wrinkled his nose. He'd take them out just as soon as he'd finished eating his kebab.

He opened a window in the front room, letting a bit of fresh air into the flat. He stood by the open window for a moment, hoping to feel a cool breeze, but the evening was stinking hot.

Disappointed, he removed the white, plastic carrier bag that had been looped over his arm as he stomped around the coffee table. The couch creaked as he lowered his ample backside onto it. Bloody sofa. It was a tatty brown velvet thing that sagged in the middle and was covered with food stains. He'd inherited it from his mum years ago.

Craig kicked off his trainers and put his feet up on the coffee table. Sometimes he missed his ex-girlfriend, Kelly, but right now he was grateful she wasn't here to complain about his smelly feet like she used to.

He pulled out a can of Coke from the carrier bag. The steamy heat from the kebab had condensed against the cold can. He wiped it against his jeans to get rid of the water droplets.

He popped the ring pull and took a long drink. The fizzy liquid instantly cooled his throat and quenched his thirst. That was better. He'd needed that. He was sick of summer already. It was far too hot outside. It was all right for places like Spain. They had air conditioning, so you could fry yourself under the sun all day and then go back to your nice cool room and have a good night's sleep. Tonight he'd have to sleep in a stuffy bedroom, sweating like a bastard.

In his opinion, summer was overrated.

Craig didn't bother with a plate. He pulled out the plastic carton containing the extra-large kebab and chips. He left his double cheeseburger on the coffee table. If he couldn't manage it now, he'd have it as a snack later.

He screwed up the carrier bag and dumped it on the floor next to his trainers. He wrinkled his nose. What was that awful smell?

He sniffed the kebab. No, it wasn't that. He looked suspiciously down at his feet… Maybe Kelly had had a point.

He decided to change his socks after dinner, settled back

into the sofa and grabbed the remote control, while trying not to drop any of the kebab's contents onto his lap.

There were some benefits of living alone. He always kept the remote balancing on the arm of the sofa so it was within reach whenever he wanted it. It used to drive him nuts when Kelly would leave it by the television. What was the point of a remote control if he had to get up and walk to the television to change the channel anyway?

He pressed the red power button and groaned as the news appeared. Changing the channel brought up male athletes in Lycra, limbering up by the side of the track for the men's running. Craig stopped chewing. God, that Lycra left nothing to the imagination. How was he supposed to eat while watching them parade around with it all hanging out?

He quickly changed the channel again. There was some kind of reality show on ITV. That was better than nothing, so he left it on and listened to some silly old bint singing her heart out.

He sniffed again. That smell was getting worse. It smelled of blocked drains. A prickling sensation crawled over his skin. That was how it had started in the newsagent's – a subtle smell like this that got worse and worse until … No. He shook his head. He was being paranoid. Imagining things. He would empty the bins tonight. And if that didn't solve it, he would have to get on to the council, get them to sort it out.

He took a large bite of his kebab, and the juice from the meat trickled down his chin. He wiped the greasy drips away with the back of his hand. It might be messy, but it tasted bloody handsome.

Craig took another swig of coke then belched loudly. He shovelled the last of his chips in his mouth, stifling a yawn. He was so sick of this hot weather. It made him feel tired all the time.

He dumped some of the lettuce from inside the kebab - he

didn't want that filling him up - and polished off the kebab in one final large bite.

He had just put the polystyrene container back on the coffee table and reached for his cheeseburger when there was a knock at the door. Craig dropped the burger back on the table and got to his feet heavily. Who the hell could that be at this time of night?

Craig waddled down the corridor towards the front door. That was funny. His front door had a glass panel, which meant he could usually see the shadow of whoever was outside. But there was nothing there. No shadow, no silhouette. Nothing.

Craig had tried to get the council to replace the door. Anyone with an ounce of common sense would realise a glass-panelled door was a security risk here on the Towers Estate, but common sense was probably asking too much from the council. Technically, it was a housing association now, but there wasn't much difference between them and the council in Craig's opinion.

He opened his front door, keeping the chain on because you never really knew who you might come up against on the estate.

Craig was a big bloke, so he wasn't as vulnerable as some. But there was no point in being careless. Size didn't mean much when knives were involved. Lots of the kids on the estate carried some sort of weapon. Knives were common. Craig had even heard rumours of certain gangs carrying guns. With those kinds of nutters about, a bloke couldn't be too careful. Sometimes size could actually make you a target.

He pushed the door as far as the security chain would allow, and peeked through the crack.

There was no one there. His eyes scanned the empty corridor.

He closed the door, so he could remove the security chain, then he opened the door fully and stuck his head outside.

Nothing.

A movement to his left caught his eye, and he jerked his head inside. His fingers gripped the door, ready to slam it shut, when he realised it was just a cat.

The tabby cat sat back on its haunches and stared back at Craig with huge green eyes. The cat kept its distance, eyeing Craig warily before disappearing into the stair lobby.

Craig blew out a breath and grinned. Why was he so jumpy tonight? It was to be expected after what happened at the newsagent's, he supposed. Because of Vinnie Pearson.

Craig shook his head and went back inside, slamming the door behind him. It was probably kids, having a laugh, knocking then running away. Well, next time they rang, he wasn't going to answer.

Feeling stuffed and uncomfortable, he wrapped his arms around his belly as he waddled back into the lounge. He went to sit down on the sofa, reaching out for his burger at the same time, when he noticed something odd.

A movement outside.

Craig blinked and stood up slowly. He moved towards the window.

Although Craig had a ground floor flat, there was only a small patch of grass outside, and he didn't normally see people walking by. Most people tended to use the path. Every now and then he'd see a couple of kids kicking a ball around during the day, but even that was pretty rare. Especially after Craig had sworn at them and told them to bugger off.

Craig stared out at the shadows. The council had put up a number of lights after complaints by the residents, but most of them had been vandalised, which gave the grounds around the block of flats an eerie, shadowy appearance.

He couldn't see anyone out there. Maybe he'd imagined it. He really needed to relax.

He was just about to turn away and get back to his burger

when he noticed there was something propped up against the window.

It looked like a sheet of paper. He picked it up. It was A4-sized and it had been laminated. It was blank on one side. Craig turned it over and saw that there was a message written on the other side.

Warning.

Toxic gas. Suicide committed inside.

Do not enter. Call 999.

And there was a bloody skull and crossbones printed at the bottom of the sheet.

Craig looked outside again, staring into the darkness.

What the hell was going on? That wasn't there earlier. He would have seen it.

He frowned and tried to remember the last time he'd looked at the window. Was it there when he opened the window earlier? He hadn't really been paying attention. It could have been there for a while.

The smell … It washed over him again, worse now.

His breath caught in his throat. There was no mistaking it now. It was the same smell…

He had to get out of here.

He spun around, faster than he'd ever moved before. He knew what effect that gas would have on him. He didn't have long. He needed to get out into the fresh air.

His life depended on it.

But Craig Foster didn't get very far. There, standing in the doorway, was a figure dressed in black. He wore some kind of mask and looked like something out of 'Call of Duty.'

Craig's heart nearly jumped out of his chest. He willed his arms and legs to move, but they remained frozen, like big useless lumps of flesh. He stayed rooted to the spot as the man in black approached him.

Now, the man was so close Craig could see the darkness

beyond the distorted eye-piece of the mask. The man said, "Hello, Craig. Are you ready?"

Craig bent double as the acrid gas washed over him and made him want to gag.

Craig's lower lip wobbled as he asked, "Ready for what?"

"Justice, Craig," the masked man said. "Are you ready for Justice?"

CHAPTER THIRTEEN

THE KILLER HAD TO TAKE off his gas mask in the stairwell before he left Bexley House.

No one would pay any attention to a man dressed in dark clothes walking down the street in this neighbourhood, but even the self-absorbed residents around here might notice the gas mask.

He shoved it into his black holdall and chucked the bag over his arm. He looked like a normal middle-aged man heading to the gym. Innocent enough. Nothing about him stood out. There was no reason for anyone to remember him.

He pushed open the swing doors and left the flats, sucking in the warm, clean night air and smiling to himself. He'd done a good job tonight.

One down. Four to go.

Vinnie Pearson had made it almost too easy, getting his four friends to descend on the newsagent's. Not knowing that that was what the killer wanted all along. He wasn't sure if they had all been involved in the riots last summer, but it didn't really matter. They'd all gone along with Vinnie, prepared to trash the newsagent's. And it wasn't the first time for any of them. They all deserved it.

They were all crying out for justice.

Killing them with the gas in the shop would have been too easy. That would hardly have been a worthy punishment. He wanted them to be afraid. To know that he was coming for them, hunting them down. To know that there was no escape.

They deserved to suffer.

The killer slipped his right hand in his pocket and touched the cool smooth surface of the mobile phone he'd taken from Craig Foster's dead body.

He strolled along under the rustling plane trees that lined the road. He could hear a few lairy shouts from the punters in the pub in the distance. The warm weather always brought out that type of person.

He narrowed his eyes. A group of men stood outside the pub, laughing, joking and waving their pint glasses around. It was all very amiable now, but how long would that last? Someone would say the wrong thing at the wrong time and it would all kick-off.

The happy revellers turned his stomach. He turned away.

They had no idea. They weren't bothered what kind of depravity went on right under their noses as long as it didn't affect their sad little lives.

Dante had once said, "The hottest places in hell are reserved for those who maintain neutrality."

The killer needed a drink, something to stop the shaking. His hands were trembling uncontrollably. This was unexpected. Was it some kind of delayed reaction?

He couldn't believe he'd actually done it. He'd performed the execution. He turned Craig Foster's flat into a gas chamber. Rather fitting and thoroughly deserved.

The killer had done his research. He knew Craig Foster deserved this. He'd stolen things and trashed honest businesses, just wandering in and taking what he wanted. Scum of the earth.

So why was he still shaking?

This wasn't right. He should be feeling good. Craig Foster had it coming.

The killer rubbed a hand across his face. He couldn't wipe the image of Craig Foster stumbling to his knees out of his mind.

For some reason, the line from the Wilfred Owen poem, *Dulce et Decorum est*, ran through his mind on repeat.

He didn't want it to. He tried to shove it away, to block it out, but it kept coming. Those words…

"He plunges at me, guttering, choking, drowning."

The poem was about the effects of mustard gas in World War I. He'd read it at school, but he hadn't thought about it for years.

The killer had stood there, wearing his gas mask with the hydrogen sulphide filter, and watched the life fade from Craig Foster.

And he'd felt something.

A horrible feeling of self-doubt. A feeling that he might be wrong.

He shouldn't doubt himself. How many years had he been planning this? How carefully had he arranged everything? There was no time for second thoughts now.

This was his purpose.

He was right. What he was doing was right. This element of doubt sneaking into his brain contaminated his thought process. He wasn't thinking logically. He was questioning things, things he knew for certain.

The killer entered the Duke's Head. The scent of beer and stale sweat wrapped themselves around him, but he could still smell it. The sulphur. The stench of Craig Foster's death.

He manoeuvred his way through the rowdy crowd of

drinkers who were celebrating a heady day of summer, so rare in England. The Olympics had been going well and there was a strange feeling settling on London, the complete opposite of this time last year, one of camaraderie.

It was hard to believe that only last summer fires had raged, businesses had gone under and lives were destroyed. How quickly people forgot.

At the bar, the killer ordered a double whiskey and took it off to a corner. There weren't any spare tables, so he stood by the window, staring out as he sipped his drink.

He knew what would make him feel better. He dropped his black holdall on the floor. Kneeling beside it, he rummaged through the contents, taking care that no one inside the pub could see into the bag. The last thing he wanted was for someone to spot the gas mask.

The killer pulled out a battered black notebook. He ran his fingers across the worn leather surface and smiled before zipping up the bag. As soon as he held the book in his hands, he felt a feeling of calm and renewed sense of purpose wash over him. He was doing the right thing.

He opened the book and looked at the quotes he had neatly printed out on the pages over the years. On the first page, he had copied a quote from Leonardo da Vinci, "He who does not punish evil commands it to be done."

The killer closed his eyes, savouring the peaty taste of the single malt on his tongue, and let the words roll over him, willing them to sink into his consciousness.

On the next page of his notebook he had printed in capitals the words of Winston Churchill from the War Office departmental minutes from 1919, "I AM STRONGLY IN FAVOUR OF USING POISON GASES AGAINST UNCIVILISED TRIBES."

The killer took a deep, calming breath. Craig Foster was nothing if not uncivilised.

He deserved everything he got. If someone like Winston

Churchill thought it was the right thing to do, then he was worrying about nothing.

He was too hard on himself. It should never be easy to take another life. To stand there and look that person in the eye as their life slipped away wasn't pleasant, but he owed it to them.

He passed the sentence, which meant he should be the one to kill them.

The fact was that if he was unable to do that, to look them in the eyes as he took their lives, then perhaps that person didn't deserve to die after all, and that would change everything.

The killer wasn't crazy. He wasn't one of those people who thought they could change the world on a grand scale. He didn't think people would remember him, or write about him after he was dead. There wouldn't be any articles or TV shows. He didn't want that anyway.

There weren't many people in this world whom history would remember. He didn't expect to be able to change the way people thought.

It was hard to change society, but if everybody tried to change small events, if people stood up for their ideals, it could start something. It could start a ripple … and that ripple would spread.

The killer turned to the third page of his notebook where he'd copied out the thoughts that passed through his mind as he planned his campaign for justice. His eyes scanned the dark, squashed text, looking for his favourite quote from Dante. He knew them all by heart, but there was something about seeing them written down, something reassuring.

All too often, people were content to sit back and do nothing, even when confronted with the most awful degradation of society, as long as it didn't impinge on their everyday comforts.

He wasn't like that.

He was doing the right thing. He was standing up for something he believed in.

The killer drained the last of his whiskey and headed outside.

Yes, he was doing the right thing, and he wasn't going to stop.

CHAPTER FOURTEEN

AFTER THE DEBRIEFING, MACKINNON HEADED over to Fiona Evans' house in Twickenham to drop off Tim Coleman's card.

Fiona let him in and led him into the kitchen where her daughter sat at the kitchen table scribbling furiously in a Disney colouring book. The little girl was so busy making sure the blue crayon she was using to colour the princess's dress stayed within the lines she didn't look up when Mackinnon entered.

"Hello, Anna," Mackinnon said.

Her eyes flickered upwards for a moment, and she smiled shyly before returning to her colouring. "Hello."

"Come on, sweetheart," Fiona said. "It's time for bed."

Anna pouted and dropped her blue crayon on the kitchen table. "Oh, just a little while longer."

Fiona shook her head. "No, it's bedtime. I'll come and tuck you in after you've cleaned your teeth."

Anna gathered her crayons together, putting them back in the pencil case slowly, all the time looking at her mother with a doleful expression. When that didn't work, she tucked the colouring book beneath her arm and shuffled out of the kitchen.

Fiona turned to Mackinnon. "I was just about to open a bottle of wine. Would you like a glass?"

"Thanks."

As Fiona set two wine glasses on the scrubbed pine surface of the kitchen table and took a bottle of white wine from the fridge, Mackinnon fumbled in his pocket for the agency card.

He put it down on the table in front of him. "His name is Tim Coleman, and he works as a carer. I don't know much about the agency, or whether he'll be suitable, but I knew you were looking for some extra help with Luke."

"Thanks, Jack. I appreciate it. It's really hard to get someone you trust."

Mackinnon pushed back from the table a little. "He did say that the agency worked with the NHS in some cases."

Fiona smiled and looked down at the card. "I'll give the agency a ring and check them out." Fiona poured a generous measure of Chardonnay into both of the glasses. "Money is not such a problem now," she said.

Mackinnon looked up at her. "It isn't?" Immediately his mind was full of all kinds of scenarios. Had Bruce stashed some money somewhere?

Fiona pushed one of the glasses across the table to Mackinnon and gave a twisted smile. "My parents are well off," she said. "Bruce didn't want to accept their money. He wanted to support us himself. But now..."

Fiona sighed and sank down into a chair, propping her elbows on the kitchen table and resting her head in her hands for a moment before taking a long sip of wine.

"Things weren't exactly easy in the months before Bruce died. Luke was attending a clinic that promised us the world and cost us a fortune. We were struggling financially, to be honest. My parents offered to help, but Bruce was stubborn.

"And you know what a police officer's salary is like. I wasn't working, and it wasn't easy to make ends meet. I wanted to accept the money from my mum and dad, but Bruce wouldn't hear of it."

Mackinnon took a sip of the ice cold Chardonnay and wished it was a beer. He wasn't a big fan of white wine, but on a warm night like tonight it was at least refreshing. He couldn't understand it. If Fiona's parents were offering to give them money to pay for Luke's rehabilitation, why would Bruce risk everything for a bribe?

He'd gambled on his career. He understood Bruce may have had his pride, but surely accepting some money from his in-laws would have been a better option than taking dirty money from a drug dealer.

Mackinnon was lost in thought as he stared down, watching droplets of water trickle through the condensation on the outside of his glass.

Fiona reached out and touched his hand. Mackinnon's eyes flickered up from the wine glass and met hers. There was something in the familiarity of the gesture that made him feel uncomfortable.

Mackinnon pulled his hand away, picked up his glass and swallowed the rest of the wine. "Thanks for the drink. I'd better get back. We're in the middle of a busy case at the moment."

Fiona sat back in her chair. "You're going back to work tonight?"

"Trawling through paperwork, not much fun. Chloe is not going to be happy," Mackinnon said, not really knowing why he felt the need to mention Chloe. "But I guess you'd know what it's like being married to a police officer."

"I didn't realise you were married," Fiona said. Her gaze

fixed on Mackinnon's left-hand.

"I'm not, but I live with Chloe. Well, not all the time. She lives in Oxford, so I spend a lot of my time driving between London and Oxford. It's not easy but we make it work."

He was rambling, but he didn't want to send Fiona the wrong signals.

"Right," Mackinnon said, standing up. "I'd better be off. Thanks again for the wine."

"Any time. Thanks for dropping off the card. I'll give the agency a call tomorrow."

As Mackinnon was about to leave, Fiona lay a hand on his arm and said, "Thank you for thinking of us. You're a good man, Jack."

Mackinnon was lost for words.

At the end of the driveway, he looked back at the house and saw Anna staring at him from one of the top floor windows.

"I think someone else wants to say goodbye." Mackinnon nodded at the window and grinned, waving back at the little girl.

Fiona stepped out of the doorway and then peered up at the window.

Anna quickly disappeared from view behind a swishing curtain.

Fiona rolled her eyes. "She's supposed to be in bed. I thought she'd been too quiet."

As Mackinnon walked back to the train station, he considered why he'd been so quick to bring up Chloe. He wanted to help Fiona and her children. He felt he owed them something. But the last thing he wanted to do was give Fiona the wrong idea about his visits.

It hadn't been that long since Bruce died, so perhaps she wasn't even thinking that way. Perhaps he'd been reading too much into things.

CHAPTER FIFTEEN

CHARLOTTE GOT BACK TO HER flat at just after eight p.m. She then spent the next hour checking the place was secure.

She had fallen into a routine now and could do a circuit of the flat in one thirty-minute sweep.

An hour a day. Half an hour before leaving in the morning and half an hour after returning home. First she did a loop of the whole flat, checking nothing had been moved, then she moved on to the balcony doors and checked each window in turn, running her fingers along the frames, making sure everything was just as she'd left it.

At eight twenty-five she had almost finished when she remembered that she'd missed the window in the sodding bathroom.

Now she would have to start all over again.

Thirty anxious minutes later, she poured herself a glass of cranberry juice and laced it with a hefty slug of vodka. She liked to think it was practically healthy with all that vitamin C making up for the alcohol.

She knew she should cut down because it had gotten to the

point where she needed a couple of drinks every night to get to sleep and that wasn't good.

She sighed and took a sip, enjoying the sharp, dry taste of the cranberry.

It had been a long day, but she wanted to do a little research. She opened up her beat-up old laptop. The fan started making an awful noise almost immediately, a kind of whirring, almost a groan. It wouldn't last much longer. Great. More expense. It was expensive enough living in London without all these little extras.

Over the past few weeks, she'd been thinking of moving. A fresh start, a new job, a new home.

She looked around her living room, fit to bursting with one armchair, a two-seater sofa and a little coffee table. She'd be able to afford something bigger if she moved away from London.

She'd been thinking about fresh starts a lot recently, thinking it might help with all the strange habits she'd been developing. She attended counselling for a little while, under duress. Her GP had been quite insistent it would help. It hadn't. The only thing she'd gotten out of it was a name for her weird behaviour: OCD.

But knowing what it was didn't make it go away.

Starting over, in another part of the country, would give her a chance to put all this crap behind her.

She took another sip of her drink, still no closer to coming to a decision. Glancing down at her laptop, she saw that the computer had finally booted up. She clicked on the browser icon and muttered a prayer, hoping it didn't crash on her as it did fifty percent of the time.

Forty-five minutes and a number of Google searches later, she closed the lid of the laptop and sat back in disbelief. She couldn't believe people were making a profit from suicide. How could people make money from something like that?

She'd forgotten all about her vodka and cranberry.

She'd discovered sites where people sold gadgets to make sure the gas acted quickly and couldn't escape before they killed the subject.

They called them exit hoods.

Charlotte pushed the laptop away from her. She'd seen posts on forums where desperate people declared their intent to kill themselves, even giving dates and times. And people were actually encouraging them, telling them how brave they were and that they were doing the right thing.

She wondered what their families would think if they knew.

So far, the information they'd gathered for the victimology hadn't indicated why Syed Hammad may have wanted to take his own life. They had spoken to people who had seen him every day, and so far, no one had said that Syed Hammad had been depressed let alone suicidal.

She picked up her drink and carried it to the window. She leaned on the windowsill, staring out at the East London skyline. There were so many people out there, some of them feeling desperate, helpless.

In this morning's briefing, DC Webb had said he could not understand how people could be so selfish.

But she could. She understood what it was like when you hadn't slept properly for weeks, when you never felt safe, not even for a moment.

She drained her glass. Maybe it was time for that fresh start.

CHAPTER SIXTEEN

PC STEWART ALLAN AND PC Rhonda Jones were called out to investigate the disturbance at Bexley house. PC Allan knocked on the door of flat number nine.

"The complaint came from number nine, didn't it?" PC Allan asked his colleague.

PC Jones rolled her eyes. "Yes. Don't tell me you've forgotten already."

She pushed in front of him and rapped on the door again, louder this time. Finally, the door was opened by a little grey-haired old lady. She beamed up at the officers.

"Come in. Come in," the old lady said.

They entered a hallway that was decorated with pink floral wallpaper and a deep pink carpet. Small tables and cabinets lined the side of the passageway, each with a dozen trinkets and statuettes of ballerinas balanced on top. PC Allan edged his way carefully past the precariously balanced ornaments.

"It's a very warm night," the old lady said. "Would you like a cup of tea?"

"That would be lovely," PC Allan said as he followed her into the sitting room.

The two officers sat down on an overstuffed sofa, and the old woman bustled off to make some tea.

PC Allan yawned and noticed PC Jones glaring at him. They should really have asked about the disturbance straightaway, but he was gasping for a cup of tea.

He stretched out his legs and tried to arrange the cushions behind him to get comfortable.

PC Jones shot him another look. She didn't like him much. He could tell. She was new and eager. Far too eager, in his opinion. It was all business with her. She hadn't yet learnt to slow down and actually talk to people. Ten years as a PC in this area had shown him just how important it was to create a rapport with the community.

They sat in silence until the little old lady brought the tea.

PC Allan smiled widely as he caught sight of the custard creams balanced on the tea tray.

The little old lady began to pour the tea and said, "You must be boiling in those uniforms. It is such a stifling evening. We must be due for a thunderstorm, don't you think?"

PC Jones frowned and pulled herself forward, struggling not to sink back into the cushions. "Could I take your name please, madam? And the details of the disturbance?"

The old lady pursed her lips and handed PC Jones a cup of tea.

PC Allan smiled at the little old lady as she handed him his cup. "What a charming tea service," he said, holding up the cup and admiring the delicate rose pattern and gold rim on the saucer.

The old lady beamed. "I am rather fond of this set. It was a wedding present, so it's over fifty years old. Would you believe in all that time I've only lost one saucer?"

"Er, yes. Lovely, I'm sure," PC Jones said. "But if we could talk about the disturbance? That is why we are here."

PC Allan took a bite of a custard cream. It was no use. He'd never worked with anyone with less people skills.

"Oh, yes," the lady said. "Of course. My name is Barbara Stanley, and I have lived here for over forty years."

"That's a long time," PC Allan said. "You must have seen a few changes."

PC Jones narrowed her eyes again. And before Barbara Stanley could answer, PC Jones balanced her biscuit on the saucer and said, "What time was the disturbance?"

"It would have been about an hour ago." Barbara Stanley took a sip of her tea. "Yes, that's right. I remember now. I looked at the clock because my quiz show had just started."

"And what sort of noise was it?" PC Jones asked with her pencil poised above her notebook.

"Shouting, a man's voice. He sounded very distressed, as if he was pleading for something."

"A man's voice?" PC Jones lowered her pencil. Her shoulders sagged.

PC Allan knew exactly what PC Jones was thinking. They had probably been dragged out here to investigate a man cheering an Olympic event on television. Still, it had to be checked out.

"It seems quiet enough now," PC Jones said.

"Yes," Barbara Stanley said. "I haven't heard another peep out of him."

PC Jones flipped shut her notebook, not even trying to hide her annoyance. But PC Allan wasn't annoyed. He liked the old lady, and it wasn't just because she'd given them tea and biscuits.

"We'll look into it now," he said, putting his cup and saucer back on the tray. "Do you know which flat the noise came from?"

"I'm pretty sure it was coming from the flat opposite me. A young man lives there. But I'm afraid I don't know his name. It's not like it used to be around here. When I moved here forty years ago, I knew every single one of my neighbours."

PC Allan got a sudden whiff of an unpleasant odour. It smelled like the drains were bad. He tried not to wrinkle his nose. He didn't like to mention it. The flat was spotless. The carpet had Hoover lines, and the polished surface of the coffee table gleamed. He presumed the smell was coming from outside.

As Mrs. Stanley took them to the front door, the smell seemed to get stronger. Mrs. Stanley gave a little cough.

"My goodness. I don't know what that smell is. It's not normally like that," she said, looking embarrassed.

She opened her front door and then pointed across the hall to a blue door. "It's that one. I'm sure the noise came from there."

She reached for the glasses that were hanging on a chain around her neck and perched them on the bridge of her nose. "Oh, that's very odd." She squinted across the hallway.

PC Allan followed her line of sight. There was a white notice stuck to the door. He frowned. That hadn't been there when they arrived. At least, he didn't think so. He looked back at PC Jones, who looked as concerned as he did.

His heart was thumping as he made his way across the corridor. He wasn't close enough to read the scrawled writing, but he already knew it was bad.

Even from Mrs. Stanley's doorway, he could see the skull and crossbones clearly.

PC Allan suppressed a shiver as he read the note.

He turned quickly. "We need to evacuate the building."

"Oh, my." Mrs. Stanley raised a hand to her mouth. "But what about Mr. Cecil?"

"Mr. Cecil?" PC Jones frowned. "Who is that?"

"My cat," Mrs. Stanley said as if it should be obvious. "I can't leave him."

"Bring your cat. Be as quick as you can and get outside. I'm going to tell the other residents." PC Allan began to walk towards the stairwell. "I'll meet you outside and explain further."

PC Jones nodded. "I'll call it in."

When he was sure all the flats were empty and all the residents were standing outside, PC Allan decided to take a look around the side of the building.

As the flat was on the ground floor, theoretically he should be able to peer in through the windows.

Leaving PC Jones to look after the residents and field their questions, he headed for the dark alleyway that ran along the side of the building. Soon the emergency services would be here along with someone more senior to take charge. He needed to get a better idea of what was happening. Perhaps they would need to evacuate the other blocks of flats in the area, too. It was hard to make a decision when he didn't really know what he was dealing with.

He walked across the flowerbed, zigzagging his way through the shrubs. He squeezed past a prickly bush and snagged his shirt. After he'd freed himself from the thorny branch he walked slowly to the back of the building.

By his calculations, if the flat was the same as Mrs. Stanley's, the window at the back should look into the sitting room.

His stomach flipped over as he saw another note propped up on the inside of the window, identical to the one on the front door. The same skull and crossbones. The same "DANGER. KEEP OUT" printed in capital letters.

The windows were double glazed, but despite that, he thought he could still smell that awful rotten stench. He knew what it was now. He'd been told about it during training a couple of years ago. Hydrogen sulphide gave off a character-istic smell of rotten eggs.

It was probably a suicide.

He took a step back from the window, and then a horrible thought crept inside his mind. What if the owner of the flat was still alive?

What if he could save him?

PC Allan moved closer to the window, leaning his forehead against the cold glass. The lights were on inside the flat, but he couldn't see anything. The light from the television flickered, giving the domestic scene an eerie feel.

His breath was steaming up the glass.

He wiped away the fog with the sleeve of his jumper and looked again. His eyes searched the room. There was a half-eaten takeaway burger on the coffee table. A brown, tatty sofa sat back against one wall.

Then he saw the body.

It was mostly hidden by the sofa. PC Allan swallowed. All his training had taught him not to enter the scene unprotected. The specialist team would be here soon.

In the distance, sirens sounded. PC Allan ran back around the side of the building, ready to tell the team the location of the victim. But he had a horrible feeling they were too late.

CHAPTER SEVENTEEN

EVIE CHARLESWORTH SAT AT HER desk at seven a.m. the following morning, cradling a cup of coffee, steaming hot, black with one sugar, just the way she liked it.

She squinted at the Excel spreadsheet on her screen. She was happy to work with whichever system the senior investigating officer was comfortable with, and DCI Brookbank liked Excel.

Personally, she preferred i2 charts. But in her job she needed to be flexible.

She scanned the columns on the spreadsheet. Each column had its own heading – date, time, location, victim age, victim occupation, known associates and so on.

They had set up a timeline of the event and a family tree for the victim. As most of Syed Hammad's family lived in Pakistan that hadn't been easy. Most of the information in the timeline had come from interviews of the people in the shops either side of Syed Hammad's newsagent's. This morning, Evie had to work on the victimology and try to tease out threads of associations. Although they didn't have any suspects identified, and Syed Hammad's death was still being treated as a suicide, it was still essential to identify who else had been there at the time.

Yesterday, she'd been working through Syed Hammad's phone records, trying to cross reference the numbers and draw up an association chart, but so far she hadn't found any link between Syed Hammad and the youngsters who had been found in the shop.

Perhaps when they'd managed to identify the rest of the gang of youths from the CCTV or old-fashioned questioning, she might have more luck. It would certainly make her analysis easier. Evie sighed and took a sip of her coffee. She could do with a bit of luck.

She checked her watch. She didn't have long until the morning briefing.

Evie was required to attend the morning and evening briefings, and it was her job to keep the charts updated so the senior investigating officer always had the most up-to-date information to hand. Luckily so far, Brookbank was proving to be relatively forward thinking. Evie didn't think she would have any trouble with him. On her last case, she had worked with an older SIO, and she'd left that job feeling demoralised. Unfortunately, some people still viewed analysts as paper pushers, and were reluctant to use them to their full potential.

An analyst's role was so much more than typing and displaying pretty charts. When analysts were used to their full capacity, they helped to steer and direct the inquiry.

Evie heard a low whistle from the desk directly behind her. She turned around.

The Holmes indexer, Emmie Foxall, gestured for her to come over. "Evie, take a look at this."

Evie wheeled her chair towards Emmie's desk, and Emmie shuffled along so that Evie could see the screen.

"Have a look at this, Evie. What do you make of it?"

Emmie grinned and took a sip of coffee from her yellow Tweetie Pie mug.

Evie moved closer to the computer screen. Small details unearthed during the course of an investigation could change the whole direction of the case. It wasn't all about getting a list of suspects. The details formed the fabric of the case and were essential for a successful prosecution.

Evie stared at the screen. "Another suicide. The same method. The same gas."

Evie stood up, her coffee forgotten. "The DCI needs to hear this. Right now."

CHAPTER EIGHTEEN

THIRTY MINUTES LATER, MACKINNON ARRIVED at Wood Street. He filed into the major incident room with the rest of the team, and immediately saw that DCI Brookbank would be heading this one.

The DCI shuffled through his notes at the front of the room. DI Tyler leaned on the desk beside him, looking like he was trying to attract the DCI's attention.

Charlotte walked into the room, yawning. Followed by DC Webb, with his hair perfectly gelled, obviously trying out a new style. He had to be almost forty, but there was something about him that gave him the appearance of youth. Although that was probably more to do with his personality than his looks.

DC Collins was the last member of MIT to enter the room. He sat down in a chair beside Mackinnon. "I've not missed anything yet then?"

Mackinnon shook his head. "Not started yet."

"There's something big going down apparently," Collins said. "Something they've picked up from Holmes."

DCI Brookbank cleared his throat and looked up from his notes. "Right then," he said and cracked his knuckles. "Let's get started. First up, we have some new information. There has been another suicide involving hydrogen sulphide at a flat on the Towers Estate."

DCI Brookbank paused, but the room was silent.

"There was only one casualty, the suicide victim, Craig Foster. All the other residents in Bexley House were evacuated." Brookbank tapped a key on his laptop, and the screen behind him flickered as the suicide note was projected onto its white surface.

DC Webb whistled, but no one said anything for a few moments. They were all struggling to make sense of it.

The suicide note was exactly the same, word for word, as the one found on Syed Hammad's body.

"It's important to remember," Tyler said. "This doesn't necessarily mean... That is to say, we shouldn't jump to conclusions." He met Mackinnon's gaze.

Tyler stood up and turned to face the rest of the team. "DC Webb has been looking into it, and he's found suicide kits freely available on the Internet. Signs, instructions and notes that people can print off and use."

Everyone's attention focused on DC Webb, who looked slightly uncomfortable. "Ah, yes. There are. Ready-made suicide notes."

"That's a little ghoulish," Charlotte said.

"As far as I can tell," DC Webb said, "they seem to be doing a roaring trade. Exit hoods, step-by-step instructions. Anything a suicidal punter could want."

"That's sick." Charlotte's voice was sharp.

DC Webb shrugged. "It takes all sorts."

"And if this isn't a suicide?" Mackinnon asked.

DCI Brookbank didn't reply. He exhaled heavily and stared

back at his team, seemingly expecting one of them to come up with the answer.

"It doesn't add up," the DCI said finally.

Tyler spoke up, "Look, let's not get carried away. We know you can get all types of copycats. These things can be almost contagious. They happen in clusters."

"But that usually happens among people of the same age group, people who have something in common," Mackinnon said. "What does Syed Hammad have in common with the victim from last night?"

Tyler threw up his hands. "That's what we have to find out. We've still got to work out the victimology. There's no link to Syed Hammad so far, but that doesn't mean we won't find one if we look closely enough."

"Maybe they were both members of one of these Internet forums," Collins said. "That's got to be worth looking into."

DCI Brookbank nodded. "Craig Foster had a laptop. We'll find out what sites he visited and what, if any, Internet forums he posted on."

"DC Brown." DCI Brookbank turned to face Charlotte. "I'd like you to go to the hospital today. We need to question Vinnie Pearson and Robbie Baxter as soon as possible."

Charlotte nodded.

Mackinnon didn't envy Charlotte that task. Robbie Baxter may only have been fourteen, but they'd had dealings with his family in the past. Both of his older brothers were serving time for armed robbery, and his mother had a particular hatred of the police.

As Brookbank continued with the briefing, Mackinnon wrote Craig Foster's name and Syed Hammad's name on a piece of paper, with a line linking the two. Was it really possible both deaths were suicide? Two deaths from hydrogen sulphide inhalation in the same week? Could it be a coincidence?

He didn't think so. There had to be a link. They just needed to find it.

CHAPTER NINETEEN

AFTER THE BRIEFING, DC CHARLOTTE Brown spent the rest of the morning at the hospital, getting absolutely nowhere. Every single doctor she spoke to told her the same thing. Neither Vinnie Pearson nor Robbie Baxter was up to answering any questions.

She hadn't managed to catch a glimpse of Robbie yet, but Vinnie Pearson looked in perfect health in her opinion. He had even given her a cheeky smirk as she stood in the doorway to the ward. A scary-looking junior sister, with a hairy mole on her chin, had blocked her path. Charlotte had pleaded for just a couple of minutes, but the sister had crossed her arms and shook her head. She was adamant that Vinnie did not want to talk to the police at the moment, and the doctor had said he wasn't strong enough for questioning.

He looked strong enough to Charlotte. He was strong enough to laugh and give a regal wave when the nurse had sent Charlotte packing.

Charlotte insisted the junior sister call the doctor, but he was unreachable, apparently. He was probably playing golf somewhere with one of the surgeons.

Even though she hadn't managed to talk to Vinnie, his condition cheered her. Medically, he would be fit for questioning soon and there wouldn't be anything he could do to get out of it then.

She couldn't believe the cheeky bugger had waved to her as the junior sister ushered her out of the ward. His laughter followed her all the way down the corridor. It was hard to imagine someone who laughed that much had tried to take his own life.

Charlotte should probably have given up and gone back to the station, but she still held out a little hope. She asked one of the nurses to contact Dr. Sorensen. Dr. Sorensen had been very helpful on a previous case involving contaminated heroin in the area, and Charlotte hoped she might be able to help her out a little bit here, too.

She was in luck. Dr. Sorensen was on duty, and within ten minutes, she was striding along the corridor toward Charlotte. A flicker of recognition passed over her face.

"Dr. Sorensen, I'm not sure if you remember me. I'm DC Charlotte Brown," Charlotte said.

Dr. Sorensen nodded. "Of course. Sorry to keep you waiting." The doctor rubbed at the creases in her forehead. "It's been a busy morning. We've been trying to patch up a man who jumped off a roof."

"Suicide attempt?"

"No. I don't think so. He was high at the time. Apparently he told his friends he was going to fly to Battersea."

As Dr. Sorensen delivered her words with a straight face, Charlotte wasn't quite sure how to respond. Luckily she didn't have to as Dr. Sorensen continued, "What can I help you with today?"

"Two young males were brought in with hydrogen sulphide poisoning."

"I heard about that. Do you know how it happened?"

"We're still looking into it," Charlotte said. "At the moment, it's looking like a suicide and the kids got exposed accidentally. Wrong place, wrong time."

Dr. Sorensen nodded. "Not a very nice way to go. We had a memo on hydrogen sulphide suicides issued about a year ago. Everyone thought it could become very common. From what I've read, there have been a few cases in the US, but it's very rare here."

Charlotte stepped to the side, moving out of the way of a cleaner who slopped a mop along the hallway, humming to herself.

"Well, Vinnie Pearson appears to be getting better, although apparently he isn't strong enough for questioning yet. I've just seen him and he looks pretty energetic to me." Charlotte pulled a face. "Do you know how Robbie Baxter is getting along?"

"No, but I can find out," Dr. Sorensen said and headed inside the ward to speak to the nurse at the nurses' station.

As Dr. Sorensen spoke to the nurse in a low voice, Charlotte looked anxiously round for the junior sister. She didn't want to get Dr. Sorensen in trouble. She probably should have mentioned the fact that Robbie Baxter's doctor had said he wasn't up to talking to the police yet. But Charlotte only wanted to see him. She was quite prepared to wait to ask her questions. She just hoped that wait wouldn't be very long.

Dr. Sorensen returned from the nurses' station and said, "He's in the next ward along. Linden Ward." She began to walk down the corridor. "This way. I'll show you."

As Charlotte followed her, Dr. Sorensen said, "Robbie's mother is around somewhere. She's probably just gone to get a cup of coffee. She's been here all the time. They have arranged accommodation for her in the nurses' block, but I don't think she has used it."

Charlotte hoped Robbie Baxter's mother wasn't around. Ivy Baxter was a skinny woman with a mouth that never stopped. Her two older sons were inside for armed robbery, not that Ivy would admit they were at fault. According to Ivy, her sons had been set up by the officers who had investigated the case. Ivy Baxter had a deep-seated hatred of police that she had instilled in her sons from a very young age.

As Dr. Sorensen led Charlotte into Linden Ward, which smelt of boiled vegetables, Charlotte was glad Ivy Baxter was nowhere to be seen.

They approached Robbie Baxter's bed, and Charlotte could see immediately he wasn't doing as well as Vinnie Pearson.

Robbie was small for his age, but today he looked even smaller. With his eyes closed and his pale cheek resting against the white pillow, he looked very much like the child he was. Who would have believed the police had a list of complaints about him as long as Charlotte's arm?

Charlotte heard a beeping sound that she assumed was one of the many machines in the ward. Then she heard a muttered curse from Dr. Sorensen, who was digging around in the pockets of her white coat.

"I'm sorry. I'm going to have to go and take this." Dr. Sorensen held up the small black pager.

"Sure," Charlotte said. "I'll just hang around here and wait until Robbie's mum turns up."

To Charlotte's surprise, Dr. Sorensen didn't object. She gave a brief wave of her hand and left the ward, leaving Charlotte looking down at Robbie Baxter.

His eyelids fluttered but he didn't wake. He had dark circles like bruises beneath his eyes. It was hard to imagine him full of life and mischief. Charlotte would never have put Robbie Baxter down as the type to be involved in a suicide pact. But that was stupid. There was no such thing as 'a type.' Robbie had had a hard life, and had as big a reason as anyone to want to end it. Maybe it had been a joint suicide pact… Maybe…

"Get away from him!" The shrill voice made Charlotte turn.

Ivy Baxter stood behind Charlotte. She looked faded as if all vitality had been sucked out of her. She may once have been an attractive woman, but the years hadn't been kind. She had nondescript, mousy hair and wore no make-up to hide her blotchy complexion. Her pale lips quivered with rage.

"I'm Charlotte Brown. I –"

"I don't care who you are, love. Just get away from my boy." Ivy Baxter's eyes flashed with anger. She didn't try to keep her voice down. She didn't care if she disturbed any of the other patients.

Charlotte tried again. "I'm Detective Constable Charlotte Brown, City of London police."

Ivy Baxter's face twisted into a sneer, but Charlotte carried on before she could interrupt, "I have reason to believe your son may have been part of a suicide pact."

The words seemed to puncture Ivy Baxter. She crumpled. Her shoulders folded inwards as she pressed her hand to her chest. "He wouldn't…"

Charlotte looked away from the woman and stared down at Robbie. She'd been way out of line. Ivy Baxter was a first-class bitch, but nothing excused how Charlotte had just delivered that news. She should have taken her somewhere private, given her tea and sympathy first, not just blurted it out like that. What was wrong with her?

"I'm sorry," Charlotte said. "I know it's –"

"What do you know about it? You're talking bollocks. Why would I believe you? This is your lot trying to cover up a chemical spill. I've heard about this kind of thing, and I wouldn't put it past you bastards to try and lie your way out of it. One of your bosses probably came up with this cock-and-bull story to stop anyone claiming compensation."

The idea that a mother could be thinking of compensation, of financial benefit, when her son lay in a hospital bed was repellent, but the tremor in Ivy's voice and the way she looked at Robbie as she spoke, told Charlotte more than words ever could.

"He'll wake up," Ivy Baxter whispered. "Then he'll tell me what happened."

Charlotte left the ward in an irritable mood. She came here for answers, but got nothing. If anything, she had made matters worse by getting Ivy Baxter all riled up.

Charlotte left the inpatient area of the hospital and entered ENT outpatients, wondering if the signs really pointed to the exit. It seemed like she had been walking around in circles. She turned right, following another of the little brown exit signs, when she heard someone calling her name.

She turned to see Dr. Sorensen.

"I'm sorry I had to leave you," Dr. Sorensen said. "Did you have any luck?"

Charlotte shook her head. "Unfortunately not. Robbie Baxter's mother didn't have any information, or at least, she didn't have anything she was willing to share."

"Have you got time for a coffee?" Dr. Sorensen asked. She pushed up the sleeve of her white coat and looked at her wristwatch.

Charlotte smiled apologetically. "I'm afraid not. I really need to get back to the station."

"Maybe the next time you're here? I'm sure Vinnie Pearson will be up to answering your questions soon."

Charlotte sighed. "He looks well enough to me already. I'm pretty sure he's taking advantage of the situation."

Dr. Sorensen smiled politely as two nurses passed them in the corridor. She said, "He isn't my patient. But…"

Charlotte frowned and waited for Dr. Sorensen to continue. Maybe she would get some information after all. Maybe Vinnie had spoken to his doctor, told him what happened.

Dr. Sorensen shoved her hands in the pockets of her white coat and lowered her voice. "I think he's scared of something, or someone."

"Has he said anything? Told you who he's scared of?"

Dr. Sorensen shook her head and bit her lip. "Not to me, but the nurses have noticed he is very anxious, and he keeps asking about security. It's probably nothing… But I thought it was worth mentioning."

Charlotte thanked Dr. Sorensen then continued on her way to the exit, through the winding corridors, following the little brown exit signs.

Her mind was completely occupied with one question: just who was it Vinnie was scared of?

CHAPTER TWENTY

KATHY WALKER KEPT HER SMILE fixed in position as she secured the last of Mrs. Cutler's rollers. The smile took a huge effort. She'd felt bad all day. Of course, that was what she deserved for drinking half a box of cheap white wine last night.

"There, all done, Mrs. Cutler," she said, beaming at the old lady in the mirror. "We'll leave those rollers in for twenty minutes. Can I get you a drink while you wait? Or something to read?"

Mrs. Cutler asked for a cup of tea, white, one sugar, and a magazine.

Kathy handed her a dog-eared copy of Marie Claire then headed out back to the little kitchenette to make the drink. She got two mugs out of the cupboard, put a tea bag in the pretty blue one for Mrs. Cutler and put two heaped spoonfuls of instant coffee in her own chipped mug. Heaven knows she needed the caffeine.

Kathy glanced up at the clock on the wall as the kettle boiled. She'd have to spend ten minutes with Mrs. Cutler after the rollers came out, but then she'd have half an hour free before her next appointment.

As Kathy reached for the kettle, she noticed her red and chapped hands. She looked down at them in surprise. How did those wrinkly, red fingers belong to her? She was getting age spots, too. Forty, single and still living in the area where she grew up. What would her sixteen-year-old self say if she could see her now?

She'd been full of ideas when she left school. Hairdressing was going to be a stepping stone. She planned on getting trained then going off on a cruise ship and seeing the world.

So much for dreams.

She didn't even get to do much exciting stuff in the way of hair styling these days. Most of the women who came to the salon had kept the same style for years, and had no intention of changing.

Still, Kathy thought, looking on the bright side, at least her next client was under sixty. She might be up for something a little bit more exciting than a shampoo and set.

As Kathy poured boiling water into the mugs, she tried to ignore the fact her hands were shaking. Why on earth did she drink so much last night? But she knew the answer to that already: Because she was alone. So she'd sat there on the sofa, drinking glass after glass of wine and getting more and more pissed until she'd been singing along to Whitney Houston. She flushed at the memory. God, she was like Bridget bloody Jones, except older and fatter and with no sign of Colin Firth on the horizon.

Not that she hadn't had any chances with men. But with all of them she'd managed to push them away, telling herself she didn't want to settle down and have kids. After her crap childhood, she worried she'd be a terrible mother, and she wasn't prepared to take the risk. There was no way she wanted to screw up another generation. She was pretty sure her brother felt the same way.

He lived over on the Isle of Dogs, but he often popped in to check up on her. He'd been popping in even more frequently recently, which Kathy knew was due to whatever was going on between her brother and Mitch Horrocks, the owner of the cafe down the street.

Not that her brother would admit there was anything going on. Stuart hadn't even told her he was gay. Although she'd have to be bloody blind not to notice. Still, it wasn't any of her business. She just wished he'd pick someone nicer than Mitch Horrocks.

Kathy took the tea through to Mrs. Cutler and did a quick check on the rollers, asking if she was comfortable. Mrs. Cutler said she was fine, gave Kathy a quick smile, then returned to her engrossing magazine article on celebrity cellulite.

Kathy looked up as she heard the door open. Crap. She hoped that wasn't her next client. She'd been banking on twenty minutes between clients to get her head straight.

Kathy let out a sigh of relief when she realised it was only Stuart.

Mrs. Cutler peered at Stuart over the pages of her magazine. Clearly, Mrs. Cutler didn't find celebrity cellulite as interesting as potential gossip. Kathy waved to her brother and gestured for him to follow her out of the back of the salon.

Stuart entered the kitchen. His floppy, fair hair fell down over his eyes.

"You need a trim," Kathy said.

He pushed his hair back and gave her a grin. Kathy was closer to Stuart than anyone in the world. She supposed their shared, crappy childhood had forged the strong bond. It wasn't possible to live through something like that without consequences.

She narrowed her eyes as she noticed Stuart's hunched shoulders. There was definitely something bothering him.

"What's wrong?"

Stuart scowled. His forehead creased just like it used to do when he'd been a little boy. "Nothing."

Kathy should've known better than to pry further. But it wasn't in her nature to leave things alone. There was definitely something bothering him, and he must want to confide in her, otherwise why would he be here in the middle of the day?

"Tea?" Kathy offered, reaching for the kettle.

Stuart shook his head. "No, thanks. I haven't got time. I just wanted to see if you're all right."

Kathy put down the kettle. "Of course, I am. It's not that busy today." She flushed. Could Stuart tell she was hungover? Did he think she had a problem?

"After what happened to Syed, I thought you might still be a bit shaken up."

"Oh, I'm all right," Kathy said. "But it's horrible to think he was just one door along feeling so depressed that he…"

Stuart put a hand on her arm and squeezed.

"Are you sure you don't want that tea?" Kathy asked, blinking rapidly and turning her back so Stuart wouldn't see the tears brimming in her eyes.

"No, thanks. I'm going to pop along the road and see how Mitch is doing. It can't have been nice for him either, especially with his mum." Stuart hunched his shoulders again. It was almost as if he were trying to make himself smaller, unnoticed.

Kathy supposed she should be glad Stuart had taken an interest in someone. She wanted him to be happy, of course she did. But why did he have to pick Mitch?

That bloody man was always in a bad mood about something and never had a nice word to say to anybody.

Kathy folded her arms across her chest. "I'm quite sure Mitch is fine."

"What do you mean by that?"

Kathy shook her head. "He isn't exactly the sensitive type, is he? I can't imagine he was bothered by what happened to poor old Syed."

Kathy was pretty sure Mitch wouldn't be bothered by anything that didn't directly affect him.

"Don't be like that, Kathy. Of course he'll be bothered. His old mum was up there. He was so worried she was going to get hurt."

Kathy only just managed to stop herself from rolling her eyes. Everyone in the street knew that Mrs. Horrocks was as tough as old boots and as mean as a snake.

She decided to take a chance, while Stuart had his guard down. "I know you… like Mitch… But you could do better, Stuart." She saw the dark look on his face and continued quickly, "You deserve better."

"I don't know what you mean." Stuart's voice was cold. "I'm just going to check on an old friend and his elderly mother."

Mitch Horrocks had gone to the same school as Kathy and Stuart, but they'd never exactly been friendly. In the ten years that Kathy had run the salon, she'd seen Mitch Horrocks nearly every day, and every day he looked meaner and grumpier than before.

Kathy chucked her remaining coffee down the sink. She wasn't going to get anywhere with Stuart now. The shutters had come down.

"I know you, Stuart." Kathy shrugged. "I just want you to be happy."

Stuart jerked his chin and zipped up his jacket even though it wasn't cold outside. "I'll give them your regards."

CHAPTER TWENTY-ONE

1982

THERE WERE SNIGGERS BEHIND him. But Junior didn't turn around.

Mr. Lockwood stalked between the desks. The English teacher walked with a slight limp because his left leg was an inch shorter than his right. He wore a stacked heel on his shoe, but it didn't seem to help. It would have earned any other teacher a rude nickname, but Mr. Lockwood put the fear of God into every child in the class.

He paused at the front of the classroom, next to the black-board, and stared out at his pupils until they all stopped fidgeting.

"Open your books, page fifty-two," Mr. Lockwood said.

Junior flipped through the pages of his copy of Lord of the Flies until he reached page fifty-two. His fingers felt thick and clumsy. He could feel Mr. Lockwood's eyes on him, and he felt the flush of blood rise to his cheeks.

"You can start us off, boy," Mr. Lockwood said.

Junior peered up at the teacher through his overlong fringe. He shook his head slightly. Mr. Lockwood couldn't mean him. He knew Junior was no good at reading aloud. He got flustered and mixed up his words.

But it was no good. Mr. Lockwood was staring directly at him. For a fraction of a second, Junior considered slamming the book closed and running out of the classroom, but the teacher's eyes scared him. Junior said a silent prayer. Please let him pick someone else.

"What are you waiting for, boy?" Mr. Lockwood's voice boomed around the classroom.

There was no point delaying the inevitable. Junior lowered his head and licked his lips. He pointed his index finger at the line of text, hoping it would help to keep the words in order.

Junior's voice shook as he began to read.

There were some titters of laughter from the boys who sat in the back row, but Junior tried to ignore them.

Junior managed to get to the end of the paragraph, but he had to repeat himself three times to get the final sentence right.

His old English teacher, Mrs. O'Brien, had told Junior it wasn't his fault. She said he had dyslexia, which made it hard for him to read, but it didn't make him stupid. His mother said Mrs. O'Brien was a silly old woman who didn't know her arse from her elbow.

When Junior stumbled over the start of the next paragraph, Mr. Lockwood interrupted. "That's enough. We will give someone else a chance to read now. Good effort."

Junior smiled. He heard somebody hiss, "swot." But he didn't care. He didn't like those children anyway. They teased him about his clothes and the way he talked. They never let him join in any of their games at break time. He didn't need them. He didn't need friends. He was learning now and doing well in school. It finally made sense. He might not have friends but Junior understood how to make his teachers happy, and that made his life much easier.

Everything was better now that Junior knew that he had to obey rules. Rules were very important and terrible things happened when they weren't followed. Just like in this story. He wished the other children would shut up. He liked this book, and he wanted to know what happened at the end.

Junior was thinking about the rules he would set if he were on the island and in charge, when Mr. Lockwood dropped his copy of Lord of the Flies onto his desk and slapped his hand on the cover, sending a cloud of chalk dust into the air.

"Homework," Mr. Lockwood said. "Man has a capacity for evil. Moral integrity must be upheld to control this evil and maintain a civilised society. Discuss."

Mr. Lockwood didn't look at Junior as he spoke, but that didn't matter. Junior knew those words were a direct message for him.

CHAPTER TWENTY-TWO

PRESENT DAY

FIONA EVANS STRAIGHTENED the neck of her blouse and looked at herself in the mirror.

Christ, she was nervous.

It was ridiculous. Surely it was supposed to be the other way around. The interviewee should be nervous, not her. She glanced at her watch and then walked through into the sitting room, peering out of the window. No sign of him yet.

She perched on the edge of the sofa and turned at the sound of Anna's light footsteps. She said nothing, but sat down beside Fiona's feet and began brushing her doll's hair.

Anna liked to be close to Fiona all the time. She didn't trust Fiona not to disappear like her father.

Fiona turned to look out of the window again. Although it was practical, she didn't really want a male carer for Luke. It would be strange having a man around the house again. A man she didn't know. It would have been different if Bruce was still alive.

But that was silly. Even if Bruce was still here, he would have been at work and she would be dealing with this situation on her own.

Unable to sit still any longer, Fiona got up and walked into the kitchen. She'd put Tim Coleman's CV on the granite worktop. She pulled it towards her and began to read it for the tenth time.

On paper, Tim Coleman sounded perfect.

Fiona hoped he was. She hoped his caring for Luke would ease some of the pressure on her shoulders and give her more time to spend with Anna. Sometimes Anna got the raw deal. Luke's special needs meant that sometimes Anna's needs were overlooked. Fiona thought some extra bonding time would help to reassure Anna, make her realise Fiona wasn't going anywhere.

Fiona jumped as the front doorbell rang. She shook her head. What on earth was wrong with her? She needed to get a grip. She walked towards the front door, feeling her stomach churn.

She had considered asking Jack Mackinnon to be here during the interview. He'd been so kind and so understanding, and it would have just helped to have a friendly face around. But she didn't want to bother him. It was a bit of an imposition, and she never wanted to feel like she was a burden.

It was funny, now that Bruce was gone, she understood him more than she ever had when he was alive. She understood why he'd wanted to do things himself and why he hadn't wanted to rely on anybody else's money.

Although Fiona readily accepted financial help from her parents, she didn't want to burden anyone emotionally.

She opened the front door and saw a man in his mid-thirties with light brown hair. He looked friendly enough as he smiled at her. "Mrs. Evans?"

"Yes. You must be Tim? Please come in." Fiona felt Anna grab onto her legs. She pried off one of the little girl's arms and took her hand.

"Thanks." Tim stepped inside.

Fiona took his coat and noticed her hands were shaking as she hung it up. "Anna, why don't you go and play for a little while so mummy can talk to Mr. Coleman?"

Anna pouted. The little girl's lower lip wobbled, and for a moment, Fiona thought Anna might launch into a full scale tantrum. What would Tim think of that? He wouldn't be very impressed with her if she couldn't handle Anna, let alone a child with Luke's problems.

Thankfully, Anna decided to behave on this occasion, and with one last pout, she headed off to play with her dolls.

Fiona led Tim through to the kitchen. "Can I get you a tea or coffee?"

"Coffee would be great, thanks," Tim said, looking around the kitchen. "Lovely house."

"Thanks." Fiona switched on the kettle, glad she could keep her hands busy and focus on something mundane while she was doing the interview. "Your CV looks very impressive. I thought we could have a bit of a chat first, and if things go okay, I could take you upstairs to meet Luke. If that's okay with you?"

"Sounds good to me."

They chatted for a while, and as they did, Fiona felt herself relax in his company and within minutes she was certain Tim Coleman would be the right person to look after Luke.

For the first time in ages, Fiona actually felt hopeful for the future.

CHAPTER TWENTY-THREE

JOANNE JAMES SLID INTO THE driver's seat of her shiny, silver VW Golf, a seventeenth birthday present from Daddy. She rearranged her bright pink Juicy Couture tracksuit bottoms. She'd just had a spray tan, and she didn't want streaks.

Joanne carefully reached for the gear stick, taking care not to smudge her freshly painted nails.

Before she pulled away, she checked her mobile phone for the fifth time that hour. "Bastard," she said. Bloody Vinnie still hadn't phoned. She wasn't stupid. She knew that the police might monitor his calls, but he could have found some way to get in touch. He didn't even know that she had made it out okay! All things considered, she'd got off pretty lightly. She'd had a nasty cough, but that was practically gone now.

Come to think of it, how did she know Vinnie was okay? She'd seen Craig Foster clamber through the broken window and she'd followed. She hadn't actually seen Vinnie get out. Maybe he'd been arrested? But, no, that was silly. Vinnie always landed on his feet.

She just had to accept he wasn't interested. Bastard. She glared down at her phone.

When she got his Facebook message last week, she'd thought things might be back on again. They'd dated on and off for six months last year. Then out of nowhere, Vinnie dumped her. She hadn't seen it coming.

Joanne had tried to move on, she really had. None of her friends understood what she saw in Vinnie. To them, he was just a waster.

Thanks to her father, Joanne had never had to work a day in her life. She'd tried college and half-finished a beauty training course, but she'd never really stuck to anything because she didn't have to. Why work when she could spend that time having lunch with her friends and having a good time?

Then Vinnie had come into her life and made her see how predictable and boring her life had become.

With Vinnie, things were exciting. He was a bad boy. Her friends called him her bit of rough. They'd all expected the relationship to last a few weeks before Joanne got bored. But it didn't work out that way. It wasn't her that pulled the plug.

She was used to being the one who walked away from her exes. The fact that Vinnie Pearson thought he could drop her like that really pissed her off.

She'd been really down after he'd dumped her. Tears, ice-cream, lying in bed all day – the works. She hadn't had her hair or nails done in over a month.

Her dad had been beside himself with worry. But as the weeks passed, she'd slowly started to put her life back together. She'd even gone out on a couple of blind dates her friends set up. They were nice enough, but none of them matched up to Vinnie. They were all too strait-laced. One was an estate agent who had spent most of the evening talking about local house prices. He couldn't have been more boring if he'd tried.

Then Vinnie had sent that message on Facebook, and she'd thought he missed her and wanted to see her again.

Of course, she'd said yes. Vinnie wanted her to come along on one of his jobs. They were exciting, and no one really got hurt. She'd been determined to show Vinnie that he could trust her, that she was up for a laugh.

When he'd broken up with her, he'd laughed and called her daddy's little Essex princess. By going along with Vinnie on this job, she intended to show him just what sort of person she really was. That he could rely on her.

She hadn't thought anything would go wrong. Like Vinnie said, shop owners were insured. It didn't bother them. She didn't do it for the money, of course, but the buzz was exciting. She liked the power.

She crunched the gears as she pulled away from the parade of shops and glanced at the gold Omega watch on her wrist. Her dad had bought it for her 18th birthday.

Damn, she was going to be late for dinner. Mum was doing shepherd's pie.

She put her foot down as she came up to the pedestrian lights and crossed just as they turned from amber to red.

"Green," she said aloud, even though there was no one else in the car.

She took the next right turn and hurtled over the mini roundabout. The tyres screeched as she turned into Finch Lane.

Finch Lane was lined with hawthorn bushes and long wild grasses, which made it hard to see cars coming in the other direction.

She recognised the opening beats of a song she liked on the radio. Rihanna – fantastic! Joanne looked down at the radio and reached for the volume control to turn it up.

Her eyes only left the road for a fraction of a second. But that was long enough.

When she raised her head, she swore. In front of her, a stationary black Volvo blocked the lane.

Joanne slammed on the brakes. The squealing sound sent cold shivers down her spine.

The car was sliding sideways, out of control, and for one terrifying moment, she thought she was going to smash into the car. But her car screeched to a halt a few metres from the side of the Volvo.

That had been close. Far too close. She sat there for a moment, her hands still gripping the steering wheel, breathing heavily. Then she wiped her sweaty palms on her tracksuit bottoms. The radio was still blaring out Rihanna's latest song. Joanne reached out a shaky hand and turned down the radio.

The silence was only broken by the sound of her own breathing. She couldn't hear any traffic. She was too far from the main road.

She focused on the Volvo.

It didn't look damaged. She couldn't see anyone inside. She flung open the door and the warm green scent of the summer's evening washed over her. She took a couple of deep breaths and headed over towards the car.

What sort of bloody idiot would stop in the middle of a road? She stalked up to the car ready to give the driver a piece of her mind. You got all sorts of people driving along these country lanes, lots of old people bumbling along. It was probably some old granddad who'd stopped to look at his map, unaware he was blocking both lanes.

But there was no one in the driver's seat.

Confused, Joanne looked around. What the hell? What kind of idiot would leave their car in the middle of the road? They hadn't even pulled it over to the verge, for God's sake. A few hundred yards back, there was a small lay-by. So why hadn't they stopped there?

She pressed her hands against the smooth metal of the driver's door and peered inside. But there was nothing inside the car to give her any clue to the driver's identity. On the back seat, there were a couple of bottles of cleaning fluid, but nothing else. Had they run out of petrol? Broken down?

She swore and turned around, thinking she'd have to go back and go the long way round that would add another fifteen minutes to her journey. She heard the hoarse cawing sound of crows, roosting in the trees above and shivered.

She was glad of the long summer evenings. This was not an experience she would want to have after dark. It was creepy enough now. She never realised quite how isolated it was in this area before. There were no other houses. And very few cars took this route. The lane only led to the tiny village of Finch Hill.

Joanne pushed her hair back from her face and grabbed the bottom of her velour top, fanning herself. She was sweating. That was going to ruin her spray tan. Annoyed, she turned to head back towards her own car.

She froze. There was someone standing next to her car. A man, dressed in black.

Her heart flipped over in her chest. Who was it? The driver of the Volvo? Why did he just stand there like that? Why was he next to her car?

The sun, low in the sky, made her squint. She raised a hand to shade her eyes.

Don't let him know you're scared, she told herself. Keep your distance, and you'll be all right.

"Is this your car?" she called out. "Do you need some help or something?"

The man in black didn't answer, but shifted his position so

he was facing her. At least, she thought he was. The sun made it hard to see him properly.

"I could call the AA for you? Or the RAC maybe?"

Her heart was really thundering now. She looked back at the Volvo. Perhaps she could jump inside and drive the hell away from this weirdo who wouldn't speak. She could do it. The Volvo's keys were in the ignition.

As soon as she'd thought of keys she patted down her pockets. Shit. She'd left her keys in the ignition of her Golf, too.

And she left her phone in the car. A lot of good that was. Great. Just bloody great.

She looked again at the Volvo. Could she do it? But what if it didn't start? What if he really had broken down?

She edged forward, walking toward the passenger side of her Golf. If she could get inside quickly, she could push down the locks, then climb over into the driver's side and get away.

The setting sun had made it impossible to see the man clearly, but when she moved closer he stepped forward, too, and that was when she saw his face.

She let out a strangled scream, and her hand smacked over her mouth.

Oh, Jesus. He was wearing some kind of mask, with big, scary eye sockets that made him look like some kind of mutant fly.

It was a gas mask, she realised. But why on earth would he be wearing one of those?

But she didn't have time to wonder why. She lunged for the passenger door. Her fingers felt clumsy as she grasped the handle. She could sense him coming for her, but she didn't dare look up.

She threw herself into the car, pulled the door shut. The hard metal edge of the door connected with her ankle bone.

When she finally heard the door slam shut, she clambered over the handbrake to press the locks.

Thank God. She climbed into the driving seat, trying to slow her breathing. She'd made it. Now all she had to do was drive home and get away from this nutter.

Not bothering to fasten her seatbelt, Joanne turned the key, shoved the gearstick into first and stamped on the accelerator. The engine roared, and the masked man took a step back, out of the path of the accelerating Golf.

Joanne sped along the country lane, barely slowing down for the twists and turns. She had lived in Finch Hill all her life, and she knew this road like the back of her hand. She knew every bend, every bump in the road, so she flew down Finch Lane, determined to get away.

The breath caught in her throat as she jerked the steering wheel, narrowly missing a baby rabbit at the side of the road. One of the wheels connected with the grass verge, and the car seemed to tilt to the side. She only just kept the Golf from tumbling into the ditch that ran along the side of the lane.

She couldn't wait to get back to the safety of the village. She glanced in her rearview mirror. There was no one there. She was safe.

Perhaps she should call her dad. She wanted to make sure the police caught that weirdo. She didn't want to give him enough time to get away. She reached for her iPhone, which she always kept in the little holder in front of the gearstick. But she fumbled the phone, and it slipped from her grasp, falling into the passenger footwell.

Shit. She wasn't about to slow down so she could pick it up. She was better off driving as fast as she could and getting out of there.

Joanne checked the rearview mirror again. There were no headlights behind her. She felt the tightness between her shoulder blades ease. Thank God. Maybe she had overreacted.

Maybe the masked man had been going to some kind of fancy-dress party. But he must have known how scary he looked. As soon as she got home, she would tell her dad and get the freak reported to the police.

A large popping sound made her jump. The noise was loud enough to send her heart thumping in her chest again. The car slowed and swerved to the side of the road. Joanne pressed down on the accelerator, but the car pulled to the right side of the road and made an awful grinding sound.

Oh, God, she'd blown a tire. Had she run over something sharp? Had she damaged the tyre when she hit the verge? Or had the man in the mask done something to her tyre?

She tried to keep the car straight, to keep driving, thinking she just had to get to the main road to be safe. But the car was going slower and slower, and the grating noise was getting worse and worse.

What could she do now?

She had to call for help. She pulled over to the side of the road and glanced behind her. She looked through the rearview mirror, then checked over her shoulder just to make sure.

There was nothing there. Nothing but an empty lane and rustling trees.

She fumbled in the passenger footwell until her fingers closed around the smooth case of her phone. She smiled. She was less than a mile from home, all she had to do was call her dad and … Joanne looked up.

Framed by the passenger window, the masked man stared in at her.

The thick plastic eye protection distorted his features. Despite the distortion, she could see the burning fury, the hatred, in his eyes.

At that moment, Joanne James knew she was going to die.

CHAPTER TWENTY-FOUR

OBLIVIOUS TO WHAT HAD HAPPENED further down the lane, Laura Vincent steered her Astra around a bend in Finch Lane. She hated this road, particularly at dusk. It was so hard to see the oncoming traffic. She usually drove slowly, but she was already late. Again. Her husband had left an angry voice message on her phone, telling her he'd picked up two-year-old Gracie from his mother's two hours ago. And where the hell was she? He went on and on, complaining that she treated his mother like an unpaid babysitter.

Laura had been working late. It wasn't as if she'd been out partying or having fun. But he didn't seem to understand that.

Laura's mobile rang again. "For God's sake," she muttered under her breath, "I'd get home quicker if he would just leave me alone."

She reached over to her leather handbag, which was sitting on the passenger seat, and tried to locate her mobile phone. It was playing some silly tune from Gracie's favourite TV show.

She looked down. Where the bloody hell was it? She had too much junk in her bag. She could never find anything.

She dumped the bag upside down, emptying the contents out onto the passenger seat, and her eyes fixed on the glowing light of the phone's screen.

As she reached across further to grab it, from the corner of her eye she saw a flash of silver. It took a moment to realise the silver VW Golf was in front of her, on the wrong side of the road. She hesitated for a fraction of a second, before dropping the phone, gripping the steering wheel with both hands and stepping on the brake as hard as she could.

But her reactions weren't quick enough. The front of her car slammed into the VW Golf.

After the impact, Laura sat there, dazed and panting for breath.

Her head had hit the steering wheel. The bloody airbag hadn't inflated. For God's sake. As she tried to reach across to unclip her seatbelt, a searing pain radiated out from her shoulder. She gasped and tried to keep as still as possible. Remaining motionless was the only thing that stopped her screaming out in pain.

Sobbing with effort, she reached out for her mobile phone with her uninjured arm and dialled 999.

CHAPTER TWENTY-FIVE

PC ANDY GREEN STEERED THE road policing unit's BMW estate into Finch Lane, keeping his lights on full beam so he could see the road ahead. PC Mark Cameron sat in the passenger seat, his eyes scanning the road on the lookout for the accident.

Control had reported an incident involving two vehicles on this narrow, winding lane. PC Green felt a twisting in his stomach. It was impossible to predict how serious these kinds of accidents were going to be. They never knew what state people would be in when they got there.

He just hoped they'd had their seat belts on.

As they reached a turn in the road, Green slowed the car, and they both caught sight of the red Vauxhall Astra with its crumpled bonnet and the silver VW Golf with a huge dent in its side.

The Astra was an old model, but the Golf was only a year old. The Golf sat on the wrong side of the road. Cracks resembling a spider's web, radiated out from the centre of the Astra's windscreen.

Worryingly, there was no immediate sign of the car's occupants.

Green brought the police car to a stop a few feet away from the traffic collision, and Cameron radioed control to let them know they were at the scene.

At first glance, the collision didn't look too bad. They'd seen a hell of a lot worse.

Both men climbed out of the BMW and surveyed the scene. Their first priority in a case like this was the hazards from other cars. This was a quiet lane, which helped. But they would still need to temporarily close the road.

They approached the red Vauxhall first, and Cameron's stomach clenched when he saw the baby on board sticker. Please, God, no kids tonight.

A woman sat in the driver's seat of the Vauxhall. Her hands still gripped the steering wheel, and she barely seemed to notice their presence. A trickle of blood ran down from a cut on the bridge of her nose. She would have a hell of a bruise tomorrow.

There was a baby-seat in the back, but no sign of a child. Thank God.

PC Green knocked softly on the glass, and the woman blinked at him then tried to wind down the window. It wouldn't open.

Green opened the door.

"That car was in the middle of the road," the woman said in a shaky voice. "I didn't have time to stop. I didn't have a chance. I just turned the corner, and it was sitting there in the middle of the road."

Cameron could see the panic in her eyes. She was in shock.

"Are you hurt?" Green asked.

"Is the other driver okay?" she asked. "I haven't been able to get out of my car. I've hurt my shoulder. I couldn't open the door. I can't even take my seatbelt off."

"We'll soon get you out," Green said.

"It wasn't my fault. I mean, why would they stop in the middle of the road like that?" she asked, her eyes wide and fixed on PC Green's face.

Green moved a little closer, and Cameron knew he was getting close to see if she'd been drinking.

Green looked back at Cameron and gave a barely detectable shake of his head. They had worked together long enough for Cameron to know what he meant. There was no trace of alcohol on her breath.

Cameron nodded and stepped back. Her injuries didn't seem as serious as they might have been. Green could handle it. He moved on to check the occupant of the VW Golf.

After Cameron had checked out the VW Golf, he hurried back to his colleague. In the background he could hear the distant wail of sirens.

PC Green frowned as he saw his colleague marching towards him.

"What is it?" Green asked. "Fatality?"

Cameron nodded. "But it's worse than that. We're going to need some more units."

CHAPTER TWENTY-SIX

WITHIN HALF AN HOUR, THE road was closed in both directions. Police cars, two ambulances and two fire engines were parked up behind the accident site. A group of officers, some wearing high-visibility jackets, gathered a safe distance from the cars.

PC Mark Cameron swallowed nervously and leaned back against the smooth cool metal of his BMW estate. PC Andy Green approached him and asked again if he was all right. Cameron just nodded. He didn't really want to talk about it. He didn't want to think about what could have happened if he hadn't spotted the sign.

He'd put his hand on the driver's door and had reached for the handle when, just in time, he'd seen the note on the window, warning about the gas inside.

All his training had taught him not to try and get the victim out himself. But it hadn't taught him how hard it was not to help.

The pale-faced young girl had been sprawled across both front seats. In all likelihood, she had been dead within seconds of breathing the gas. During training they'd been told that death occurs very quickly. But that didn't make him feel any better.

They'd asked the controller to call more units, and advised the fire brigade of the situation. The fire and rescue service were now here, dressed in protective suits and wearing special breathing apparatus. They had monitoring equipment which could detect the levels of toxic gas. One of the problems in these types of situations was that they couldn't rely on home-made notices to identify the gas. They had to wait for substance identification by the specially trained fire crew.

They'd attempted to establish the downwind hazard area by attaching a strip of crime scene tape to the edge of a fence-post to determine the wind direction. Evacuation of any nearby residents would be down to the fire commander, but luckily this area was only sparsely populated. When the safety officer arrived, he set up a cordon around the site and made everyone move back from the scene.

Cameron's role was to maintain the scene logs and make sure that no members of the public could stumble into danger. No doubt there would be some reporters down here soon, and then his job would be to keep them away as well.

SOCOs were already in attendance, photographing the scene. All the first responders had to wear gas-tight decontamination suits, so everything was taking much longer than usual. The girl's body would have to be stored in a special body bag and taken back to the morgue.

Cameron shivered. The poor kid. She'd looked so young. What made someone like her want to end it all?

Cameron raised his head to the heavens as a light rain began to fall. This was his first toxic suicide. He hoped it would be his last.

CHAPTER TWENTY-SEVEN

POLICE INDEXER, EMMIE FOXALL, HAD endured a really bad start to the day. First, she'd overslept, somehow managing to sleep through the alarm on her mobile phone. A fast shower, without washing her hair, followed by a cereal bar gobbled down instead of breakfast and she was almost back on schedule.

Until she got in her car, and the bloody thing wouldn't start.

She'd had to beg her boyfriend to use his Jeep. Shiny and red, it was his pride and joy. As she backed out of the drive, he chewed on his nails. The fear on his face was almost comical. Emmie knew his concern wasn't for her but his fancy Jeep.

She deliberately ignored his frantic expression as she crunched the gears before driving off. She managed to crunch the gears three more times on the way to work. She'd passed her test with a manual, but that had been a long time ago.

When she finally got to work, she found someone had been using her coffee mug and hadn't washed it up. Squirting it with fairy liquid, Emmie gave it a good scrub.

Nothing was safe in this place. She'd expected staff working in a police station would respect other people's property, but she'd had a whole bag of Maltesers go missing from the fridge last Friday, and now some cheeky bugger was using her mug. She didn't really mind it being used, but they could have at least washed it up!

Emmie made her tea just how she liked it – really strong with a dash of milk. Evie, the crime analyst she'd been working with, called it builder's tea.

Evie was working a later shift today, so for now, Emmie had the area to herself. She fumbled around in her desk drawer and fished out a packet of paracetamol. She popped a couple of the small white tablets from the foil packet and swallowed them, chasing them down with a sip of hot tea. Then she took a deep breath and looked down at the amount of work she had to get through today.

Emmie loved her job. It suited her perfectly. She loved putting everything into place and making order out of chaos. She had an extra-wide computer monitor, so she could look at whole spreadsheets at a glance, taking in all the information at once.

Before she got started on her actual indexing work, Emmie decided to take a quick look at the overnight stuff first.

She scrolled through the list of events and singled out items of interest. Her fingers gripped the computer mouse more tightly when she read the account of the incident in Finch Lane.

Another suicide. Another case involving hydrogen sulphide.

Emmie copied the details to her screen and chewed her bottom lip as she read the report.

Another hydrogen sulphide suicide – could it really be a coincidence?

If it was, it was a bloody big one. Emmie reached for the phone on her desk.

CHAPTER TWENTY-EIGHT

"THERE'S BEEN AN IMPORTANT DEVELOPMENT," DI Tyler said, then paused to get everyone's attention.

Collins put down the document he'd been reading.

"There's been another suicide, involving hydrogen sulphide." Tyler waited until the murmurs around the room died away. "This one's a very different set up – a car in a country lane." Tyler pointed to a map of the county taped to the whiteboard behind him.

"Finch Lane, Essex," Tyler said. "An eighteen-year-old girl called Joanne James. DS Webb, I want you to speak to the family."

Webb pulled a face. No one enjoyed dealing with bereaved parents, but Webb was particularly prone to putting his foot in it.

"We need to find out if she had any association with Craig Foster or Syed Hammad... Maybe she got the information the same way they did... A website... A forum... And we need access to her computer."

"Right," DC Webb said, writing furiously in his notebook.

"The circumstances are very different." Tyler loosened his tie and looked down at the floor. Even from across the room, Collins could see the furrows crease Tyler's forehead. "But all of these suicides have one thing in common…"

He had everyone's attention. Tyler set down a sheet of A4 paper on the desk in front of him and took a deep breath. "It's the same suicide note."

Collins could almost hear the cogs turning in the room as Tyler shook his head. "We can't jump to conclusions."

"Did Joanne James sign her suicide note?" Mackinnon asked.

"What?" Tyler shook his head, distracted. "No. It wasn't signed."

"Just like the others…" Charlotte said, turning to Mackinnon.

"I already said that," Tyler snapped.

"That's got to mean something," Mackinnon said. "None of them signed the note. Don't you think that's strange?"

"It doesn't mean anything." Tyler leaned forward, resting his palms on the desk. "It's probably because they printed it from the same website. People never bother to write anything anymore. They probably didn't think about signing anything. DC Webb found sites with every last thing you could possibly want if you wanted to end it all… Step-by-step instructions, tips on how to tidy up your affairs to make it easier for the people you leave behind and…" Tyler paused for emphasis and poked the desk with his index finger before delivering his killer line, "And he found websites with suicide notes – all ready to print out."

Collins had seen the websites himself, but it still didn't make sense. It was so impersonal.

"Did anything look suspicious about the death?" Mackinnon asked.

"It's still early days," Tyler said. "The car was found in the middle of the road, not parked at the verge like you might expect." Tyler shrugged. "That's unusual, but I'm still waiting on further details."

After DI Tyler wrapped up the impromptu briefing, Collins got on the phone. The technical team was still working on the CCTV footage from Syed Hammad's shop. They still hadn't managed to extract anything useful. Although they had promised to get in touch as soon as they had something to show the major investigation team, Collins thought it couldn't hurt to give them a little nudge.

As he waited to be put through to Troy Wilson, who hopefully would be able to help, Collins chewed on the end of his Biro. These multiple suicides made him uneasy – not just because of the death of three people who had their whole lives ahead of them, but because there was something about this case which didn't feel right.

Collins' first experience of suicide came when he was at school. The father of a boy in his class jumped off the roof of a multi-storey car park. He could never understand how anyone could put their kids through something like that.

It might be un-PC to think it, but the way Collins looked at it, it was selfishness.

He still remembered the boy's name – Frankie White. He'd been a happy enough kid beforehand, with a gap-toothed grin, and he'd been the best football player in the class.

Frankie had been in the last year of primary school when it happened, and after his father's death, he'd started to wet himself. At the age of ten, there weren't many things more humiliating than wetting yourself in the classroom.

Collins and Frankie had gone on to separate secondary schools, and Collins had no idea what had happened to the boy, but he still thought of him every now and then when suicide cases like this came up. He wondered what happened to Frankie. He could be married with kids by now... Or...

Collins dropped his pen on the desk as Troy Wilson came on the line.

"So, you want images. Reference number?" Troy Wilson asked in a bored tone.

"Er…" Collins fumbled through the paperwork in front of him. "It's images from the CCTV from the newsagent's on East Street. DCI Brookbank's the SIO."

Troy Wilson sighed heavily. "If you don't have your reference number, I can't help you."

"Hang on. Hang on," Collins said. "It's here somewhere." Bloody numbers – everything was numbers these days. "Ah, here it is," Collins said, extracting a slip of paper from the pile. "It's reference 721 – XCG."

Collins held his breath.

"We've not finished that one yet," Troy Wilson said. "I'll call you when it's done."

"What? You've got to be joking. This is urgent."

"Not according to my file it isn't," Troy Wilson said.

Collins had no idea what Troy Wilson looked like, but he imagined him sitting in a computer chair, wearing thick nerdy glasses and sporting sweat stains beneath his armpits, a smarmy, self-satisfied smile plastered on his face.

"Now you listen to me," Collins began.

"No, I don't have time for this. We have managed to get copies of a few stills from the footage, but we're having to do the whole thing in batches as no one uses this kind of software anymore. None of our systems are compatible. If you only knew how long it has taken us…"

"All right, all right. Can I at least look at the stills?" Collins asked. "They might give me something to go on."

On the other end of the line Troy Wilson hesitated. "The images are still a bit fuzzy, so don't come down here expecting miracles."

"Just a little bit of cooperation would do," Collins muttered.

"What was that?"

"Nothing. Be with you in five minutes."

A few minutes later, downstairs in the computer labs, Collins saw Troy Wilson in person for the first time. He may not have had sweat stains under his armpits – he moved too slowly to ever build up a sweat – but he'd definitely pictured the self-satisfied smirk correctly.

"I thought you said five minutes." Troy Wilson said and folded his arms.

Collins sighed. He'd been cornered by DCI Brookbank on the way down. Despite that, he'd only been ten minutes, tops. Rather than point that out, Collins swallowed his retaliation and sat down in a computer chair next to Troy.

"Sorry," Collins said and then focused on the computer screen. "Is this it?"

Collins could sense Troy glaring at him as he looked at the screen.

Troy narrowed his eyes. "It's the best we have so far."

Collins leaned forward. It wasn't bad, better than he'd been expecting anyway.

It showed the inside of the shop floor. The edge of the till was just visible on the right-hand side as the camera was set up behind the counter.

It was a black-and-white image. Newspapers and magazines lay scattered on the ground. There was an overturned chair, and chocolate bars lay around the body of a young boy.

Collins pointed at the boy. "That's Robbie Baxter. I'm sure of it. He's still in hospital."

Troy grunted, showing just how interested he was.

Collins searched the image for the other kid they had in hospital. He sat slumped against the wall. The image was slightly pixelated but Collins was sure it was Vinnie Pearson.

There were three other figures in the shot.

One was a girl with dark hair and a slim figure, wearing a tracksuit. Definitely a new lead. Next to her, a boy lay curled up and half hidden by the counter.

Collins' eyes focused on the final figure. This one was male, fat and down on his hands and knees. It wasn't the best angle but …

Collins frowned and leaned closer. "Christ…"

"What? Is it helpful?"

Collins stood up. "Can you print me a copy? And then email me the image. Right away."

Troy tapped a few keys, and the printer next to him churned out a copy. "I haven't got your email…"

Collins dropped a card with his contact details onto Troy's desk next to the keyboard. Collins picked up the printed copy and walked out of the room, his eyes fixed on the image.

"Oh, no trouble, at all," Troy Wilson grumbled under his breath. "At your service. No need to thank me."

Collins' mind was reeling as he took the stairs two at a time. He needed to get back to the briefing room quickly and confirm he wasn't seeing things.

It wasn't a good picture really, only a side-on view, but Collins was sure he recognised one of the people in the shop.

The fat one.

It was Craig Foster, he was sure of it.

The implications were huge. Craig Foster had survived the gas in the shop, but the second time he hadn't been so lucky. Had this been a suicide that messed up the first time? But then why not do it in his own flat in the first place? Why do it in a newsagent's of all places? Why with Syed Hammad?

Collins slowed his pace, his breath coming a little bit faster.

If it really was a suicide pact, then Craig Foster had decided to make a second attempt separately… Collins entered the briefing room.

What did this really prove? Only that DI Tyler was probably right. It probably was a joint suicide pact gone wrong, and Craig Foster had made a second and successful attempt.

Collins walked across to Mackinnon's desk and stuck the print out under his nose. "It's a still from the CCTV at the newsagent's. It's –"

"Craig Foster," Mackinnon said. "Jesus." He took the image from Collins and studied it.

Collins leaned back against Mackinnon's desk. "Well, I guess it was a suicide pact, and Craig Foster was successful the second time. God knows how they got together in the first place. I mean Syed Hammad and Craig Foster are hardly the obvious candidates…"

Collins trailed off as he noticed Mackinnon staring at him. "What?"

Mackinnon tilted his flatscreen computer monitor so Collins could see it. On the screen was a head and shoulders shot of a dark haired girl, smiling for the camera.

Collins took a deep breath. The girl was the spitting image of the girl from the CCTV still.

"Collins," Mackinnon said. "That's Joanne James."

CHAPTER TWENTY-NINE

IT WASN'T THE CLEAREST PICTURE, but even DI Tyler couldn't deny the resemblance between the CCTV still and the photograph of Joanne James provided by her devastated parents.

"So it's either a suicide pact, or we've got some weirdo knocking them off one by one." Tyler scratched the side of his nose with a pen.

"We need to talk to the other kids," Mackinnon said. "It's too late for Joanne James or Craig Foster, so we've got to talk to Robbie Baxter or Vinnie Pearson and..." Mackinnon leaned forward to point out the figure curled up next to the counter. "And whoever this is."

The as yet unidentified young man, slumped on the floor beside Robbie Baxter's feet, could hold very valuable information.

Tyler nodded. "If we can't talk to Robbie Baxter or Vinnie Pearson directly yet, we need to talk to their friends and family. It's ridiculous. Surely one of them should be up to a quick chat by now. I'm not talking a full scale interrogation, just a few questions."

Then Tyler turned back to Mackinnon and Collins. "We don't have much time. We need to find out who this other person is."

Tyler didn't say anything more, but both Collins and Mackinnon understood the implication. Two of the people who had survived inhaling the gas at the newsagent's were now dead. Whether by their own hand or someone else's.

It could be only a matter of time before the other kids in the photograph suffered the same fate.

CHAPTER THIRTY

1982

JUNIOR STOOD IN THE kitchen wiping up the plates after dinner. With his skinny legs, scraped knees and freckles, no one could have guessed he'd grow up to be an Arbiter of Justice.

He and his mother were working as a team. After Junior wiped up a plate, he would set it on the kitchen counter, and his mother would pick it up and put it in a cupboard. They didn't speak but worked in a happy kind of silence.

The front door banged shut, and Junior froze.

His mother glanced in the direction of the door, and for a moment an unguarded expression of fear gripped her face. She recovered quickly, smiling as she took the tea towel from Junior's hand.

"I'll finish off here, Junior. You get to bed before –"

"Before what?" The man filled the doorway. He was easily one of the largest men Junior had ever seen. He swayed from side-to-side, and his eyes were bleary from drink.

He looked at Junior's mother, and then blinked down at Junior, his eyes struggling to focus.

He slapped a hand against his leg. "Call this a welcome?" His voice boomed out, echoing around the kitchen.

He spread his thick, muscled arms wide. He expected Junior to hug him.

Junior glanced at his mother, who nodded encouragingly. He moved forward hesitantly, then looked back again at his mother.

She smiled, offering reassurance. "Go on, Junior."

"What are you waiting for, boy?" The man's huge, red face loomed in front of Junior.

"Hello, sir," Junior said as he moved his arms around the man's waist.

Junior called him sir because he felt that was right and respectful. It was what he called his school teacher, but he felt the man's body tense, and Junior knew he'd said the wrong thing.

The man reared back, roughly slapping Junior's arms away. "Why don't you ever call me father? I took you on, didn't I? There aren't many men who would be prepared to do that."

Junior didn't really know what the man meant. He didn't need anyone to take him on. His mother had always looked after him perfectly well. She'd done a good enough job without this man.

"You'd better get off to bed, Junior." He felt his mother's hands clasp his shoulders. "School tomorrow." She began to manoeuvre him around the man's bulk, into the safety of the hallway.

"He should call me father," the man growled.

But Junior got lucky. The man was already distracted,

moving towards the other end of the kitchen and sniffing the air. "What's for dinner?"

Junior fled upstairs. He learned it was better to stay upstairs when the man was around. Junior shut his bedroom door and kneeled beside his bed. He lifted the edge of the mattress and pulled out his black notebook.

He didn't use it like a diary. He liked to write down phrases and quotes he thought sounded important. When he felt anxious, he would flick through the pages of the notebook, and it made him feel better.

He lay back on the worn, blue bedspread covering his single bed and clutched the notebook to his chest.

He couldn't stop thinking about what might be going on downstairs. It was impossible to concentrate on the writing inside the notebook, but the feeling of the smooth leather binding under his fingers was still reassuring.

He could hear his mother's pleading voice, trying to calm the man. But it wouldn't work. After he'd had a drink, nothing calmed him down.

Junior tried to block out the noise, screwing shut his eyes and muttering over and over, "I hate him."

Distracted by his chanting, he didn't notice the door open inch-by-inch until it creaked loudly. Junior's eyes flew open, but it was just the little girl.

She'd turned up a few weeks ago, the same time as the man. She was very small, and she didn't even go to school yet.

Mother said she was a strange one because she didn't talk. She might not be old enough for school, but she should have been talking by now.

The little girl stood in the doorway. She didn't enter the room, but as the sound of crashing furniture came from downstairs, her eyes widened in terror.

Junior held out his arms.

The little girl hesitated for a few seconds, and then ran to Junior's side, flinging herself onto the bed.

With the tiny girl huddled up beside him, Junior tightened his grip on the notebook and stared at the ceiling as his mother's screams began.

CHAPTER THIRTY-ONE

PRESENT DAY

"ARE YOU SURE I agreed to help you with this?" Derek asked, his face flushed and sweaty. He lifted a paving slab from the pile and awkwardly carried it across to the makeshift patio.

"Yes, you agreed last weekend," Mackinnon said, taking the paving slab from Derek.

As Mackinnon laid the paving slab on the ground, Derek grumbled under his breath, "You must have asked me when I was drunk. I would never have agreed to this if I'd been sober."

Mackinnon straightened and massaged the small of his back. He hadn't thought laying a new patio in Chloe's garden would be such hard work.

"This was a stupid idea," Derek said. "It's too hot for this kind of work."

It was hot. Hot for England even in July. Derek's dog,

Molly, sat under the shade of an apple tree. Molly's tongue lolled out of her mouth as she sat there panting and looking at both men as if they were crazy. As it was the hottest day of the year so far, she was probably right.

Derek yanked up another paving slab. It slipped through his hands, and the slab landed on his toes. He let out a strangled curse.

"This is not fun," Derek said. "You told me this would be fun." He lowered himself into a garden chair and pulled off his trainers.

He held up his left foot. "Look at that. I bet it's broken."

Mackinnon took a look. It was a bit red. "Stop being such a baby. Unless it swells to at least half the size, you're not getting out of this."

Derek groaned and got to his feet. "And I'm sure you mentioned something about food. I thought we were having a barbecue."

Derek slipped his trainers back on. "You got me here under false pretences. You said we would cook some burgers, drink some beers and that this little patio would take half an hour."

Derek looked up at the clear blue sky and wiped the sweat off his forehead with the back of his hand.

"I'm getting too old for this," Derek said as he picked up the paving slab and carried it across to Mackinnon.

"What are you talking about? You're only thirty-seven."

"Yeah, well I feel older. And this isn't fun."

"You've already said that."

"And I'm hungry."

"You said that, too."

Mackinnon looked down at the half-completed patio. He wiped the sweat from his face on the sleeve of his shirt. "Chloe will be back soon. She is getting the stuff for the barbecue."

"You said that an hour ago."

"She must have got waylaid. She'll be here."

D. S. BUTLER

"When? I'm beginning to think you made up the barbecue idea just to get me here."

Mackinnon set down the next two paving slabs then paused, trying to catch his breath. How could it be so hard for two men to lay a patio? He was glad Chloe wasn't back yet to see just how pathetic their attempt was.

Mackinnon laid the next stone slab and glared down at it. What the hell? There was a three-inch gap. "Derek, are you sure you measured this?"

"Yeah, why?"

Mackinnon pointed to the gap.

"Oh," Derek said. "I don't know how that happened. You must have distracted me."

Mackinnon shook his head. "Fantastic."

"It's not my fault. I don't work well on an empty stomach. You should have done it yourself."

Mackinnon shrugged. "Never mind. I've got a few extra paving slabs. We can just extend it."

"Brilliant."

"Come on. We're almost there. We've done well today."

Mackinnon looked down at the paving. It wasn't too bad. He reached for the spirit level and grinned in satisfaction. At least it was level.

"I can't believe you roped me into this," Derek said. "It's a Saturday. The day of rest."

"That's Sunday."

"Saturday, Sunday. Whatever. Both days should be relaxing."

"Yeah, well, the only reason you agreed to help me was because you wanted to get out of visiting Liz's parents."

Derek scowled because he knew Mackinnon was right.

"I've only been dating Liz for three weeks. That's far too soon to meet her parents."

"Why didn't you just tell her that? Tell her the truth?"

Derek looked at Mackinnon as if he were crazy. "Don't you know anything about women?"

At that moment, Chloe came out into the garden carrying a bottle of beer in each hand.

"Oh, my God." Derek scrambled to his feet and took one of the beers from Chloe. "I could kiss you for that. Jack has had me sweating over this patio for hours without a break."

Chloe grinned and passed the other bottle of beer to Mackinnon. "That's how I like my men – doing hard physical labour while I shop."

Derek flopped back into a garden chair as Chloe inspected her new patio. "It's looking good." Then she frowned. "But there seems to be a gap here."

"It's all under control," Mackinnon said. "We decided it needed to be a little wider. All part of the plan."

"Oh, okay."

Mackinnon gulped down half the bottle of ice cold beer in one go. Jesus, that tasted good.

Katy wandered into the garden, a paperback book in her hand, fanning herself. "Have you finished yet?"

"Nearly," Mackinnon said.

"Are we having the barbecue soon, Mum?" Katy said. "I'm starving."

Derek jumped to his feet, suddenly finding some energy from somewhere. "I'll do it," he volunteered. "We've nearly finished the patio. I'm sure Jack can take it from here." He smirked at Mackinnon.

When Mackinnon finally laid the last stone and the patio was complete, he wandered towards the sound of sizzling sausages and the smell of charred burgers.

Derek was waving the spatula around while he chatted to Sarah. Mackinnon's stomach rumbled. He was so hungry the sight and smell of the food was far more interesting than what

Derek was saying, but his ears pricked up at the mention of an iPod.

"What are you talking about?" Mackinnon asked, leaning down to pluck another beer from the ice box by Derek's feet.

"Sarah says her iPod's broken. I told her I can get one for –"

"Oh, no you don't," Mackinnon said and turned to Sarah. "You can get a new one from a shop just like everyone else."

"I know what you're thinking, Jack." Derek said. "But it's not dodgy. I know a guy who is –"

"She doesn't want it."

Sarah pouted. "Oh, but Derek can get one so much cheaper than they sell them in the shops."

Mackinnon shook his head. There was a reason for that. Derek was a good friend, but he wasn't without his faults. The main one being an ability to lay his hands on things cheaply. Mackinnon wasn't an idiot. He knew Derek's so-called friends, and there was no way he would let Derek sell a dodgy iPod to Sarah.

"No," Mackinnon said. "Now pass me one of those burgers."

Derek rolled his eyes, shoved a blackened burger in a roll and handed it to Mackinnon.

Derek put another burger in a bun and took it over to Chloe, who was stretched out on a sun lounger.

"Thanks, Derek. I could get used to this." She raised her sunglasses and grinned up at him.

Mackinnon sat down on the seat beside Chloe. Molly, Derek's border collie, walked over to them wagging her tail.

Mackinnon broke off a piece of sausage and leaned down to give it to Molly.

Derek yelped. "Don't give her that. I told you she has a sensitive digestion."

"She's a dog. She eats meat."

"Only specially prepared meat," Derek said.

The sun was setting; golden rays filtered through the trees and above them a red kite swooped gracefully home to roost.

"I can't believe you two managed to finish the patio in one afternoon," Chloe said as she polished off her burger. "I bet those stone slabs were heavy."

Derek nodded, holding his beer on his stomach as he leaned back in the garden chair. "It wasn't too bad," he said. "I mean, I had to motivate Jack. He's not really one for manual labour. I had to crack the whip a bit."

Chloe took one look at Mackinnon's face and giggled.

Mackinnon just shook his head. Derek, who had reclined the garden chair so he was practically lying flat, fanned himself with one hand and balanced the beer on his protruding belly with the other.

"How heavy are they?" Katy asked.

"They weigh a ton," Derek said. "It's a good job I'm in shape."

Katy frowned. "You look shattered."

"I'm just resting my eyes."

A few minutes later, the sun was down, and the food was finished. Molly had curled up by Derek's feet. Mackinnon felt a wave of contentment wash over him. Derek liked to wind him up, but there was nothing like watching the sunset after a hot summer's day. They didn't get enough of them in England.

Mackinnon looked over at Chloe as she laughed at something Derek had said. Katy sat on the floor, stroking Molly's soft fur. Yes, Mackinnon thought, this was pretty much a perfect evening. It didn't get much better than this.

CHAPTER THIRTY-TWO

1982

JUNIOR BLINKED INTO THE darkness.

He'd been dreaming about a trip to the seaside with his mother. He'd had an ice-cream cone with a flake, and they'd paddled in the sea. It had been a good dream, and Junior didn't want to wake up yet. He snuggled back underneath the duvet, burying his head in the pillow, trying to get back to sleep.

But it was no good.

The out-of-tune singing interspersed with curse words was too loud. Too loud to be coming from downstairs. That meant the man was up here.

For a moment, Junior didn't dare move. Would the man come into his bedroom?

Junior slowly eased himself out of bed and snuck across the room on tiptoes until he reached the door.

Peering out into the hallway, he could see that the little

girl's bedroom door was slightly ajar. The man stood at the top of the stairs teetering on the top step.

"Come here, child." The man lunged forward.

For a horrifying second, Junior thought the man was talking to him, but then he noticed the little girl was outside by the staircase, too. She had pressed herself back against the wall.

Junior held his breath and dared to open his bedroom door another inch.

Clutching her forearm, the man pulled the little girl towards him and gave her a sloppy kiss on the cheek. The little girl was rigid, not understanding why this man would wallop her one minute and kiss her the next.

Her bony knees were shaking beneath her white cotton nightdress, and her big round eyes looked huge in the dim light.

Annoyed with her reaction, the man shook her by the arm. "Idiot child. Say good night to your daddy."

The little girl was silent. Her lower lip wobbled.

"Come on. You can say it. Say daddy… D…A …"

The girl started to cry.

"You pathetic little bugger. You're not right in the head. No wonder your mother dumped you on me."

She tried to pull her arm away.

"Don't you move. I'll tell you when you can go back to bed. Do you understand?" He slapped the back of her legs.

"Do you understand?" he roared. He clamped his meaty hands on her tiny shoulders and shook her like a rag doll.

The little girl wasn't Junior's real sister. She'd turned up at the same time as the man, and mother said he was an older brother now. He might not be her proper brother, but he still didn't like to see somebody making her cry.

Junior shivered in the doorway. His bare feet were exposed to the draft whistling around the house.

He inched a little further forward.

The man was still standing by the top step. He let go of the little girl's shoulders, and she fell to the floor, sobbing. He staggered, then grabbed the banister.

That gave Junior an idea.

Junior was as quiet as a mouse as he moved forward.

The little girl saw him creeping up behind the man. She jumped in surprise and took a little step backwards, but the man was so drunk he didn't even notice.

Junior put a finger to his lips.

The drink had made the man immune to the cold; he only wore his trousers and a white vest. The red flush on his face increased as he sang an old-fashioned song Junior didn't recognise. But the singing was good because it meant the man was less likely to hear him.

Junior winced as a floorboard beneath his bare foot creaked. He was so close now.

He raised his arms an inch at a time.

So close, almost touching.

His hands were shaking. He shot a glance at the little girl. She wanted him to push. He could read it in her eyes.

Junior bit down on his lip. It was now or never. He couldn't change his mind and turn back now, even if he wanted to, because the man would catch him and would be sure to give him a beating.

Junior shoved against the man's back with all his might, grunting with the effort.

Time seemed to stand still as the man moved forward only slightly. He seemed to hold on at a perilous angle before, finally, he fell. As the man tumbled down the wooden stairs, his arms flailed. He was trying to get a grip on the bannister and break his fall, but it was no good.

He landed in a crooked heap at the bottom of the stairs.

Junior felt dizzy. He put one hand on the banister to steady himself and stared down at the man's body.

The man didn't get up.

Junior turned to the little girl and smiled. "He fell. That's what happened. He fell down the stairs because he had too much to drink."

The little girl fixed him with her solemn gaze, then nodded.

Junior moved towards her quickly. "We'd better get to bed so mother doesn't see us."

The little girl put her tiny, cold hand into Junior's and said, "J ... Junior."

"Yes?" Junior asked, squeezing her hand and trying to warm it with his own.

But the little girl didn't say anything else. She ran off to her bedroom, and Junior clambered into his own bed with his heart beating like crazy.

Just a few seconds later, his mother found the man's body crumpled at the foot of the stairs.

Junior smiled as her agonised wails rang out through the house.

CHAPTER THIRTY-THREE

PRESENT DAY

ESTELLE PUMMELLED THE small of her back with her fists, trying to relieve the ache.

Bloody Tyrell. She tried to hoover the flat this afternoon but had to give up after a couple of minutes. She couldn't carry on. Her back ached so much.

Tyrell was such a lazy bastard. Surely it wouldn't kill him to run a duster around the flat now and again, or help with the hoovering. It wasn't as if he had a job to keep him busy.

She glanced at the clock. He was supposed to be home by now. He'd promised Estelle a nice evening, just the two of them, to make the most of the time before the baby arrived. She wouldn't be surprised if he'd completely forgotten. He was probably holed up with his mates somewhere, playing Xbox games. He'd come home eventually, stinking of booze and full of apologies.

Estelle leaned forward, trying to stretch out the ache in her spine, then flopped down on the sofa.

She couldn't wait for the baby to be born. Her mother kept going on and on about how hard it would be. She constantly told Estelle that Tyrell needed to pull his weight.

As if she didn't know that herself! It was all very well saying that, but getting Tyrell to actually help out more was an impossible task.

The worst thing was that Tyrell didn't even argue. He just solemnly nodded and agreed with her, promising to help her out more and do better from now on. But it was all words. He never changed.

Estelle tried to bend forward and massage her feet, but the huge bump got in the way. Her feet were so swollen they wouldn't even fit in her slippers anymore.

She chucked a cushion over the top of them, to try and keep them warm, and settled back on the sofa.

She reached for the TV remote control. She would have to entertain herself as it didn't look like Tyrell was about to turn up any time soon. But as she pressed the red button on the remote, she heard his key in the lock.

She struggled to her feet and walked through the doorway, meeting him in the hall.

"Hey, babe, how you feeling?" Tyrell looped an arm around her shoulders.

"My back is killing me, and I've had nothing to do all day but watch TV. I couldn't even do the hoovering because my back ached so much."

"Don't worry about that. I'll do it tomorrow," Tyrell said. "Now, come in here and sit down. I've got a surprise for you."

He handed her something the size of a pack of cards. It had a smooth, sleek black case. As her hand closed around it, she frowned.

A phone. She held it in front of her, dangling it between her thumb and forefinger. "What planet are you on, Tyrell? We can't afford this with the baby coming. We've still got so much stuff to get: the cot, the pram …"

"Yeah, yeah, don't worry about that stuff, babe. I'll handle it."

Estelle stared at him.

Tyrell moved back, creating distance between them. "Don't you like it?"

"Of course, I do. I just think, with the baby on the way, there are more important things to spend money on right now."

"Look, I said I'd take care of you, didn't I?"

"I know. I'm not trying to argue…"

"It sounds like it to me."

Estelle shook her head. "I just think we should be more careful with our money."

"I don't understand you. I get you a present, and you turn it into an excuse to nag."

"I'm not nagging." Estelle felt tears prick the corner of her eyes. "I just…"

"Oh, give it a rest," he said and slumped back into the cushions on the sofa.

Estelle blinked back the tears. She hated crying. It was the stupid bloody hormones making her emotional.

"Enough of the waterworks," Tyrell said. "I can't handle this."

He picked up the remote control and flicked through the channels on the TV. "There's sod all on."

"I know." Estelle sniffed. "There's been nothing on all day. And I've been stuck in on my own."

Tyrell sighed. "I'm sorry, all right. But you've got to relax and trust me. I'll make sure you and the baby are okay."

He put a hand on her stomach. "All right?"

She put her hand over his and gave him a tearful smile. "Yeah, all right. I don't mean to nag. I just worry, you know?"

"Why don't you choose a DVD? We can have a nice evening in, and I'll pick us up a takeaway. What do you fancy?"

"I'd love a Chinese," Estelle said.

Tyrell nodded. "Right." He leaned over and kissed her on the cheek, then grabbed his front door keys off the coffee table. "I won't be long."

After Tyrell left, Estelle looked round the room. She'd never paid much attention before she got pregnant, but now she thought the room was looking tired. It desperately needed decorating.

She moaned to her mum the other day about it, and her mum said it was something to do with nesting, wanting everything to be perfect before the baby arrived, but Estelle thought she was just sick and tired of living in a dump.

It was mostly Tyrell's junk that made the place look so messy. He didn't believe in putting anything away. He left odds and ends scattered over surfaces, which of course made it harder to dust and clean. Magazines and newspapers were piled on the floor in the corner of the room.

She eased herself off of the sofa. Christ, she didn't even remember what it was like to be able to get up out of a chair without an effort.

She walked into the kitchen, intending to get some plates and knives and forks out ready for the Chinese, and rested her hand on her stomach.

In response, she felt the baby move inside her and give a little kick.

She put both hands on her stomach and smiled. It would be all right once the baby was here.

CHAPTER THIRTY-FOUR

THE ARBITER OF JUSTICE STOOD on the pavement outside Tyrell's flat, watching his phone intently, focusing on the red flashing light.

He liked that name. He'd considered writing to a newspaper, and signing his name like that. He wasn't so keen on the label the newspapers had currently saddled him with. The Masked Man. It didn't have the same ring to it as the Arbiter of Justice. But names weren't really important. Actions were what counted.

Tonight he couldn't fill his mind with stupid ideas about names. He needed to be on the ball. It wouldn't be as easy this time. The flat was on a higher floor, so he wouldn't be able to seal all the windows from the outside. He stared up at the illuminated windows. The killer smiled. Good. If the lights were on, Tyrell should be home. Even from down here, he could see that the windows were double glazed. They should keep enough gas inside to do the job.

He needed to be flexible, to be able to change his plan at a minute's notice. That was the path to success.

He rested the heavy black holdall on the floor next to him and mentally ran through his checklist. He had his small toolkit to work on the lock. He preferred to make his entrance unannounced. Of course, he could ring the doorbell and force his way in, but he liked the element of surprise.

Ideally, to get the gas to work quickly, he would use an enclosed space. The bathroom or kitchen perhaps? Of course, it might not be that easy.

He could never have forced Craig Foster into the bathroom. The sheer size of him prevented that. The boy would have overpowered him. He'd needed a huge amount of gas to fill Craig Foster's sitting room.

Tyrell Patterson was much slimmer than Craig Foster. In fact, he was almost scrawny. But the killer knew not to underestimate his opponent. People could summon an incredible amount of strength when they felt cornered or endangered.

So the killer would have to think on his feet. It didn't matter where or how. It only mattered that justice was served.

Tyrell might be strong enough to smash the door down, especially the cheap doors they tended to fit in these flats, but the gas would overpower him within seconds. There wouldn't be time for him to escape.

The killer leaned down to pick up the black holdall. It was time.

CHAPTER THIRTY-FIVE

INSIDE THE FLAT, ESTELLE CHECKED her watch. It only took five minutes to walk to the Chinese takeaway, so allowing for five minutes each way, with a ten minute wait for the food order, Tyrell should have been back within twenty minutes.

But that didn't take into account the fact there was a pub next door to the Chinese. Tyrell was bound to have popped in there for a pint. He probably wouldn't be back inside of an hour.

Estelle poured herself a fresh cup of tea and then walked back along the hallway, stopping at the door to the nursery. She smiled. The little room was painted yellow and Estelle's mother had paid for the new carpet. The soft plushness felt lovely under her bare feet.

The smell of new paint was still strong, so she decided to open the window. Tomorrow she would leave it open all day. She'd managed to get the paint on special offer from B&Q so it had been a bargain really. At least the baby's room was ready. Tyrell was meant to be getting the cot and the pram, but he didn't want her to buy it from Mothercare because he said he knew a bloke...

That obviously meant he knew a bloke selling knocked off stuff. Either that or some cheap rubbish from China that might not be safe. She was getting seriously concerned that when the baby turned up they wouldn't have anywhere for it to sleep. She sighed and took a sip of her tea.

Maybe when the baby arrived, Tyrell would change. People said kids made you change your outlook.

But with Tyrell ... Well, Estelle would believe it when she saw it.

She looked down at the little brown, fluffy teddy bear propped up against the wall. It had been a gift from her mother. The baby's first toy.

She switched off the light in the nursery and walked back into the sitting room.

As she passed through the doorway, she blinked. A man, dressed in black and wearing a hideous black mask, stood in the centre of the room.

At first she couldn't move. She couldn't do anything. Finally, the adrenaline spiked in her system, and she screamed, dropping her cup of tea, which sent the scalding liquid splashing up her legs.

She barely noticed. Her hands protectively covered her belly, and she turned and ran awkwardly, down the hallway towards the front door, screaming.

But the masked man got to her before she reached the door. She felt him push his way past her as he sped along the hallway and out of the door.

CHAPTER THIRTY-SIX

THE KILLER TOOK THE STAIRS three at a time. He needed to get away right now.

Christ, the woman was pregnant, ready to burst. What was she doing there? It was Tyrell's flat. Why hadn't he been there?

The killer felt his throat tighten. She looked massive. She must've been practically full-term.

He'd been so close ... No, he couldn't think that. He shook his head, trying to shake the image of the woman with her hands clasped around her belly. He didn't know anything about her. She might be just as bad as Tyrell Patterson, but the child was an innocent. And he'd been about to ...

He reached the bottom of the stairs and tore off his mask, stuffing it into his black holdall.

He wanted to wait to see if Tyrell turned up. How could he have got it so wrong? It didn't make sense. Tyrell was supposed to be there. He couldn't wait around here for Tyrell, though. The pregnant woman would probably be on the phone to the police by now, and he didn't want to be in the vicinity when they turned up.

He kept walking. He didn't want to attract unnecessary attention, so he willed his shaking legs to slow down. He felt vomit rise in his throat and ducked into an alleyway and threw up in the gutter.

Panting, he leaned back against the rough brick wall. He stayed there for a few moments, waiting for the nausea to pass and for his breathing to become regular. A sound nearby made him turn sharply, but it was only a cat scavenging through the rubbish. A tom cat on his nightly rounds.

He rubbed a hand over his face and thought about his mother. What would she have said if she had known what he'd been about to do?

He closed his eyes as he imagined his mother's disapproving face and a painful memory hit him. Even now, it still hurt when he remembered. She'd only done it for his own good. Mother had wanted him to have children. She only wanted what was best for him.

It happened when Junior was working at the council. It was his first job, and he was basking in the satisfaction of finally earning a wage and contributing to the household.

Money-wise things were always tight now. After the man had gone, they'd struggled to get by on his mother's wages from her cleaning jobs, but they got through it. And now Junior was working, he was bringing in money, too.

His mother was still working. She cleaned at Canary Wharf, travelling up there early every morning, but soon she wouldn't need to. Junior had plans. Soon his mother wouldn't be cleaning up after anybody else's mess.

He'd realised something was wrong as soon as he got in from work.

He hung his jacket on the coat stand by the door and looked down the hallway to the kitchen. His mother sat at the table. There was nothing unusual in that, but there was something about her stillness that made Junior frown.

Normally, as soon as Junior got home, she'd get up, put the kettle on and take some biscuits out of the cupboard, but today she just sat there.

Junior walked into the kitchen and set the envelope containing his wages down on the table. "There you go, Mother. That should help with the housekeeping this week."

His mother raised her head slowly and looked up at Junior, studying his face as if she were searching for something.

"What is it, Mother?" Junior asked. "Is something wrong? Has something happened to –?"

"That boy called for you again, five minutes ago."

Junior flushed.

"I told you I didn't want you to see him anymore, Junior. I've heard things. I've heard rumours."

Junior's palms began to sweat, and he wiped them against the legs of his trousers. "But, Mother, they are just rumours, started by a bunch of nasty gossips. They're making things up. He's a nice boy."

Junior looked down at the table. He couldn't meet his mother's eyes. He needed to tell her something. He'd been building up the courage for months, but he was terrified of how she would react.

"Mother, I… I need to tell you something… There's something you should know …"

His mother set her palms flat against the table. "Before you start, Junior, there's something I want to tell you."

Junior swallowed, surprised by his mother's change in the conversation. He looked at her, bewildered, and nodded. "Okay."

He didn't know how he was going to get the words out anyway. It was so difficult.

His mother picked up the cup of tea by her side. It looked like it had gone cold. The brown tannin had stained the edge of the cup. She put the cup back down again without drinking and began to tell her story.

"There was a boy at my school, and I know things are different now, times change, but I want to tell you about him."

Junior pulled out a chair and sat down.

"It happened when I was sixteen. He was in the same year as me, so he was roughly the same age. He was caught with another boy in the locker room." Junior's mother paused then licked her lips. "He was caught doing unnatural things. Do you understand me, Junior?"

Junior said nothing.

She moved her cup in front of her and studied the tea rather than Junior.

"And then a terrible thing happened to him. He killed himself. He swallowed a whole bottle of his mother's sleeping pills."

Junior finally found his voice, "But that's terrible. If only he had talked to someone… If he'd had someone to confide in…"

His mother's smile tightened as she stroked the scrubbed pine table with the palm of her hand.

"His family must have been devastated …" Junior dared to raise his eyes and look at his mother's face.

His mother folded her arms and said, in a grim voice, "It was for the best."

"For the best?" Junior's voice was hoarse.

His mother nodded. "A dead son was preferable to a queer one." She stood up and curled her hand around her cup. "The tea's cold. I'll make a fresh pot, shall I?"

CHAPTER THIRTY-SEVEN

KATHY WALKER STOOD IN THE hallway of her flat and debated whether to go into the sitting room. Her brother had come for dinner, which he tended to do at least once a week.

Mitch must have spotted Stuart's van because he turned up shortly after Stuart. Mitch never paid social calls. So it was quite obvious there was something going on.

Kathy had made some excuse about needing to finish off something downstairs in the salon, to give them a chance to talk privately, but that had been half an hour ago.

Feeling guilty, she moved closer to the sitting room door. She could hear low voices coming from inside. Of course it was her sitting room. She shouldn't feel like a gooseberry in her own flat. She raised a hand to the door knob, then changed her mind and let her hand drop. She'd give them a bit more time and make a cup of tea first.

She bustled about the kitchen taking her time over preparing the tea. She leaned back on the counter to drink it. It had been a long day. All she wanted to do was kick off her shoes and sit down in her sitting room and put her feet up.

Why was she lurking in the kitchen? It was ridiculous.

With her cup of tea in one hand she approached the sitting room door and pushed it slightly ajar.

Mitch and Stuart were both sitting on the sofa, but thankfully they were just talking. In fact from the look on Mitch's face, it looked like they were having quite a serious conversation. Mitch looked thoroughly miserable, but then again, he always looked miserable.

What did Stuart see in him?

"I think you should tell your mother about us," Stuart said. He kept his voice low, but Kathy could still hear the desperation in his tone, and it made her hate Mitch Horrocks.

Who did he think he was, treating her brother like that?

Mitch folded his arms and shook his head emphatically. "No."

Stuart looked away for a moment, then turned back to Mitch and said, "She adores you. What are you afraid of? Are you ashamed of me? Of us?"

"Of course, not," Mitch said.

Stuart slapped the palm of his hand against the arm of the sofa. "I'm sick of it. Either you tell your mother, or we forget about the whole thing."

Kathy mentally cheered her brother. That's right. Show him that you won't be messed around.

Silence followed. She put her hand on the door knob, but hesitated, waiting to see if Mitch would reply.

Mitch muttered something quietly. As Kathy leaned forward to try to hear what he said, she tilted her cup, spilling her tea and burning her fingers.

She winced and wiped her wet hand on the legs of her jeans.

"Don't make me choose between you," Mitch said quietly.

Stuart exploded with anger, gritting his teeth as he turned to face Mitch. "Why the hell shouldn't I?"

Mitch sighed heavily and looked down at his hands resting in his lap.

"Because you'll never win," he said.

CHAPTER THIRTY-EIGHT

FIONA EVANS TOOK A SIP of wine and smiled.

Things had really improved since Tim Coleman had started to look after Luke.

Fiona had been able to spend so much more time with Anna during the day. And for the first time, she found herself without anything pressing she needed to do in the evening. That had really helped her unwind.

She could actually settle down in the evening and have a glass of wine, watch some TV, or read a book. God, she'd forgotten how much she loved to read.

She loved having Tim around. She thought having another man around the house might be difficult, but he'd made everything so easy. They'd started having a glass of wine together, after he'd finished for the day, and she loved having adult conversations for a change.

It was remarkable how good it felt to chat to somebody about day-to-day things, rather than kids TV programmes or Barbie dolls!

This week Tim had taken Luke to an appointment at the

rehab centre where they worked on Luke's muscle tone. As Anna went to nursery, Fiona had a whole morning free. She'd gone shopping, treated herself to a piece of carrot cake in the John Lewis coffee shop. It was so silly, but being able to do small things like that made such a difference.

The only downside to this free time was the extra time it gave her to think because her thoughts naturally went to Bruce.

She still missed Bruce, of course. She lay awake in the evenings, remembering, but during the day things were getting bearable. She had to think of the future, for her and the children, and the future was looking brighter. And it was all thanks to Tim.

CHAPTER THIRTY-NINE

THE FOLLOWING MORNING, THE BELL above the door rang out as Charlotte entered the hairdressing salon. Compared to the warm, bright sunshine outside, the salon was cool and dark. Charlotte took a moment, waiting for her eyes to get accustomed to the dim light.

It wasn't busy, and at first, she didn't see anyone in the salon at all, then she noticed a middle-aged lady sitting in one of the chairs in the back corner of the room. The woman had her face buried in a magazine, and her hair was in tufts, coated with tinfoil.

"Hello," Charlotte said. "Is Kathy about?"

"She's out back somewhere," the lady said, without looking up from what Charlotte could now see was a cross-word puzzle.

Charlotte walked through the salon, passing the mirrored walls and the holders containing hairbrushes and combs. There were adjustable seats in front of each mirror. Maybe they got more use during busier times.

Charlotte walked past the till towards a white painted door

at the rear of the room. She gently rapped on the door. "Hello, Kathy?"

The door opened and the petite, elfin face of Kathy Walker appeared. "Just give me a minute," she said. "I'll be right with you."

True to her word, Kathy bustled out the back room a few seconds later. "Okay, my love, what can I do for you? Perhaps, we could give you a few highlights. I'm not sure that dark colour suits you very much."

Charlotte swallowed the insult. "I'm not here for my hair. I'm DC Charlotte Brown. I spoke to you the other day, after the gas incident in the newsagent's."

The smile slid from Kathy's face. "Ah, yes, of course. Sorry, I didn't recognise you at first. It was all a bit of a palaver that day. There were so many people coming and going, you know?"

Charlotte nodded. "No problem. I've got some photographs to show you. I'd like to know if you can recognise anyone."

Kathy visibly recoiled. "It's not Syed, is it? I don't want to look at pictures of a dead body."

"It's nothing like that," Charlotte said. "It's just images from the CCTV footage of the newsagent's, but no dead bodies, I promise. There were kids inside at the time, and we would like you to help us identify them if you can."

Charlotte noticed the lady with the tinfoil hair had turned around in her seat and was looking at them curiously.

"Perhaps we'd better do this out the back," Charlotte suggested.

Kathy nodded. "Yes. Come through. Ten more minutes for that colour, Irene," Kathy called over her shoulder to the tin foil lady.

Kathy led Charlotte into the small kitchenette. There was space for a couple of chairs, a tiny table and a sink. A small window looked out onto the backyard, which was full of cardboard boxes.

Kathy noticed her looking. "They're my brother's. He does deliveries. Sometimes they pay him extra to take away the packaging. He'll take it to the tip tomorrow."

Kathy pulled out a chair. "Let's have a look at these photos."

Charlotte pulled the prints from a brown envelope and spread them out on the table. "We're looking to identify any of the kids."

Kathy got up from her chair. "What am I like? I forgot my reading glasses. Won't be a minute."

She headed back into the hairdressing salon, and Charlotte took the opportunity to have a look around. She peered out into the backyard at the cardboard boxes.

They couldn't have been stored here long. At the first sign of rain, the boxes would turn into a soggy mess.

She could go out there now, have a bit of a nose around, and she'd probably find out that Stuart Walker was doing something he shouldn't be. But you had to choose your battles in this job.

Kathy Walker seemed nice enough. Although, Charlotte was willing to bet this salon was suffering. People still needed haircuts, but with hair dye for sale in Boots and every other chemist on the high street, why would you pay sixty quid to get it done at the salon?

It might be different if you were rolling in money, but for most people it made sense to take the cheaper option. Charlotte had been colouring her own hair raven black since before she joined the police. Her own hair was a boring light brown. She'd gone through a bit of a Goth phase at university and never really grown out of the black hair.

Charlotte's mother was always dropping hints about her hair colour and suggesting it might be a good idea to get out in the sun and get a bit of colour in her cheeks. Chance would be a fine thing. The weather was glorious today, but it always seemed to be glorious when she was at work. When the weekend rolled around it would probably be raining again.

Kathy came back, wearing red-rimmed reading glasses. "Sorry about that. Where were we?"

Charlotte pushed one of the images across the table, so Kathy could get a better look at it.

She peered down. "Right, well, they're not all kids, are they? That one's ginormous," she said, pointing out Craig Foster.

"No, they're not all kids." Charlotte supposed she must be getting old, referring to Craig Foster as a kid. "He was twenty-one."

Kathy looked up. "Was?"

Charlotte said nothing.

Kathy looked back down at the picture. "Oh, God."

"Do you recognise anyone?"

Kathy nodded. "I think so. We had some trouble last year, at the time of the riots. It was nowhere near as bad as it was in Tottenham, Croydon or some of those other places.

"A friend of mine owns a beauty salon over Croydon way, and her place was completely wrecked.

"But we did have a bit of trouble here with this group of youngsters," Kathy pressed her finger to the print-out. "I'm pretty sure they were behind it."

Kathy looked down at the table and swallowed hard. Tinny pop music trilled out of the radio on the window sill.

"Stuart was able to chase them away before they did any real damage, but I did have a broken window, and the rioters were attempting to get inside. It was a very scary night, I don't mind telling you. Plus, the fact we couldn't get the police to help."

"I think the police were under great demand that night,"

Charlotte said.

"I know that, but... I pay my taxes," Kathy said. "And when I needed them, they weren't there."

Charlotte could have gone into the debate about funding. The lack of resources, reduced numbers of officers. The last couple of years had been pretty tough. But she didn't have time to try to explain.

"Do you know any of their names?" Charlotte asked.

Kathy pointed to Robbie. "I know that little bugger ... Sorry, pardon my language, but his name is Robbie Baxter. His mother is quite well known around this area." Kathy grimaced. "They're not a very nice family. Both of Robbie's older brothers are inside."

Charlotte nodded. "Anyone else?"

"I don't recognise the girl. I haven't seen her before. But this is Vinnie Pearson." Kathy nodded. "He's a troublemaker. He's the leader of their little gang. He and his friends completely trashed the cafe along the road."

"What about him?" Charlotte pointed at the unidentified member of the gang.

Kathy squinted at the image. "It's not the best picture is it? But I'm pretty sure I recognise him." Kathy tapped the image with a long, pink, painted nail.

"Tyrell Patterson. I've known him since he was a little boy. He's Vinnie's right-hand man. They've been inseparable since they started school."

"Tyrell Patterson," Charlotte repeated, writing the name on the back of the photo. "Do you know where he lives, or where I might find him?"

Kathy shook her head. "Sorry, I've no idea."

Charlotte slipped the lid back on her pen. "Thanks for your help, Kathy."

She smiled. Finally it looked like they were getting some-where. Now all they had to do was find Tyrell Patterson.

CHAPTER FORTY

CHARLOTTE GOT BACK TO WOOD Street station just in time for the briefing. There was a bit of buzz in the station because the CCTV was finally ready to view.

DI Tyler stood at the front of the room, with the remote control in his hand, and attached the projector to the laptop.

"While I'm setting this up, I want to bring you all up to speed," Tyler said. "The external expert we brought in believes that all the suicide notes were printed using identical printers. Also, we have the post-mortem report back on Syed Hammad. It concludes he was killed by a blow to the head, and not by inhaling the hydrogen sulphide gas."

Charlotte slid into the seat next to Mackinnon. Had Syed's death been an accident? Had Syed set up the buckets and glass vials and then fallen, hitting his head? Or had someone killed Syed before moving on to target the kids?

"Okay," Tyler said. "Let's take a look at this."

He adjusted the projector, so the light shone on the blank, white screen attached to the wall. A jerky picture came into view. It was black-and-white and jumped a little. White splodges danced around on the screen, giving the impression of an old-fashioned horror movie.

As the shop floor became clear and the gang of kids could be seen, Charlotte held her breath. There was no question about it – the kids were trying to get out. They were panicking. Charlotte clenched her fists as she saw little Robbie Baxter crash to the floor. Joanne James tripped over him as she tried desperately to open the door.

Charlotte remembered what David Oakley, the SOCO, had said when they looked around the crime scene. The door bolted behind them. Someone had locked them in.

Watching them trying to get out was gruesome. Although the footage had no audio, she could see their mouths open in silent screams, panicking and desperately trying to escape. Charlotte wanted to tear her eyes away.

But she couldn't.

The fact she thought of them as kids was a sign she was getting old. The eldest was only twenty-two, and little Robbie Baxter was only fourteen. He really was a kid.

The CCTV footage came to a juddering halt, and Charlotte knew without a doubt those kids had not been trying to kill themselves.

There was silence in the room.

Tyler cleared his throat, then said, "Not a very pleasant thing to watch. They weren't trying to kill themselves." He folded his arms and leaned back against the desk. "They were trying to get out."

CHAPTER FORTY-ONE

MACKINNON SPENT TWENTY MINUTES ON the phone to Ivy Baxter before she agreed to let him talk to Robbie. She insisted he could only have five minutes as she didn't want Robbie getting upset.

Five minutes was better than nothing, and Mackinnon was determined to get some answers.

Mackinnon decided against taking one of the squad cars. It was usually quicker to use public transport.

Construction workers had put hoarding up, blocking the pavement by the Red Herring pub. The driver of a black cab blasted his horn after a pedestrian stepped into the road without looking. It was a close call, but the office worker who'd almost been mowed down didn't seem too bothered as he gave the retreating cab the finger.

Mackinnon turned right into Gresham Street, walking past numerous glass-fronted buildings. A little further along the road, the pavements widened as he approached St Anne and St Agnes. A woman in a business suit sat on the bench outside the church, eating her lunch in the sunshine. It made Mackinnon remember how hungry he was. He glanced at his watch. He could pick up a sandwich on the way, and still get to the Baxters' in plenty of time.

He decided to take a detour and took a left by a set of pedestrian lights and walked past the central criminal courts, craning his neck to look up at the golden Lady of Justice perched on top of the Old Bailey.

He took another left and entered George's cafe. George made the best bacon rolls in London. Mackinnon ordered a roll and a coke to go. He normally ordered coffee, but it was just too hot for that. He didn't envy George, red-cheeked and sweating behind the counter, but despite the heat, George was his normal cheerful self.

Mackinnon ate as he walked, savouring the taste of crisp bacon. When he got to the city Thameslink he boarded a number twenty-five bus going towards Ilford. He got off at Fieldgate Street and started to walk the short distance to the Baxters' house.

Mackinnon strolled along Queen Street in the warm sunshine, glad he'd left his jacket back at the station. His phone started to ring, and he fished it out of his pocket. The number flashing on the screen was Ivy Baxter's.

Mackinnon loosened his tie and leaned back against the brick wall to answer it. "Hello?"

"Are you there yet?" Even over the phone Ivy's voice sounded brusque and demanding.

"I'm almost there," Mackinnon said.

"Well, you'll have to wait outside," she said. "I'm getting Robbie McDonald's for his tea. The little bugger won't eat anything else. I don't normally spoil him, but under the circumstances... Anyway, I've told him not to open the door to anyone, especially not the police, so don't try and talk to him before I get back."

Mackinnon tightened his grip on the phone. "I wouldn't dream of it, Ivy. How long do you think you're going to be?"

"I'm in the queue now."

Mackinnon heard a muffled sound, as though Ivy Baxter had put her hand over the receiver.

After a brief silence, her muffled voice continued, "I shouldn't be any longer than ten minutes, but you mind what I said. You don't speak to Robbie unless I'm there."

She hung up.

Mackinnon sighed and stuffed his phone back in his trousers pocket. He carried on walking slowly. There wasn't any point rushing now.

He did understand Ivy Baxter's mistrust of the police. It was something deep-seated that had grown over a number of years. Her two sons were serving time for armed robbery, and Mackinnon had heard on the grapevine that Ivy's father had been in and out of prison all of her life.

Getting angry at Ivy Baxter wouldn't help. It was annoying to be kept hanging, but if he got some information out of Robbie, it would be worth it.

Families like the Baxters would cut off their noses to spite their faces. Even if their lives were in danger, they wouldn't confide in the police. Mackinnon knew it was only Ivy Baxter's fear for her son that had convinced her to let Mackinnon speak to him.

It only took Mackinnon another two minutes to reach Newton House, where Ivy Baxter lived with Robbie in a ground floor flat. Newton House had been built in the sixties. The block of flats stood on the outskirts of the Towers Estate. The surrounding grounds were well maintained, and the flats themselves were more spacious than the new-builds and highly in demand.

They had the large, old-style windows, letting lots of light into the rooms. He didn't envy the residents' heating bills, though – the windows weren't double glazed. They definitely didn't need to worry about the heating bills today. It was sweltering.

Mackinnon leaned back against the wall near the front entrance of Newton House and enjoyed the fierce sun warming his face for a moment or two, while thinking through the questions he needed to ask Robbie. If he only had five minutes, Mackinnon needed to make every minute count.

He sensed the smell gradually.

It started off so light and vague that at first he thought he'd imagined it. But it grew stronger. Much stronger.

It was one of those smells that could be easily explained away - like something rotting or drains …

But after all the cases involving hydrogen sulphide recently, he couldn't ignore it.

Mackinnon turned around to face the flats. It was a rectangular block, five stories tall. The sun glinted off the windows. Nothing seemed out of place. No signs on the windows, at least.

Mackinnon paced along the front of the building. From his reckoning he thought there must be four flats on each floor. He knew the Baxters' flat was on the ground floor, but which one was it?

According to the officers who discovered Craig Foster's body, a sign had been stuck to the window, warning of the toxic gas inside. But he couldn't see any signs on the windows. One window had net curtains and heavy floral drapes, but right in the corner there was … something.

Mackinnon rushed forward only to realise that it was a sign for neighbourhood watch. He exhaled, surprised at how fast his heart was beating.

He needed to check the back of the flats. There was a small alleyway between this block of flats and the next tower.

It obviously didn't get used much. The path was littered

with broken bricks and pieces of wood. Mackinnon carefully made his way down the side of the building, towards the blazing sunlight. At the end of the alleyway, he blinked in the bright light and turned to check out the windows on this side.

There was nothing.

He debated whether to call it in. Was it just the drains smelling particularly bad on this hot summer day?

He worked his way back through the alleyway, cursing as a splinter of wood caught on his trousers.

When he made it to the front of the building, Mackinnon's pulse spiked. The smell was much stronger here.

He definitely wasn't imagining anything.

Then he saw it: the sign propped up against one of the windows on the right-hand side of the building.

It definitely hadn't been there before. As Mackinnon got closer, he could see the word 'TOXIC' printed on it, along with a skull and crossbones.

Exactly the same as the sign found at Craig Foster's flat.

Mackinnon rushed up to the window and shadowed his eyes, trying to peer inside. He wished it wasn't such a bright day. Inside looked dark, and he couldn't make out anything except shapes.

As his eyes adjusted, he thought perhaps it looked like a bedroom. He could see a TV flickering at the far end of the room.

It looked like a boy's bedroom, decorated in blue colours. Was it Robbie's? Were these flats two-bedroom or three-bedroom?

Mackinnon fumbled for his phone. He would have to call this in and evacuate the building.

He told control the location, and that the suspected toxic gas was hydrogen sulphide. He asked for backup and a hazmat team.

As Mackinnon finished the call, he noticed that the room was not empty after all.

There, slumped in front of the TV like a pile of dirty washing, was Robbie Baxter.

Mackinnon ran around the side of the building, grabbing the first brick he stumbled across. He needed to break that window and release some of the gas before it killed Robbie. If it hadn't already.

But first he needed to make sure everybody in the building evacuated.

Christ, he hoped they had a working fire alarm system in there. Mackinnon bundled his way back around the front of the building, to the entrance door. He tried to open it, but it was locked. He pressed every single one of the doorbells, hoping to get an answer from one of the flats.

Nothing.

Surely, someone must be at home? He yanked the handle, and the door rattled. The door was old, and the security lock was just a small panel on the side of the door. With enough pressure, it might give.

Mackinnon gripped the door handle with two hands and yanked as hard as he could. He put his foot on the wall to give himself more purchase and pulled again. The door groaned. Almost there.

Then all of a sudden, there was a buzz, and the door was released. Mackinnon barely managed to stay upright as the door flew open.

He darted inside, his eyes scanning the walls for the fire alarm. It had to be here somewhere.

He found it behind the door. Mackinnon pressed the panel of glass with his thumb, breaking the glass, and the shrill sound of the fire bell rang out.

Thank God. He picked up the red fire extinguisher, which

was hung on the wall just below the fire alarm, and raced back outside, leaving the security door propped open with a brick.

Outside, Mackinnon moved towards the window, lifted the fire extinguisher high above his head, and then smashed it, with as much force as he could, into the window.

As the glass cracked, the smell of the gas released from inside was unbearable. Mackinnon gagged, then held his breath and continued smashing the glass.

He called out to Robbie, telling him to get over to the window, to get out. But Robbie remained unresponsive on the floor.

Mackinnon continued battering the splintered glass until he'd removed enough to climb inside. He gripped the window ledge and clambered inside. His trousers caught on the remaining spikes of glass sticking up from the window frame.

He was still trying to hold his breath, but his lungs felt like they would burst.

He reached Robbie quickly. The boy's face looked so pale. Was he dead already? Mackinnon heaved the boy over his shoulder and staggered back towards the open window. He needed to take a breath. He was starting to feel dizzy.

Mackinnon bundled Robbie outside.

Mackinnon kept a grip on Robbie's tracksuit top, to stop him falling head first, and lowered him to the ground. Mackinnon followed Robbie's body out of the window.

Mackinnon's head was spinning. He dragged Robbie's body further onto the grass, hoping that the fresh air would get rid of some of that toxic gas. How much did it take to kill someone? Probably not much for someone as small as Robbie.

Other people started to exit the building. Most of them covered their noses and mouths with their sleeves.

"Oh, my God," a woman said. "What's happened to the boy?"

"Gas," Mackinnon managed to say. "Hydrogen sulphide.

Very toxic. Is everybody out of the building?" He was finding it difficult to breathe. His throat tightened and he gagged.

"I think so." A man with long dreadlocks, sweeping past his shoulders, approached Mackinnon. "What's happening?"

Mackinnon didn't answer. He was too busy checking Robbie's airways were clear and trying to determine if he was breathing. He fought the need to vomit and lowered his head close to Robbie's mouth. A faint whisper of a breath touched his cheek. Robbie was still alive.

A plump woman, carrying a little Yorkshire terrier, ran coughing towards them. "Robbie? My God where's Ivy?"

She bustled forward, gently pushing Mackinnon away from Robbie's body. "I'm a nurse," she said and started to check Robbie's breathing. "What's happened here?"

Mackinnon couldn't answer. He left the nurse attending Robbie. He needed more air. Despite the fact he'd thought he'd managed to hold his breath in the flat, he really wasn't feeling very good.

He managed to stagger away in time to throw up by a brick wall.

Afterwards, he sat down on the grass and tried to take in deep breaths.

Another person exited the flat. Mackinnon was feeling so awful, he almost missed it. It was the reaction of the rest of the crowd that got Mackinnon's attention. Perhaps they thought this man was some kind of official, someone here to contain the gas, after all he was wearing protective clothing.

The man, walking briskly away from the flats, wore a gas mask and was dressed entirely in black.

As the masked man headed down the path and away from the flat, Mackinnon called out, "Hey, you. Stop. Police."

The man in the mask turned to look at Mackinnon.

Mackinnon struggled up onto his hands and knees on the grass. He obviously didn't look like much of a threat. The masked man didn't even bother to run. He just picked up his walking speed.

No one stopped him.

Mackinnon got to his feet, trying to stop coughing. If this was the man behind all the gas attacks, he couldn't let him just walk away.

Mackinnon's legs shook as he tried to follow the masked man. He bent over and rested his hands on his knees as a hacking cough ripped through his chest. Mackinnon staggered forwards. "I said stop. Police!"

The man started to walk faster. Mackinnon broke into a jog. His lungs hurt, and his chest gave a stabbing pain every time he breathed in, and now his eyes were watering too. He wiped his eyes with his sleeve.

It was like being in a dream.

The faster Mackinnon moved, the faster the man in front seemed to move. He never gained on him. By the time they got to the end of Queen Street, the man in black was sprinting.

CHAPTER FORTY-TWO

THE KILLER BROKE INTO A run. What the hell was that man doing here? He'd seen him before. He was one of the police officers looking into Syed Hammad's death.

He couldn't believe it when the fire alarm sounded. But even then he thought the gas would kill Robbie before the fire brigade arrived. He'd had to keep his mask on when he left the building. There were too many people who could have given his description to the police. It attracted more attention, of course, but at least it disguised his face.

He'd been furious when he looked back towards the building and saw the broken window. He didn't know if he'd been successful. Surely Robbie couldn't have lived through two exposures.

He couldn't believe he'd been so unlucky. If Robbie Baxter hadn't lived in a ground floor flat, that policeman would never have spotted him in time.

He clenched his fists. That stupid policeman. Why was he there? How did he know?

Did he just happen to be passing? No, that was stupid.

Perhaps if it had been a uniformed PC … but this man was plain clothed that meant he was a detective.

Did that mean the police had guessed his plans? There hadn't been anything in the papers or on the news.

He carried on running along Queen Street, trying to look casual – as if a man running in a gas mask could ever look casual. He wanted to take his mask off, so he wouldn't stand out so much, but he couldn't do that until he was out of sight of the policeman, and in an area without CCTV.

The bag he carried over his shoulder was heavy even though he'd emptied all the chemicals. He shot another look over his shoulder.

The man was still chasing him, but he looked weak, and he was gasping for breath. He didn't look like he was particularly unfit. In fact, he was tall and well built. He must've inhaled some gas and that was slowing him down. Unfortunately, it wasn't slowing him down enough.

The killer felt his chest tighten and willed the stupid policeman to give up.

Why didn't the policeman understand that he was helping him, they were on the same side?

He had to push past an elderly couple who wouldn't move out of the way quickly enough, and then he looked back. Christ, where did that policeman get his energy from? He wasn't losing him. If anything, he was getting closer.

A BT engineer was crouched beside an open green electrical box on the side of the pavement. He looked at the killer, and then did a double take. If the killer hadn't been so shattered, he would have laughed.

The sun was beating down. His black sweatshirt stuck to his skin. He rushed past two teenaged girls, who screamed at the sight of him. The little yappy dog they had on a lead snapped at his ankles.

These passers-by weren't helping. They were slowing him

down. He needed to get away, somewhere quiet. He saw the road sign for the Burdett entrance of the Towers Estate.

The sign was splattered with bird shit. The killer turned a corner, and pigeons scattered as his feet slammed against the pavement. He ran into them and raised his arm to protect his face. He hated pigeons. His mother called them rats with wings.

He looked over his shoulder once more. Shit. The policeman was only a matter of feet behind him.

CHAPTER FORTY-THREE

THEY WERE APPROACHING THE CENTRE of the Towers Estate. If Mackinnon didn't catch up with him soon, he would lose him in the alleyways that criss-crossed between the flats.

Mackinnon put on a burst of speed. The muscles in his legs screamed in response. He couldn't keep this up much longer.

The masked man stumbled, almost dropping the large bag he had slung over his shoulder, and Mackinnon managed to get closer. That heavy black holdall was definitely slowing the man down.

Mackinnon desperately tried to reach out. He was within finger-tip distance. As they rounded the corner to the next street, the man in black stumbled; the heavy holdall fell to the ground.

It was enough.

Mackinnon grabbed the fabric of the man's black sweatshirt and pulled as hard as he could, sending them both tumbling into the road.

With a thud, Mackinnon's head connected with the curb.

He wasn't sure whether it was that or the effects of the gas, but his vision faded to grey.

As the face of the man in black loomed over him, the gas mask distorting his features, Mackinnon couldn't do anything but raise a hand to try to grasp him again.

He couldn't see properly, but for some reason, he was sure the man was laughing at him.

The last thing Mackinnon heard was the distant wail of sirens before it all went black.

CHAPTER FORTY-FOUR

WHEN MACKINNON WOKE UP HE was in hospital. His head was pounding, and the light above him seemed to burn into his retinas. He tried to raise his hand to block out the light and realised he was hooked up to an IV.

His first thought was Robbie. Had he been too late?

He swallowed. Everything hurt. At least he wasn't wearing an oxygen mask, so that was a good sign.

He looked around the room. He was alone. There were two other beds set up, but no occupants. He wasn't in ICU – more good news. He leaned back on the pillow. The small effort required to raise his head and look around the room had exhausted him.

Mackinnon heard the squeak of a door hinge. He expected to see a doctor or nurse come to check up on him, but instead it was Charlotte. The dark makeup around her eyes was smudged, and she looked even paler than usual.

"You daft sod," Charlotte said. "What were you thinking?"

Obviously, he wouldn't be getting any sympathy.

"Don't nag me. I feel terrible," Mackinnon said.

"You deserve to. Did you not think? Hello? Standard operating procedure - ever heard of it?"

"Yeah, all right," Mackinnon said. He rubbed a hand over his face. He knew he was probably imagining things, but he felt like he could still smell the gas. "What would you have done? That little boy was unconscious. Would you have waited?"

"He could have been dead already, Jack. And you could have died for no reason at all. That's why we have procedure."

After a moment's silence Mackinnon asked, "Is Robbie all right?"

"I think so," Charlotte said. "Dr. Sorensen's been treating both of you, and she seems to think you'll both be okay." Charlotte moved closer and stood by his pillow. "How are you feeling now?"

"Terrible," Mackinnon said.

"That's to be expected I suppose. And if you think I've told you off, just you wait until you hear from Brookbank. He's livid, Jack."

"Fantastic," Mackinnon said. "That's something to look forward to."

His head was thumping and his throat hurt. He wasn't exactly expecting a medal, but he sure as hell hadn't expected this.

Charlotte's face softened. "Seriously though, I'm glad you're okay. Did you see anything? Get a look at him?"

Before Mackinnon could answer, the door opened again and Dr. Anna Sorensen entered, followed by DC Collins.

Collins grinned. "Sleeping beauty's awake."

Mackinnon struggled to raise himself into a sitting position. "How am I doing, Anna? When can I leave?"

Dr. Sorensen frowned. "I don't think there's going to be any permanent damage, but we'll keep you in here tonight to be on the safe side."

Mackinnon nodded. "All right. But don't tell Chloe," he said, looking at Charlotte. "I don't want to worry her, and she thinks I'm staying at Derek's tonight anyway."

Charlotte shrugged. "If you're sure."

Dr. Sorensen checked Mackinnon's IV and made a note on the chart at the end of his bed. After telling him she'd be back to check on him later and warning Collins and Charlotte to let him get some rest, she left the room.

Mackinnon slumped back onto his pillows. "What did Robbie say? Did he see anything?"

"Absolutely nothing," Collins said. "The kid was glued to his Xbox. One minute he was shooting enemy soldiers, the next minute, nothing."

Mackinnon closed his eyes.

"What about you?" Collins asked. "Did you get a good look at him? We got some witness descriptions, which basically all said the same thing. Medium height. Dark clothes. Wearing a gas mask."

"I only saw him wearing the mask. A big, clunky, old-fashioned gas mask. There was a glass or plastic visor covering the eye area. It made his eyes look all distorted. It was creepy. I think his eyes were blue, but I …" Mackinnon could feel himself start to drift.

"All right," Collins said. "We'd better let you get some rest. But before I go, you know what you did was bloody stupid, don't you?"

"Yes, thanks, Nick. I've already been told that, and I'm sure you won't be the last person to tell me."

"You're right about that." Collins grinned and looked at Charlotte. "Did you tell him that Brookbank's on the war path?"

Charlotte nodded. "Oh, yes."

"At least we got something out of it," Collins said.

Mackinnon frowned. "We did? What?"

"The masked man left his bag behind. They found you slumped on the side of the road, leaning on it. Cuddling it like a teddy bear."

Suddenly, Mackinnon was wide awake. "Why didn't you say so before?" He sat up and pushed back the sheets. "We'll need to catalogue everything. What was in it?" Mackinnon got out of bed and with one hand on the chair beside him, began to rummage through the bedside cabinet. "Where the hell are my clothes?"

Charlotte cleared her throat and turned away.

Collins laughed. "You do realise the hospital gowns are backless, Jack?"

Mackinnon's hand shot round to his back. Collins was right.

Mackinnon sat back on the bed and looked at Charlotte, who was still facing the wall. "Sorry."

Collins laughed again. "Just get back to bed, Jack. You're no good to anyone in this state. We've started to catalogue the contents of the bag. I'll fill you in tomorrow."

Charlotte backed out of the door. Her cheeks were still bright pink. "See you tomorrow, Jack."

"Make sure you put your pants on tomorrow," Collins said and got an elbow in the ribs from Charlotte.

After they'd gone, Mackinnon's mind was whirling with possibilities. What was in the bag? Would it help crack the case?

He thought he'd never be able to sleep, but the moment he shut his eyes, he drifted off.

CHAPTER FORTY-FIVE

TYRELL PATTERSON THOUGHT HIS HEART had stopped beating. He'd already had six lagers and shared a bag of weed between four of his friends when his mate, John Denver, said the words that shocked him to the core.

He grabbed John's arm. "Hang on. What did you just say?"

He had to be tripping ... It just didn't make sense ...

John shook off his arm. "Swear to God. I heard it from Rita Baxter, Robbie's cousin. There was some bloke dressed up in black and wearing a gas mask. He looked like something out of World War II. Apparently, loads of people saw him coming out of the flats."

Tyrell felt dizzy, and it had nothing to do with the six lagers. The spliff he was holding dropped to the floor.

"Hey, watch out," John said, picking up the smouldering end. "You dozy bastard. You've put a fag burn in the carpet. My mum will go spare when she sees that hole."

One of Tyrell's other friends collapsed into giggles. "It's a pothole!"

Tyrell ignored them and felt himself swaying a little as he

stared at his friends. Their faces blended into one as they stared back at him.

"You all right, Tyrell? You look a bit green, mate."

Tyrell put the Xbox controller down on the floor. He and his friends had been sitting around playing this game for hours. How could they not have told him this earlier? Didn't they realise how important it was?

He'd been sure Estelle had made it up. He'd had a couple of drinks before picking up the Chinese, and she'd been pissed at him. That was why he thought she invented that stupid story about a masked man.

He'd got her hysterical phone call, effing and blinding, calling him every name under the sun, when he'd been finishing up his third pint.

He'd been so sure she was making it up. For God's sake, a man in a mask – who would believe that?

Tyrell staggered and leaned against the wall for support.

"Bloody hell, Tyrell. What's up with you?" John said.

Tyrell's other friends had gotten bored and picked up their controllers to resume the game.

"Come on, Tyrell," John said. "Maybe you ought to call it a night."

Tyrell shook his head. "You don't understand. Estelle said a masked man broke into the flat, looking for me. I thought she was talking bollocks."

John ran a hand over his forehead and scratched his scalp. "That doesn't make any sense. What would he want with you?"

Tyrell felt sick. This had to have something to do with what went down at the newsagent's. Vinnie was still in hospital, so had the Brewertons decided to come at Tyrell instead? He pushed past John. He needed to get outside into the fresh air. He needed to work out what to do.

He careered down the stairs, stumbling as he missed the last step.

He ran out of the block of flats, into the warm July evening. How the hell could this have happened?

If they were targeting Robbie, that must mean whoever was doing this was targeting Vinnie's mates.

And if Estelle was telling the truth, they were coming for Tyrell, too. He fumbled with the phone in his pocket. The tiny display window swam before his eyes. This phone was a bunch of crap. He should have kept the fancy new one for himself. He only got it in the neck after he gave it to Estelle as a present anyway.

He punched the buttons and selected Estelle's number from contacts.

It took six rings before Estelle's sleepy voice answered, "What do you want?"

"Listen, Estelle this is important. You need to go somewhere safe. Go to your mum's."

"What the hell are you talking about, Tyrell?" She sounded furious, and he couldn't really blame her.

Tyrell licked his lips. His mouth was getting drier and drier by the second.

"This is really important. I'm sorry, babe, I'm sorry I didn't believe you about that masked man. Please, go to your mum's."

"What the hell, Tyrell. You can't just –"

"Don't worry about me," he said. "I'll call you later."

"What will you do?" Estelle asked.

"I'm going to do what I should have done when you first told me. I'm going to the police."

Tyrell hung up.

CHAPTER FORTY-SIX

TYRELL WISHED HE HADN'T SMOKED quite so much weed this evening. It went against all his instincts to enter a police station high and drunk, but this was important. Surely the police wouldn't be interested in a little recreational smoking when there was a crazy nutter, trying to gas people.

As he rounded the corner to Wood Street station, he stretched his shoulders and stuck a piece of chewing gum in his mouth to freshen his breath. He needed them to take him seriously. He couldn't go in there stinking of booze.

Tyrell stared up at the blue police lanterns hanging either side of the entrance. He had to shove his hands in his pockets to stop them shaking. After thirty seconds of standing there looking like an idiot, Tyrell climbed the steps and entered the police station.

He walked to the police officer on duty at the reception desk and leaned on the counter.

The police officer was sorting papers, putting them into different pigeonholes and didn't see Tyrell until he turned around.

"Can I help you?"

Tyrell nodded. "My name is Tyrell Patterson, and I need to speak to somebody about the gas attacks."

CHAPTER FORTY-SEVEN

CHARLOTTE'S MORNING STARTED OFF VERY well. A very scared-looking Tyrell Patterson had turned up in the early hours and handed himself in. Charlotte couldn't say she blamed him.

As DI Tyler wanted to ask him questions personally, she'd left Tyrell Patterson with a cup of coffee, half a packet of chocolate digestives and a PC to keep an eye on him.

Five minutes ago, Charlotte had rung the hospital. Mackinnon seemed to be okay. No lasting damage, thank God. Sometimes health and safety laws could be over the top, but in this case, what he did was stupid. He could have killed himself.

Mackinnon should be discharged this morning. She'd heard through the grapevine that he'd already received his telling off by Brookbank, so she imagined he was feeling pretty sorry for himself.

Charlotte glanced at her watch. Time for the morning briefing. At least they had some good news this morning with

Tyrell Patterson ready to answer questions and whatever clues the team had managed to get from the black holdall.

If Tyrell could give them some answers, they might be able to put this case to bed by the end of today. From what he'd said so far, Charlotte was worried it might be a gang retaliation. God, she hoped not.

She hoped this sort of thing didn't catch on.

DI Tyler was heading up the briefing again this morning. Charlotte moved to the front of the room where DC Collins and DC Webb were already sitting.

DI Tyler made his way into the room, carrying a pile of papers. As he lowered them onto his desk, he turned to Charlotte with a grin. "I think you've got some good news for us, DC Brown."

Good news travelled fast.

"Yes. Tyrell Patterson came into the station this morning. He is scared he's going to be next."

"Hopefully the kid can give us the information we need to catch this killer. We'll need to question his girlfriend as well, as she was the one who saw the masked man. But before we arrange that," Tyler perched on the edge of the desk, "we've got Vinnie Pearson and Robbie Baxter still in hospital. Whoever is after them might try to target them again. So I am going to organise protection."

"Another waste of taxpayers' money," DC Webb said.

Tyler ignored him. "We can keep a uniformed officer outside the hospital wards until they are well enough to leave. Then we'll transfer them to a safe house. Tyrell Patterson will go straight to the safe house."

"That will cost a sodding fortune," DC Webb said.

Tyler glared at DC Webb. "I'm well aware of that, thank you."

CHAPTER FORTY-EIGHT

IT DIDN'T TAKE VERY LONG for Charlotte to convince Ivy Baxter that Robbie should go into the safe house as soon as he was discharged. After all, she was a mother, and she knew Charlotte wasn't lying about the risk to his life. But Ivy didn't make it easy for Charlotte. Ivy Baxter was her normal bolshy self, agreeing to the safe house as if she were doing Charlotte a favour rather than the other way around.

Dr. Sorensen said Robbie could be discharged whenever the safe house was ready, but Vinnie Pearson still needed medical attention and wouldn't be discharged until next week.

So, Robbie Baxter was easy enough, but Vinnie Pearson was another matter.

She'd known Vinnie would be trouble as soon as she entered the ward.

As she approached the bed, Vinnie Pearson looked up. Charlotte could see he recognised her. His whole body tensed, his eyelids lowered slightly and the edges of his mouth turned up in a smirk.

Charlotte didn't see the point in beating around the bush.

"Vinnie, after you've been discharged, we want to keep you in a safe house for a short period of time. We think that somebody might be trying to kill you and your friends."

For the briefest moment, a flicker of fear showed on Vinnie's face, and then he was back to normal.

"Yeah like that's going to happen," Vinnie said.

She tried again, trying to convince him, telling him that Tyrell Patterson would be in the same safe house and that Robbie would be going there when he was discharged, too. But her words had no effect.

Vinnie looked straight ahead, staring at the wall rather than looking at her.

She could really do without this sort of crap. Charlotte shifted in her chair, getting comfortable, then leaned back, folded her arms and waited. She could wait it out just as well as he could.

It took only two minutes for Vinnie to start fidgeting. He shot her a sideways glance. "There's no point in you hanging around. I'm not going to change my mind," he said.

Charlotte shifted her legs out of the way as a nurse bustled past and updated something on Vinnie's chart. They both stayed silent until the nurse had gone.

"Why are you still here?" Vinnie said, clearly getting agitated.

"I thought I'd hang around until you get some common sense," Charlotte said and leaned forward in the chair. "What is it, Vinnie? Do you know who is doing this? Are you refusing help because you're scared? Is that what this is all about?"

"Of course, it isn't. I'm not scared. I just don't want anything to do with the police. I mean, how would it look?"

"Surely keeping yourself safe is more important," Charlotte said. "Would you tell me if you knew who was doing this? Have you got on the wrong side of someone? Is that why they are targeting you and your friends? Is it some kind of turf war?"

"Turf war? I ain't one of the Kray brothers. Jesus, no one told me we'd gone back in time."

Despite his tough words, Charlotte noticed his hands were shaking. Dr. Sorensen was right. Vinnie was scared of something.

He looked up and frowned. "Hang on a minute. You said my friends were being targeted. You meant Tyrell and Robbie, right? No one else?"

Charlotte took a deep breath. Vinnie was still trying to protect his friends from the police. When would it sink in that the police weren't the ones he should be worrying about? "Craig Foster and Joanne James are dead, Vinnie."

Vinnie's eyes widened. "No. You're lying. I saw Craig climb out the window myself, and the doctor here told me only Robbie and me were admitted. Joanne and Craig got away."

Charlotte shook her head. "I'm sorry, Vinnie, they were killed in separate attacks. And whoever is targeting you just tried to gas Robbie again. I want to help you. You need to trust me."

Vinnie turned away. Beads of sweat shone on his forehead. "Go away. I don't feel well."

"Please, Vinnie. Be sensible. Talk to me."

After another twenty minutes of silence, with Vinnie studiously ignoring her, Charlotte finally gave up. She pulled out her card and put it on the bedside table.

"Call me when you change your mind, Vinnie."

CHAPTER FORTY-NINE

VINNIE PEARSON SHIFTED IN HIS hospital bed. It felt like he'd been lying flat on his back forever. Even though the mattress was soft, it felt like it was pressing into his spine.

He couldn't wait to get out of here, to get away from their crappy food, the falsely cheerful nurses and the doctors who kept asking him how he felt.

Right now it was only mid-afternoon yet the two oldies at the end of the ward were snoring their heads off. Vinnie couldn't blame them. There was sod else to do except sleep.

Two other people had been discharged, and the beds had been changed this morning. That had been the most exciting part of Vinnie's day. How sad was that?

His eyelids fluttered as he drifted back into sleep, but he never seemed to sleep properly. There were always noises, people clattering about, nurses prodding and poking him, trying to take readings or samples of his blood. He couldn't get any peace around here.

The other thing that stopped Vinnie sleeping properly was

his dreams. They featured the Brewerton brothers torturing Vinnie in various ways. Before the dreams had started, Vinnie hadn't realised he was so imaginative. The dreams were terrifyingly graphic. During the last dream, Vinnie woke just before Mike Brewerton was about to rip his toenails out with a pair of pliers.

He needed to get out of this bloody hospital. He was having these dreams because he was a sitting duck in here. That lady copper must have been lying about Joanne and Craig, trying to pressure him into spilling his guts. Well, it wouldn't work.

He'd never admit it to anyone, but Vinnie was glad they'd put a police officer on the door. Hopefully the Brewertons wouldn't be stupid enough to try anything with the Old Bill sitting right outside.

Vinnie could just see a small segment of blue sky through the window at the end of the ward. It was uncomfortably hot in the hospital, but it looked like a gorgeous day outside. A day that would be perfect for taking a six-pack down to Vicky Park and getting bladdered.

Vinnie thought about Joanne James. Maybe when he felt better, he'd check and see how she was doing. She was probably well pissed off with him. Vinnie grinned. That made more sense. That's why he hadn't heard from her. She was holed up in her dad's plush gaff in Essex, moaning about Vinnie to her girlfriends.

That stupid lady copper had been trying to play him. She must have thought he was a bloody idiot.

Vinnie had closed his eyes again, preparing to drift off to sleep, when a nurse appeared by his bed.

He tried to slap her hands away as she fastened a clear mask over his mouth and nose.

"Stop that, Vincent," the nurse said. "Dr. Sorensen is

concerned with the results of your blood gases, so we're putting you on oxygen again."

The annoying elastic strap felt tight against his cheeks. He hated the mask. It kept fogging up and feeling all slimy.

But Vinnie was too tired to remove it. He began to drift.

CHAPTER FIFTY

AFTER HIS LAST ATTEMPT WAS foiled so dramatically, the police had probably expected the killer to keep a low profile for a while.

They were in for a surprise.

The police had shown their hand too early. Now he knew they were on to him, he could show them exactly who they were dealing with: The Arbiter of Justice.

He was more powerful than the police. What could they do these days with all that red tape holding them back?

Murder didn't even mean life imprisonment anymore. The police were pathetic puppets, operating with one hand tied behind their backs. No wonder the country was overrun with scum.

He wasn't stupid. He knew that getting rid of a few of these criminal low-lives wouldn't be able to change the big picture straightaway.

But he believed he could be the spark to ignite the fire throughout the country. He wanted people to realise that if they wanted justice, they had to claim it for themselves.

He'd been so hopeful after the riots, so sure that the righteous would rise up and suppress the evil.

They rose up all right, but rather than use weapons to exact their revenge, they carried mops and brooms ready to clear up the mess the rioters had left behind.

What message did that send out?

Smash our businesses, steal our property and we'll … We will clean up after you!

The killer left the men's toilets, feeling at home in his new outfit. He wore white trousers and a blue polycotton top that made up the hospital porter's uniform. It had an elasticated waist, and the legs were a little short, but no one would notice.

He'd picked up the uniform yesterday, knowing it paid to be prepared.

His collar length black wig didn't feel particularly secure, but he only needed to keep it on for a few moments. He wore thick, black-rimmed glasses, too. Despite the disguise, he lowered his head as he approached the cameras.

He strode along the corridor confidently, wheeling his bucket and cleaning trolley, smiling at two nurses that rushed past him and a porter who was heading in the opposite direction.

He approached the entrance to Vinnie's ward, noticed the policeman sitting on a plastic chair outside and ignored him as if it were the most normal thing in the world to see a policeman sitting next to the entrance.

He spotted his accomplice at the end of the corridor and gave him the signal. The killer preferred to work alone, but on this occasion a helper was invaluable.

The accomplice sprang into action. He was a homeless man of around forty, a dirty, smelly drunk. Perfect for his task.

The accomplice began to holler. He crashed into a trolley then overturned a chair. A passing nurse moved quickly to the phone, no doubt to call security, but the accomplice did well.

He grabbed the woman by the waist and twirled her around. He sang and swayed as if he were dancing.

The nurse let out a piercing scream. The officer sitting outside Vinnie Pearson's ward looked up.

The killer smiled. It was all going to plan.

The tramp twirled the woman around and around as she struggled to get free.

The officer got to his feet. He glanced at the ward behind him, then ran towards the dancing couple. "Hey, you! Stop that. Let her go."

The killer wheeled his trolley inside. He didn't have long. There were six beds, four of them occupied. The two old men at the end of the ward were too far away to see anything. But the old lady nearest the door had eyes like a hawk.

Yes. She would definitely notice something. Something would have to be done with her.

The killer walked up to her bedside, smiling. "Hello, my love. It's nearly time for your injection."

The old lady blinked at him. She must have been at least eighty, and her false teeth were in a sterilising container on the bedside cabinet. Without them, her mouth had a sunken appearance.

But she was from a generation who respected medical staff. So she didn't question him.

The killer gave her his most winning smile. This was going to be easy.

He made a show of checking the little upside down watch he'd pinned to the breast pocket of his uniform. He'd bought it from Argos. The perfect finishing touch.

"The doctor will be along shortly," he said. "I'll just close your curtains to give you some privacy."

"Thank you, dear," the old lady said as he grabbed the floral print curtains and pulled them along the rung, closing her bed off from the rest of the ward.

Perfect, the killer thought, and turned back to Vinnie Pearson's bed.

A machine stood next to Vinnie's bed, monitoring his vital signs. The killer pressed a large green button with 'Mute' printed on it. So nice of them to make it user friendly! That should give him at least thirty seconds to work undisturbed.

He allowed himself only a moment to study Vinnie. He didn't have long.

This was always the most difficult part. The seconds just before he killed were the worst. When niggling doubts plagued him.

The killer squared his shoulders. It was time.

CHAPTER FIFTY-ONE

SOMETHING BRUSHED AGAINST VINNIE'S ARM. He groaned. Not another bloody test. Why couldn't they just leave him alone?

Vinnie blinked. It was someone Vinnie recognised but couldn't quite place. He looked familiar … but he didn't remember being treated by this male nurse before.

A hand clasped his forearm. Vinnie grunted and tried to pull away. He didn't want to be bothered anymore. He just wanted to sleep.

The male nurse put a tube beneath Vinnie's gas mask and pressed down hard. Vinnie reared up. Christ that hurt. What kind of a nurse …

Vinnie's heartbeat spiked.

What was going on?

This wasn't right. This person wasn't helping him …

Vinnie's mouth was filled with the foulest air imaginable. It was heavy, putrid and clogged up his lungs. He gasped for more oxygen, but took in more of the sick gas.

An explosion of pain crushed his chest. Why wasn't anyone helping him?

Vinnie tried to scream, but no noise came out of his mouth. He tried again, this time emitting a squeak muffled by the gas mask.

The man stood above him, eyes blank as he pushed the mask tightly against Vinnie's face, so Vinnie had no choice but to breathe in more of the foul-smelling gas.

As Vinnie looked up he realised where he'd seen this man before.

It was the man who'd told him about the phones. The man who'd set him up.

Now, Vinnie understood what was happening. He was being murdered.

As Vinnie slipped into the blackness, he didn't notice the man lean down close to his ear, and he didn't hear him whisper the word, "Justice."

CHAPTER FIFTY-TWO

"HE'S KILLING THEM OFF ONE-by-one," Collins said to Charlotte as they left the emergency briefing.

Charlotte ran a hand through her hair. "Vinnie was no angel, but no one deserves to die like that. And I don't understand how someone could just walk into the ward. With all those witnesses – why can't anyone give us a good description?"

"He's clever. The officer on the door was only gone for a couple of minutes."

"He shouldn't have left."

"A woman was screaming for help. He …"

"I know why he left, Nick. I'm just saying he shouldn't have. It was a set-up. The killer paid the homeless guy to make a scene. And we have nothing to go on. No useful witness statements. No CCTV."

"I wouldn't say we have nothing. From the homeless guy's statement, we know he's medium height and build and has an East London accent …" Collins faltered under Charlotte's glare. "Yeah, I suppose when you think about it, it's not much to go on."

Charlotte exhaled heavily. "No, it's not much at all."

She was glad DI Tyler said there would be a minimum of two officers at the safe house.

She couldn't believe Vinnie was dead. Maybe she should have tried harder to get him to talk. There had definitely been something bothering him. She could have stayed with him for longer, been more persuasive.

But she hadn't.

Charlotte had been pissed off with his tough guy act. She thought they still had time. She never would have guessed the killer would attempt something like this in the middle of a busy hospital.

"Are you okay, Charlotte?" Collins said.

She looked up and nodded. "I'm fine."

They strolled along the corridor. Charlotte stopped at the vending machine, punched in the numbers for black coffee. "Have you told Mackinnon?"

"Not yet," Collins said. "There isn't anything he can do. He may as well enjoy his bed rest with the lovely Chloe to attend him."

Charlotte shook her head. "He isn't staying in Oxford with Chloe. He's at Derek's, and I bet that isn't quite the same as having Chloe look after him."

"I didn't have Derek down as the Florence Nightingale type," Collins chuckled. "I'll give Mackinnon a ring, let him know what's going on." Collins collected his chocolate bar from the vending machine, then said, "If we could work out why someone is targeting these kids, then we would have something to go on."

Charlotte picked up her coffee, cursing as some of the hot liquid spilled on her fingers. She leaned back against the smooth surface of the vending machine and listened to the hum of the machine.

"I don't know. The owner of the cafe, Mitch Horrocks is a bit weird. He hates that gang of kids."

Collins nodded and said, "He's definitely odd. Maybe we should have another word with him, and I want to have another chat with Pete Morton, the manager of the mobile phone shop. He's definitely hiding something."

They both turned as DC Webb walked towards them with a face like thunder.

"What's up with you?" Collins asked.

DC Webb didn't look at him. He turned to the vending machine and punched in the numbers much harder than necessary.

Collins and Charlotte exchanged a look.

DC Webb slapped his palm against the vending machine as if that would help it along. "My prime suspects. The Brewertons. I've just had it confirmed that they are currently on holiday in sunny Florida. I've been trying to track them down for ages." DC Webb looked down at his feet and shook his head. "Bloody Florida."

"They could have arranged for someone else to do it on their behalf?" Collins suggested. "A holiday in Florida makes a nice alibi."

DC Webb shook his head. "It's another dead end. We're getting nowhere fast."

The three of them stood there in silence. DC Webb blew over the top of his plastic cup.

Charlotte said, "We have to talk to Tyrell Patterson and Robbie Baxter again. They must have some idea of who is doing this. They are the only two people who were in that newsagent's who are still alive. Surely they must see the only way out of this mess is to talk to us."

"I hope so," Collins said. "I really do."

CHAPTER FIFTY-THREE

THE KILLER WALKED SLOWLY FROM the tube station, weaving in and out of the rush-hour crowds. There were so many people, all of them in their own little worlds, with no idea he was claiming justice on their behalf.

He walked slowly along the main street, enjoying the warm evening air. He pulled his mobile phone out of his pocket and touched the icon on the screen to launch his tracker app.

He smiled at the red flashing light that appeared on the screen. Perfect.

At the time, after that fool of a policeman had messed up Robbie Baxter's justice, the killer had been furious. But now, he saw that things had worked out far better than he'd planned.

Almost like divine intervention.

Tyrell Patterson had given his phone to his girlfriend, so he would have been very hard to track. If Robbie Baxter hadn't been in the safe house, Tyrell Patterson might have been safe right now.

But he wasn't safe.

The killer smiled and shook his head. His mother always said things had a funny way of working out for the best.

Obviously, Tyrell Patterson giving his girlfriend the phone wasn't something he'd anticipated. It wasn't the killer's fault. Who would have suspected that a selfish lowlife like Tyrell Patterson would be willing to give his fancy new phone to his girlfriend?

He might have actually believed that Tyrell Patterson had something good in him, buried deep down, until he'd found out about the safe house.

What kind of man would run off to a police safe house to save himself, leaving his wife and unborn child to look after themselves?

Men like Tyrell Patterson deserved the most severe type of justice.

He crossed the street at the pedestrian lights and passed the Tesco Express, then turned left into a narrow side street.

That was better. It was quieter here, away from the crowds. It wasn't the most direct route to the safe house, but it was quieter and there would be less CCTV in the back streets.

He checked his phone again, noting the position of the flashing red light. Not far now. He turned right, into yet another narrow lane and looked around. A couple of shops and a restaurant backed onto the lane, but they had fences up, so he would be hidden from prying eyes. It was quiet and just about big enough for a car. It was the perfect spot.

He turned and walked to the end of the lane. A broad building stood on the opposite side of the road. A grey, square box – it didn't look very impressive. It didn't look like a fortress.

He bent down, pretending to tie his shoelaces as he surveyed the long street. There were a few parked cars, but no marked police cars.

They'd brought Robbie Baxter here so it must be some kind of safe house. There was no obvious police presence. But they were hardly likely to advertise the fact that this was a police safe house.

The exterior of the building was understated, chosen purposely to blend in. Inside, it was probably set up like Fort Knox.

The killer smiled. It didn't matter. There was more than one way to skin a cat.

CHAPTER FIFTY-FOUR

ESTELLE FLUNG DOWN THE MAGAZINE. It was no good. She couldn't concentrate. She couldn't think of anything but Tyrell. How could he do this to her? She really thought the baby would make him grow up.

It was ten in the morning, but Estelle hadn't showered or dressed yet. What was the point? She didn't have anywhere to go.

Her mother sat in an armchair opposite her. She peered at Estelle over her glasses, and set down her newspaper and the pen she'd been using to fill in the crossword.

"Don't look at me like that," Estelle said. "It's not his fault."

"If you say so," her mother said.

"I don't know why you've got it in for Tyrell," Estelle said. "He's always been perfectly polite to you."

Her mother folded her arms and gave Estelle a sharp look. "It's not the way he treats me that I'm worried about. How will he look after you and the baby when he can't even look after himself properly?"

Tears burned behind Estelle's eyelids. She pinched the bridge of her nose. She knew her mother was right but she could really do without the "I told you so."

Her mother shuffled forward in her armchair, perching on the edge of her seat. "I'm worried about you, Estelle. You're still my little girl."

Estelle sniffed. "Why did it have to happen now? I don't even know what he has done."

Even as she spoke, Estelle knew it was something to do with Vinnie Pearson. He was always getting Tyrell into trouble. It was pathetic. For God's sake, they were meant to be grown-ups.

Her mother eased herself out of the armchair and walked over to Estelle. "You put your feet up. I'll make you a nice cup of tea."

Estelle raised her legs and rested them on the sofa. "Can I have a biscuit with it?"

Her mum grinned. "I'll see what I can rustle up."

Estelle tried to wedge a cushion behind her back. It seemed like she could never get comfy these days. Something always ached. She settled back, then realised the television remote control was on the other side of the room.

Crap. She heaved herself up and swung her legs down from the sofa.

Then, from the corner of her eye, she saw a movement.

It was him. The masked man.

No, it couldn't be. She must be seeing things. She opened her mouth to scream.

He put his finger to where his lips would be if they weren't hidden behind that awful black mask.

How could Tyrell do this to her? Bastard. Bastard. Bastard. She clenched her fists as the anger flooded through her.

"Are you on your own?" The masked man's voice was raspy and muffled by the mask.

Oh, shit. Her mum was in the kitchen. If she saw him she'd have a heart attack.

Estelle nodded. "Yes, I'm on my own."

She moved forward quickly. "This is Tyrell's fault. It's not fair to take it out on me. I don't know anything about it." She looked over her shoulder down the hallway towards the kitchen. She could hear the radio in the kitchen where her mother was making tea.

"Look, let's go somewhere. We can talk about it outside." She put a hand on his chest to try to force him backwards, but he didn't seem to notice.

He looked over her shoulder and shook his head. "You're not alone."

"Please, please leave us alone. I've done nothing to you. I'm pregnant. My mum's in the kitchen. We weren't involved in any of this. I'm sure I can get him to sort this out, to apologise to you, or pay back whatever he owes you …"

He didn't respond.

Her hands clutched her face. "Oh, God, please, I'm sure he is sorry…"

"Words pay no debts." The voice was raspy and echoed from the mask, sending a chill down her spine.

A shrill scream sounded from behind them. Estelle's mother stood framed by the kitchen doorway, a look of horror on her face. In that split second, the masked man was distracted, and Estelle raced towards the cordless phone.

Before she got halfway into the sitting room, the back of his hand connected with her face.

Estelle staggered on her feet, shocked by the blow. She could taste the metallic tang of her blood. The anger she'd felt before was replaced by fear. She whimpered.

Her mother rushed past the masked man into the sitting room and took Estelle in her arms. "You can take whatever you want," she said gesturing around the room. "Just don't hurt us."

"Sit down." It was an order, harsh and raspy. "If you do exactly as I say, neither of you will get hurt. If you don't…"

Estelle shivered at his unspoken threat and felt a sharp pain grip her stomach.

She winced as she waddled over to the sofa. Her mother stayed close to her, muttering words of reassurance. Together, they sat huddled on the sofa, and Estelle started sobbing. How could Tyrell do this? How could he involve her mother?

The masked man bent down and put his face close to Estelle's. His eyes were distorted by the mask. Estelle flinched.

With the gas mask just inches from her face, he rasped, "Listen to me very carefully. Your life depends on it."

CHAPTER FIFTY-FIVE

THE KILLER STOOD IN THE middle of Estelle's sitting room. "You understand what you have to say?"

Estelle nodded.

Christ, she just wanted to get this over with.

She glanced at her mother. Her skin was grey and drawn. Another wave of pain clutched at Estelle's belly and she cried out.

"Very good," the masked man said. "But you'd be better off saving your acting skills for the phone call."

He handed her the cordless phone and she punched in the familiar telephone number. Surely, Tyrell would notice something was wrong. She never normally called him from the landline. She always used up the free minutes she got with her mobile phone contract.

As the call connected and she heard the ringing tone, Estelle's throat tightened.

She rocked back and forward. It would be okay. As soon as this bastard left, she would phone Tyrell again and warn him it was a trap.

When Tyrell's voice answered, her eyes filled with tears. "Tyrell, I need you to meet me."

She felt the masked man's eyes burning into her.

"You know I can't leave this place, babe."

"Please, Tyrell, I have to see you."

"It's only for a few days. I'll see you soon, I promise."

Estelle began to sob. "Tyrell, you have to …"

"Come on, babe, not the waterworks again. It's not fair. I'll see you in a few days."

Estelle looked up at the masked man. Only his eyes were visible through the black gas mask. His cold, blue eyes stared back at her. She shot a look at her mother, who sat trembling with her hand pushed to her chest. She had to make Tyrell agree to meet her.

Estelle said the only thing she had left, the only thing that would make him come, "Tyrell, it's the baby." The bitterness of the words threatened to choke her as tears streamed down her cheeks.

"What's wrong? Is something wrong with the baby?"

Estelle looked up at the masked man again, begging him with her eyes, pleading for him not to make her do this.

He walked over to the sofa and rested his hand on her mother's shaking shoulder.

Estelle had to do this. When the man left, she would phone Tyrell back and let him know it was all a lie.

"It's the baby," she said. "It's serious, but I can't tell you over the phone…"

Tyrell promised to sneak out of the safe house to meet her, and he started to tell her the address.

"I'll meet you in an hour. In the alleyway behind Viola's restaurant. It's the alleyway opposite the safe house, halfway down."

"It's probably safer to meet on the main road where –"

"No! It has to be behind the restaurant … Please, Tyrell."

"All right. I'll be there … try not to worry, babe."

Estelle couldn't reply as the depth of her betrayal began to sink in.

After Tyrell hung up, she handed the masked man the phone.

"Good girl," he said and then reached inside his black leather jacket.

Estelle's eyes widened as she saw a length of what looked like washing line. She shook her head. "What's that for?"

He beckoned her forward, holding out his hand.

She swatted it away. "No."

"Sit in the chair," he said, grabbing hold of one of the four hard-backed chairs around the dining table.

She pushed herself off the sofa, but a sharp pain shot through her, making her double up.

He waited until she straightened up and then gestured again for her to sit in the chair. When she sat down, he roughly pulled her arms behind her back and began to wrap the cord around her wrists.

"You can't do that. She's going into labour."

Estelle vaguely registered her mother's protests as the horror slowly dawned on her: He was tying her up so she wouldn't be able to warn Tyrell.

If he killed Tyrell, it would be her fault.

She struggled against the cord, and a noise that sounded like some kind of animal in pain rang out around the flat.

As the masked man sealed her lips with tape, she realised the noise had been coming from her.

CHAPTER FIFTY-SIX

THE KILLER LOOKED DOWN AT the slumped figure of Tyrell Patterson. It had been over quickly, almost too quickly.

He activated the camera on his mobile phone, and lined up the shot. It wasn't easy. His hands were still shaking, a side effect of the adrenaline flooding his system.

He had to take three photos before he was satisfied. The build-up had been so exciting, but the actual event had been an anti-climax. Tyrell hadn't put up much of a fight.

He only had one more of the gang to go now: Robbie Baxter. After that, he needed to make a plan and decide who to target next.

There were plenty of candidates needing a dose of justice. He'd be spoilt for choice.

He looked down at the photo of Tyrell and another thought struck him - there was a deserving candidate even closer to home.

He'd propped Tyrell up against a brick wall, but his head kept lolling forward. The killer grabbed a handful of Tyrell's hair. Tyrell's blotchy, swollen face made him shudder. The killer let go in disgust and pulled his hand away, wiping it on his trousers.

In the end, it had been ridiculously easy to trap Tyrell. The killer had parked in the narrow lane outside the back of Viola's restaurant. He wasn't sure how Tyrell had managed to leave the safe house and give the guards the slip but criminals could be surprisingly enterprising.

He had fed Tyrell a line about Estelle being rushed to hospital. He told him he was a neighbour of his girlfriend's mother and that they'd asked him to meet Tyrell and drive him to the hospital.

For a criminal, he was surprisingly trusting.

Tyrell jumped in the car straight away. The killer pretended he needed to get something out of the boot, and after opening it, he fed a length of tubing through the back seat and activated the locks.

It didn't take Tyrell long to realise something was wrong.

The smell gave it away, obviously he recognised it.

The killer had allowed himself a moment or two of satisfaction as Tyrell struggled to open the car door. There was no way he could escape. The killer had rigged the locking mechanism so it could only be opened from the outside.

In less than a minute, Tyrell was slumped forward against the dashboard, motionless.

The killer opened the email app on his phone to send the photo by email. He'd gotten the email address for DCI Brookbank of the city of London police from their website.

It was a shame he couldn't have sent it to that other officer, the one who'd screwed up his plans for Robbie Baxter.

After he'd sent the email, the killer headed back to the tube. He pulled his hood up, making sure he kept his face in shadow.

CHAPTER FIFTY-SEVEN

THAT AFTERNOON, MACKINNON CAME BACK to the station determined to get back to work. He was sick of sitting at Derek's, doing nothing but watching Molly doze by the radiator. Even if Brookbank had him doing paperwork and sitting at his desk all day, it was better than sitting at home feeling helpless.

He'd had a brief explanation from Collins over the phone, but he still didn't understand how the killer managed to get at Tyrell Patterson when he was in the safe house.

His chest felt tight as he climbed the stairs slowly, heading up to the incident room. He bumped into DI Tyler, who was making his way down the stairs.

"What are you doing here, Mackinnon? I thought you were supposed to be off sick."

Mackinnon paused on the stairs, glad to take a breather. "I felt better."

"Really? You don't look better."

"What the hell happened with Tyrell Patterson?" Mackinnon changed the subject.

Tyler ran a hand through his grey-streaked hair. "It's a mess. Tyrell Patterson left the safe house," He shook his head. "The fool. What's the bloody point of being in a safe house if you don't stay inside it?"

"How did he get outside, and why didn't the officers on duty notice?" Mackinnon asked.

"According to the two guards on duty, they checked up on him every thirty minutes. On their ten a.m. check he was still in bed, at ten-thirty he was gone. He left via the fire escape. The tricky little bugger disabled the alarm that was meant to go off when the door opened." Tyler leaned heavily on the bannister. "The killer sent an email to the DCI with a photo of Tyrell slumped against a wall. We found him in an alleyway within spitting distance of the safe house."

"And do you know why he left the safe house?"

Tyler nodded. "His girlfriend."

Two uniformed officers passed them on the stairs, and Tyler and Mackinnon moved back to give them room.

Tyler waited a moment before continuing. "After Patterson's body was found, we sent a routine patrol unit out to check on his girlfriend, Estelle Williams. He forced the girlfriend to phone Tyrell and arrange a meeting, then he tied her and her mother up. The girlfriend is eight and a half months pregnant."

Mackinnon scowled. "Sick bastard."

Mackinnon and Tyler began to walk upstairs slowly.

"How are Estelle and her mother now?" Mackinnon asked.

"They're in hospital. Estelle is in labour, and they've both got marks on their arms from the cord he used to tie them up, but there was no sign of any gas or any of that stuff he rigged up at the other places."

Tyler shrugged. "We had to move Robbie Baxter pretty quickly. He's at the station, for now, until we can sort something out. His mother is here, too. She's been nagging the ears off the officer looking after the family room. The woman never shuts up."

Tyler's phone began to ring as they walked along the corridor. Mackinnon stopped by the vending machine and gestured to Tyler. Tyler nodded vigorously and pointed to number seventy-two which was vegetable soup. Mackinnon pulled a face but fed coins into the machine for Tyler's drink.

Mackinnon could only hear one side of the phone conversation but it sounded like Tyler was talking to Collins. Mackinnon handed Tyler his soup, and then fed in more coins and pressed the buttons for a black coffee.

He took a sip, and looked at Tyler, trying to read his face.

Tyler beamed widely into the phone. "That is interesting. Good work," he said and hung up.

Mackinnon waited for him to elaborate, but Tyler didn't seem willing to share. He raised his cup of soup, said, "Cheers," and headed off down the corridor towards the DCI's office.

Mackinnon didn't fancy seeing the DCI. He wasn't exactly Brookbank's flavour of the month. "I thought I'd have a word with Robbie Baxter and his mum. They're downstairs in the family room, aren't they?"

"Nice try, Mackinnon," Tyler said, turning back and grinning at Mackinnon over his shoulder. "But I don't think Brookbank would approve of that. Stick to paperwork. If you're lucky, he might not notice you're back." Tyler winked, and then carried on walking.

CHAPTER FIFTY-EIGHT

AN HOUR LATER, COLLINS ARRIVED back in the incident room. His cheeks were flushed and he was slightly out of breath. He threw his jacket over the back of the chair. "I knew it," he said.

He wandered over and perched on the edge of Mackinnon's desk. "What are you doing back? Feeling better?"

"Yes, thanks," Mackinnon said. "What did you know?"

"Sorry?" Collins unbuttoned his shirt sleeves and started to roll them up.

"You just walked in and said, you knew it?"

Collins grinned and cracked his knuckles. "Ah, yes. That was all down to a brilliant piece of detective work by me." Collins scanned the incident room. "Is Charlotte around?"

"I haven't seen her ... So ...?"

"So what?"

"Are you going to tell me about this amazing piece of detective work, or do I have to drag it out of you?"

"All right, I'm getting to it. Christ, I can see you're in a great mood, after your day off." Collins wheeled over a chair and sat down. "The first time I spoke to Pete Morton, I knew he was hiding something".

"The famous Collins instinct," Mackinnon said sarcastically.

"That's right. It turns out that Pete Morton had a bit of a dodgy deal going with Syed Hammad. He'd given Hammad a box of phones, then told his boss the phones never turned up from their suppliers. Morton was panicking because he thought we'd find the box of phones and put two and two together. Of course, he insisted this was the first time he'd ever done anything like this, but then he would say that, wouldn't he?"

"But we didn't find any phones at the newsagent's," Mackinnon said.

"Exactly. We didn't find the phones because the kids had taken them. That's how our masked man has been tracking the kids. Our techies found tracking software installed on Joanne James and Tyrell Patterson's phones."

Mackinnon felt sick. "So he knew where the safe house was. He knew where they were all the time."

Collins nodded and sat back in his chair, looking pleased with himself. "Exactly. I suspect we'll find that Robbie still has his phone on him."

Collins stood up and stretched. "I'm going to go down and speak to Robbie and his charming mother. Care to join me?"

Shoving Tyler's warning to the back of his mind, Mackinnon nodded and stood up.

On the way downstairs, Collins turned to Mackinnon and said, "Ivy Baxter's been giving them hell downstairs. Still, maybe she'll be nice to you. You did save Robbie."

"I doubt it," Mackinnon said.

Ivy and Robbie Baxter had been housed in the family room, especially suited for kids. The room was decorated in primary colours. Three plump, modern, blue sofas were arranged in a

U-shape. Bright yellow bean bags were scattered around the room. There were piles of stuffed animals and a box of other toys in the corner, although at fourteen, Robbie Baxter was a little old for that kind of thing.

The room was designed to reassure children and make them feel comfortable and secure.

Mackinnon and Collins entered the room and heard the tail end of Ivy and Robbie's conversation.

"At least let me have a fag," Robbie Baxter whined.

"No you bloody can't have a fag," Ivy Baxter said as Mackinnon shut the door.

Ivy Baxter scooted forward on the sofa and smoothed back her hair. She sat with her hands clasping a tatty, designer knock-off handbag. It was printed with a generic pattern that seemed to be everywhere these days.

She wore a velour tracksuit, but it looked a couple of sizes too small. Ivy Baxter was extremely slim, which made Mackinnon think the tracksuit was designed for children. The legs of the tracksuit were too short and showed off her white socks and dark blue ballet pumps.

Robbie Baxter wore a grey hoody, dark blue jeans and a huge scowl on his face. He slumped back onto the sofa and clutched a blue cushion to his stomach.

DC Collins spoke first. "You remember DS Mackinnon. He's the one who saved your life, Robbie."

Robbie rolled his eyes and pulled up the hood on his sweatshirt as if he could shut them both out.

"If you lot had done your job properly, his life would never have been at risk in the first place," Ivy Baxter snapped, giving Collins and Mackinnon a sharp look.

Collins blinked, but Mackinnon wasn't surprised by the reaction.

Mackinnon sat down on the blue sofa opposite Robbie and

Ivy and said, "As we're finished with the pleasantries, we'd like to see your mobile phone please, Robbie."

Robbie Baxter sat up straight. "What? Why?"

Robbie looked at them, his eyes wide with innocence. Mackinnon thought he must have practiced long and hard to perfect that look. But Mackinnon wasn't falling for it.

Ivy Baxter, on the other hand, had long since given up any pretence of innocence.

"What do you want his phone for? Don't give it to him, Robbie. They're probably trying to fit you up with some piddling little crime. You'd think they'd have better things to do with a killer on the loose."

Mackinnon wasn't sure what counted as a 'piddling little crime,' in Ivy Baxter's book. He was afraid to ask.

"We believe the phone is stolen property, Mrs. Baxter," Collins said. "We also –"

Collins was interrupted by Ivy Baxter's bellow of rage as she flung herself across at Robbie, whacking him around the ear. "You little –"

Mackinnon winced.

"Mrs. Baxter, please, I'm not finished," Collins said. "We believe Robbie took the phone from the newsagent's."

Ivy Baxter shot a furious look at Robbie before Collins continued, "We believe the phone has tracking software installed and –"

"I never stole nothing," Robbie said. "I paid him for it. I gave that Syed bloke fifty quid. You can't prove I stole it."

"Hand it over, Robbie," Mackinnon said. "It's how the killer has been tracking you. Is it really worth risking your life for a mobile?"

Ivy Baxter looked pale. She put a hand to her mouth. Mackinnon thought she might be sick, and for a moment, he felt sorry for her.

Mackinnon held out his hand for the phone.

Robbie hesitated for just a moment, and then shoved his hand into his pocket. "I needed it for homework, Mum," he said. "I need to get on the Internet for school. Research and stuff."

Ivy Baxter said nothing. She just stared at the floor.

Reluctantly, Robbie pulled out the small, black phone and placed it in Mackinnon's outstretched hand. It was sleek and thin, at least half the weight of Mackinnon's phone. It made Collins' old Nokia look like something from the dark ages.

Before anyone could say anything else there was a knock and DI Tyler poked his head around the door. "Can I have a word, gentlemen?"

Mackinnon and Collins joined Tyler outside. Mackinnon handed the phone to Collins, who waggled it under Tyler's nose. "Soon we'll have the whole set," Collins said.

"Well done," Tyler said to Collins, then turned to Mackinnon. "I've spoken to Brookbank."

Mackinnon nodded. That was it then. He was going on gardening leave.

"Brookbank's perfectly happy if you'd come back to work, but solely on the condition that you're office based only, all right?"

Mackinnon was surprised Brookbank hadn't taken the opportunity to get rid of him for a few weeks. "Why does it have to be office based?"

"According to Brookbank, it's all a matter of distance. He doesn't like officers getting personally involved with the cases they work, and since you had an up close and personal encounter with our masked friend, he thinks you'll be better off in the office."

Everything about the job seemed to revolve around paperwork these days. It was Mackinnon's least favourite part of the job, but it was better than staying at Derek's and watching Molly snooze all day.

Collins left to take the phone to the evidence room, and Mackinnon headed back up to the incident room, which would be his home for the next few days. He supposed he was lucky that Brookbank was quite happy to keep the discipline in-house, which meant there would be no black mark on his record.

Mackinnon had gone against procedure, and the procedures were in place for a reason. He didn't expect to be lauded for his actions. But at the same time … Robbie Baxter might be just like his brothers, he might be an ungrateful little tyke with no respect for the law, but he was still a kid. A fourteen-year-old kid. Maybe Mackinnon should've followed procedure. Maybe he could have ended up doing more damage than good, but he went with his instinct, and he couldn't beat himself up over that.

CHAPTER FIFTY-NINE

KATHY WALKER WANDERED AROUND THE salon, trying to find things to keep her busy.

She'd already dusted all the hairdressing stations, cleaned the mirrors and swept the floor, even though it didn't need it. She hadn't had any customers since she'd swept it this morning.

She wandered over to the wide windows that looked out onto the street. She had no bookings for this afternoon, but she hoped for a little passing trade. It wasn't looking likely.

Storm clouds were gathering overhead, and there was a smell of ozone that threatened rain. No one would be in a hurry to get their hair done if it rained.

She should probably just close up, but she couldn't risk it, not if she might get just one client out of it.

It was going to be tough meeting the rent this month. The landlord had put the rent up again this year. She'd only managed to make ends meet so far because Stuart helped her out now and again. But she had to face the truth. This business wasn't making money any more. She'd be better off closing up and going to work for someone else.

As the first drops of rain started to dribble down the windowpanes, Kathy sat down at one of the hairdressing stations, staring at herself in the mirror.

Where had the time gone?

Just eight years ago, she'd been excited to be opening her new salon. A salon of her very own. Now she didn't recognise the woman in the mirror. They couldn't be her crow's feet, her puffy eyes. Even her hair was looking a bit tired and frizzy. What kind of a hairdresser was she if she couldn't make her own hair look nice? It wasn't exactly a good advertisement for her styling skills.

The trouble was, she just didn't seem to care anymore. Years ago, she would have sat down with a pen and pad and drawn out a plan of action, maybe blown up a few fliers, run some promotions, but she just couldn't be bothered. She felt like she was treading water, hanging around the same place day in and day out while other people went on with their lives. She'd seen her friends get married, have children and move away.

At least she had Stuart. They may not have been related by blood, but Kathy had always been close to Stuart.

The bell jingled as someone opened the door to the salon.

Kathy spun around on the chair, hoping to see a customer. But it was only Mitch Horrocks.

Of all the people she didn't want to see…

Still, she tried to be pleasant, if only for Stuart's sake.

"Hello, Mitch. I don't suppose you've come in for a short back and sides."

Mitch grunted and crossed his arms over his protruding stomach. "I need a favour," he said. "I need to pop out and I wondered …" He paused to look around the empty salon.

"Seeing as you don't have any appointments, I wondered if you could keep an eye on my mother for a bit."

She didn't like him. There was something about him that put her on edge, and an afternoon with his mother was the last thing she needed.

"Well, of course I'd love to help out," she said slowly, not wanting to appear rude, but desperately trying to think of a good excuse. "I was taking advantage of the quiet time between customers to give the salon a clean."

Her business might be in trouble, but she didn't have to admit that to Mitch Horrocks.

"Really? It looked like you were just having a bit of a sit down to me."

Kathy flushed. The bloody cheek.

"I'd just cleaned the mirror. I was checking for smudges." Not that it is any of your business, she thought.

"Look, don't bother if it's too much trouble," Mitch said and half turned as if to leave.

Christ, he really was an unlikeable sod. What the hell did Stuart see in him?

"All right," Kathy said. "I suppose I can spare a few minutes. How long will you be?"

"Half an hour, maximum. I've just got to pick up a few bits from the cash-and-carry. I've run out of stock and I need bacon before my evening rush. I could have sworn I picked up twenty packets last week, but they've disappeared. It's always quiet at this time, so I'll close the cafe. But I don't want to leave Mum on her own."

He paused and his dark, bushy eyebrows met in the middle as he frowned. "I'm a bit worried about her. After all that stuff at the newsagent's, she's a little on edge."

Now Kathy felt bad. It was enough to put anyone on edge, even more so if you were old and frail and stuck inside all day.

Mrs. Horrocks used a wheelchair and couldn't get around on her own. She must feel particularly vulnerable.

Kathy went behind the counter and picked up her coat. "All right. I'll come."

CHAPTER SIXTY

AS SOON AS KATHY FOLLOWED Mitch outside, the rain started to fall heavily. What had started as a light summer shower, was rapidly descending into a storm. A rumble of thunder made Kathy shiver. She locked the salon door and jogged a few steps to catch up with Mitch.

Mitch trudged beside her in silence. She wrinkled her nose when she caught sight of the sweat patch on his back. The underneath of his arms were stained yellow. Kathy kept a good distance between them as they walked the short distance to Mitch's cafe.

Mitch opened the cafe door and let Kathy enter first. "Mum's upstairs," he said. "She's expecting you."

He flicked the white and red sign on the door over to 'closed,' and then scrawled on a scrap of paper in large block-capital letters, 'BACK IN FIFTEEN MINUTES.'

He rummaged around in a drawer under the till, grabbed some blue-tac and stuck it on the back of the piece of paper. He looked up as if surprised to see Kathy still standing there.

He nodded in the direction of the internal door to the flat. "You know the way, Kathy."

And with that he was gone.

Kathy made her way over the scratched linoleum. The air was heavy with the smell of old fried food. She hesitated by the door, feeling almost nervous. It was silly really. She needed to get over her aversion to the Horrocks family, especially if Stuart started to see more of Mitch … If, God forbid, it became serious…

The stairs creaked beneath her feet as she climbed up to the living quarters.

She'd only gotten halfway up the stairs, when a shrill voice questioned, "Who's there?"

"It's only Kathy, Mrs. Horrocks. I've just come to keep you company for a bit while Mitch pops to the shops. He's run out of bacon."

She reached the top of the landing and heard Mrs. Horrocks say, "Stupid boy. He's always running out of something."

Kathy pushed open the door to the sitting room and took a deep breath. It was like stepping back in time. Delicate lace doilies sat on spindly tables. There were hand-sewn arm covers on the sofa and armchairs. She could hear the brass clock over the fireplace ticking loudly.

A large mahogany cabinet sat against the wall to Kathy's left. It displayed intricately patterned crockery. Everything was polished to a high shine. Kathy wondered absently who kept the flat so spick-and-span. She supposed it must be Mitch, seeing as Mrs. Horrocks was confined to a wheelchair.

"Don't stand there dillydallying in the shadows. Come forward, girl, so I can see you."

Kathy resisted the urge to roll her eyes and stepped into the sitting room.

Mrs. Horrocks sat in a wheelchair by the window. She had

a tartan blanket tucked over her knees. The lacy collar of her blouse came halfway up her neck and she wore a thick cardigan. Her pale grey hair was scraped back into a bun.

"So he thinks I can't be trusted on my own, does he? He sends you around to look after me?" Mrs. Horrocks gave a little shake of her head as if the very idea was ridiculous.

Kathy was beginning to feel awkward standing up. She didn't like feeling like a little child being told off. "May I sit down?"

"I suppose if you're planning on staying, you may as well."

Kathy sank down into the armchair on the other side of the room. It was the seat furthest from Mrs. Horrocks.

The light coming in from the window highlighted all the wrinkles on Mrs. Horrocks' face. Her crinkled skin didn't make her look like a sweet old lady. It made her look like a wicked old witch.

Mrs. Horrocks smelled of TCP. Kathy had never liked that smell, not since their mother had used it neat on her cuts and grazes when she was a little girl.

"Mitch asked me to come and say hello," Kathy said. "He thought you might enjoy the company."

Mrs. Horrocks raised an eyebrow, which hitched up the wrinkles on her forehead. "He thought I'd enjoy your company?"

Kathy felt heat warm her cheeks. Why did they both have to be so nasty? She had never seen anyone coming to visit Mrs. Horrocks. She'd be surprised if the woman ever had a friend in her life.

Kathy took a deep breath, then said, "Why don't I make us both a nice cup of tea?"

"Oh, that's why you've come over. You've run out of teabags, have you?"

Kathy bit her tongue. "No," she said. "I have plenty of teabags, thank you. I just thought you might like a cup of tea."

Truthfully, Kathy just wanted an excuse to spend time away from Mrs. Horrocks. She planned to drag out the tea-making as long as possible.

"Okay. I'll have mine with just a dash of milk and no sugar."

"Right," Kathy said and stood up just as a muffled thud seemed to come from the hallway.

Mrs. Horrocks heard it, too. She cocked her head to one side. "What was that? Is Mitchell back already?"

Surely it was too soon to be Mitch; he'd been gone less than five minutes. Maybe he'd forgotten something.

"I'll go and see," Kathy said and headed out of the sitting room.

"Leave the door open, girl," Mrs. Horrocks ordered.

Girl? Christ, it had been a few years since anyone called Kathy a girl.

Kathy made her way downstairs, pausing on the last step and listening, but she couldn't hear anything. She checked the cafe, but all the tables were empty and the 'closed' sign still hung on the door.

The buildings along here were more than a hundred years old, and the cafe was in the middle of a terraced row, maybe the noise had come from next door? Kathy shrugged and headed back upstairs to make the tea.

CHAPTER SIXTY-ONE

THE MASKED MAN HUMMED AS he lined up three red, plastic buckets.

He filled the buckets to the halfway mark with the first tub of chemicals. He smiled as he worked.

His next victim would make a change from the rioters, but was no less deserving.

Punishment wasn't only for the young. He'd never understood the mentality of those who believed people should be excused of crimes due to old age.

Nazis who had evaded capture for decades might look weak and frail in the photos printed by the newspapers, but did they not deserve to be punished for their crimes? Did their victims not deserve justice because the elderly Nazi had lost his teeth, his hair and gained a few wrinkles? Underneath that exterior, wasn't he still evil?

Age didn't come into it. Old or young, they were still guilty.

Some of the things kids got away with these days were

sickening, too. They needed to be taught right from wrong when they were very young.

Children could be evil. He had first-hand experience of that.

He remembered one particular occasion …

He'd stood in the playground and felt the cold wind snap at his exposed ankles. His trousers flapped against his shins.

His lower lip wobbled.

He'd forgotten how much this hurt.

It wasn't the first time Junior had been bullied, but in many ways, this was worse, much worse.

Over the years, the taunting lessened because Junior had learned not to respond.

Instead, he ignored it at the time, but he got his own back later … and when he got his own back, he made sure it was brutal.

Word spread around the school and bullies were no longer a problem.

The kids his own age might not bully him anymore, but that didn't mean they were friendly. They kept their distance.

Sometimes he felt lonely, but he managed to make friends with some of the younger kids. At least he thought he had.

At first, they'd been in awe of him. Junior had a reputation, and they thought it made them look cool by association. Stupidly, he'd thought they had liked him… When would he learn?

"What is he wearing? His trousers are skintight! Don't bend over, Junior. You might split them!" They laughed at him.

Junior tried to picture how their faces would look after he had doled out their punishments, but it was no good, he could only see their faces dimpled and flushed, laughing in cruel delight.

"You better start eating salads for lunch, Junior. If your

trousers split, the girls will see your bits." One boy cackled with laughter, and the others joined in.

If Junior was fat, then the boy taunting him had to be obese. He was definitely many inches wider than Junior. The difference was, he had school trousers that fit him.

It was stupid to get upset over trousers that were a little too small. They were made to fit ages eleven to twelve, and Junior was nearly fourteen. Mother said she would get him some new ones … When she had the money.

"Maybe he wants the girls to see his bits. Eh, Junior, is that what you want?"

"That's the only way a girl will look at them."

As they all dissolved into laughter, Junior imagined grabbing a handful of the first boy's hair and smashing his face into the wet cold pavement again and again… Until he sobbed for his mother and begged him to stop. But Junior wouldn't stop. He would grind the boy's face hard against the grit until it was bloody and raw and…

The sharp sound of a whistle made all the children jump.

Mrs. Gower, the teacher on playground duty, approached them. "What's going on here?" she asked. "I hope you're playing nicely."

"Yes, miss," the younger children said in chorus and ran off, leaving Junior standing there.

Mrs. Gower studied him. Her gaze focused on his exposed ankles and then travelled upwards, to take in the hole on the arm of his jumper. As Junior looked up into her face, he saw pity in her eyes, and he hated it.

"Are you okay, Junior? They weren't bothering you, were they?"

"Hardly," Junior said scornfully. "They're just kids."

From the way Mrs. Gower looked at him, Junior knew she didn't believe him.

Junior shoved his hands in his trouser pockets, and as the

bell rang out to signal the end of break time, he headed back to the school building, leaving Mrs. Gower and her good-for-nothing pity behind him.

CHAPTER SIXTY-TWO

KATHY CLENCHED HER TEETH. SHE was absolutely fuming. If Mitch didn't get back soon, Kathy couldn't be held responsible for her actions. She carried Mrs. Horrocks' tea back to the kitchen. Apparently, it wasn't strong enough for the old witch.

It didn't surprise Kathy that Tim Coleman left as quickly as he had. Mrs. Horrocks really was impossible. She poured the tea into the sink and watched it gurgle down the plug hole. She rinsed the cup, switched on the kettle again then folded her arms and leaned back against the kitchen counter. She glanced at the clock. Mitch had only been gone for fifteen minutes. It felt so much longer.

Kathy wasn't sure she could take much more of Mrs. Horrocks. No wonder Mitch was so bloody miserable all the time. She'd been too hard on him. She'd be miserable too if she had to live with Mrs. Horrocks.

This time, Kathy left the tea brewing in the pot for ages, and used a teaspoon to squeeze the teabags. Kathy smiled with satisfaction as she looked down at the stewed brown liquid. That should be strong enough for the old bag.

She added a dash of milk to Mrs. Horrocks' cup and gave it a quick stir. She replaced the milk in the fridge and shut the door with her elbow.

Kathy picked up the cup, ready to present it to Mrs. Horrocks for inspection. No doubt there would be something else wrong with it this time. She opened the kitchen door, and as she stepped into the hall, her foot connected with a red plastic bucket.

At first, Kathy just stared down at it. Who had put that there? It hadn't been there a moment ago when she entered the kitchen.

Her first reaction was to move the bucket out of the way. But when she bent down, she saw that the red bucket was half filled with a colourless liquid. Kathy pressed a hand over her mouth as she gagged. It smelled awful. A horrible foreboding crept over her. There had been gossip after Syed's death - talk about how chemicals had been mixed in buckets to produce the toxic gas.

But that was ridiculous. She was just being paranoid. Perhaps the bucket had been put there to catch drips. Kathy looked up at the ceiling, searching for a damp patch. But there was nothing.

Kathy turned to look down the hallway. There were more buckets …

Kathy snatched her hand away from the bucket, and the tea cup clattered to the ground. The dark brown liquid stained the carpet, but Kathy barely noticed. She didn't like this. It felt all wrong.

Someone had put the buckets outside the kitchen while she'd been inside.

Kathy took a step backwards.

She needed to get out of here. Fast.

"What on earth are you doing out there?" Mrs. Horrocks' shrill voice carried through from the sitting room. "Have you broken one of my cups, you stupid girl?"

Oh, God. How on earth was Kathy going to get Mrs. Horrocks out of here? She couldn't just leave her.

How long did they have before the gas overwhelmed them?

"Answer me, girl!"

Mrs. Horrocks' words jolted Kathy into action. She skirted around the bucket and dashed down the corridor back into the sitting room.

"How can I get you downstairs?" Kathy asked.

Mrs. Horrocks looked at Kathy as if she were mad. "What are you talking about? I don't go downstairs."

"There are buckets in the hallway. I think there is some kind of chemical in them… Like at the newsagent's. Can you smell it?"

Mrs. Horrocks swallowed and gave a single nod. "All right, but I can't walk. I can't get out of this thing." She slapped her hand against the armrest of her wheelchair.

"I'll help you," Kathy said.

Mrs. Horrocks removed the tartan blanket from her legs and Kathy could see how terribly wasted and skinny they were.

This wasn't going to be easy.

"You should get yourself out," Mrs. Horrocks said. "Go on, leave me."

Kathy ignored her and knelt down beside the wheelchair. She lifted up the foot rests, leaving Mrs. Horrocks' feet dangling above the ground.

Kathy looked up at Mrs. Horrocks. "Ready?"

Mrs. Horrocks' face was pale, and for the first time, Kathy felt a pang of sympathy for the woman.

"Come on," Kathy said, putting her arm around Mrs. Horrocks, preparing to lift her up. "We'll do it together."

Mrs. Horrocks' watery eyes focused on Kathy, and her claw-like hand gripped Kathy's arm. "I don't think I can do it."

"Of course, we can. I'm stronger than I look," Kathy said, and she hoped it was true.

Kathy pushed the wheelchair to the staircase and took a deep breath. "Just lean on me."

Mrs. Horrocks couldn't support her own weight. Kathy had to half-drag the old woman out of her wheelchair. Mrs. Horrocks winced in pain.

Kathy tried to be gentle. If she wasn't careful, she could end up dislocating the old woman's shoulder.

Mrs. Horrocks' legs dangled beneath her. They brushed against the carpet as Kathy took the first step.

After a few more steps, Kathy paused. "The smell is getting fainter. That's a good sign, don't you think?"

Mrs. Horrocks was too traumatised to reply, her eyes were fixed on the downstairs landing and her hands clutched Kathy's jumper.

By the time they reached the middle of the stairs, Kathy was shattered. Who would have thought a little old lady could weigh so much?

Kathy's arms and legs were shaking. She worried that if she attempted the rest of the stairs, they might fall. Perhaps she could do it sitting down. They could slide down the stairs on their backsides.

Kathy lowered Mrs. Horrocks to the ground, then she heard the sound of a door slamming downstairs.

Both Mrs. Horrocks and Kathy shrank back, and Mrs. Horrocks' fingers dug into Kathy's shoulder.

A low whistling tune drifted up the stairs.

Mrs. Horrocks released her grip on Kathy's shoulder.

"That's Mitchell." Mrs. Horrocks called out, "Mitchell get up here, now!"

Mitch Horrocks appeared at the foot of the stairs, sweaty and carrying two plastic supermarket bags. He stared up at them in disbelief, his eyes almost bulging out of their sockets.

He dropped the shopping bags. "What the hell are you doing, you stupid woman?"

Kathy guessed he was talking to her. "I –"

"Why have you taken my mother out of her chair?"

Before Kathy had a chance to explain, Mitch was charging up the stairs two at a time.

"There are buckets upstairs," Mrs. Horrocks said. "Did you put them there, Mitchell?"

Mitch's bushy eyebrows met in the middle of his forehead in a deep frown. "Buckets? No, of course not. I've only just got back."

"You've heard the stories about the man in the black gas mask," Kathy said, edging past Mitch. "He used buckets at Syed's. I think whoever killed Syed is trying to gas us."

"Don't be ridiculous. Syed committed suicide."

"Can't you smell it?" Kathy asked.

Mitch raised his chin and sniffed the air. "Well, now you mention it, it doesn't smell too good, but – "

"Don't just stand there looking stupid, Mitchell." Mrs. Horrocks slapped Mitch's arm. "Help us get outside."

Mitch blinked a couple of times and then did what he'd been told. He squatted down and scooped his mother up in his arms, lifting her as if she weighed nothing.

Mitch carried Mrs. Horrocks down the creaky stairs and Kathy followed.

As they rushed through the cafe towards the exit, Mitch nodded to a chair. "Bring that chair out, Kathy. Mum will need a seat."

The heavy wooden chair hit Kathy twice on the shins as

she carried it outside. She set it down on the pavement, and Mitch lowered his mother onto the chair. Then he looked up at Kathy, accusingly. "This better not be a practical joke."

Kathy ignored him and shut the door firmly behind them.

Mrs. Horrocks leaned back in the wooden chair, arranging her skirt to cover her skinny legs. She stuck a bony finger in the middle of Mitch's flabby stomach. "Stop belly-aching boy and do something useful. Call the police."

Mitch stepped back a little so he was out of the way of his mother's prodding fingers and pulled out his mobile.

Mitch raised the phone to his ear. His eyes narrowed as he looked past Kathy. "That's all I need," he said as he dialled.

Kathy looked around and saw Tim Coleman striding along East Street towards them.

Tim Coleman's eyes widened in disbelief when he saw Mrs. Horrocks sitting on a wooden chair in the middle of the pavement. "What's happened? Are you taking her to the hospital?"

Mrs. Horrocks straightened up in the chair. "No they are not. There's nothing wrong with me."

"Pity," Tim mumbled under his breath.

"Anyway, what are you doing here? Come to beg for your old job back?" Mrs. Horrocks sneered, obviously feeling better and back to her normal nasty self.

"I've come to pick up the money your son owes me," Tim said, then wrinkled his nose. "Christ, what's that awful smell?"

Mitch pressed the button to end his call to the emergency services. "They're on their way," he said. "And you," he said, pointing a finger at Tim Coleman, "can think again if you've come here to get money out of me." He turned to Kathy. "Come on we better move away from the building. It stinks."

Kathy carried the chair and followed Mitch as he carried his mother across the street. She let the sound of Mitch and

Tim Coleman's bickering wash over her. Her heart rate was slowly returning to normal. The rain had stopped, but the wind had picked up even more and whipped Kathy's hair around her face.

The traffic on East Street rumbled past them, oblivious to the potential danger. Kathy wondered if she should go and warn the other shops in the row. She turned away from the others and looked back at her own salon. There was a figure standing by the front door. Kathy's heart rate spiked and she took a step back, stumbling and almost falling into Mrs. Horrocks' lap.

"For goodness sake, girl," Mrs. Horrocks said, flapping her arms. "Watch where you're going."

"What the hell is wrong with you?" Mitch said and looked in the direction of Kathy's salon. "It's just your brother."

Kathy blinked. The wind was making her eyes water.

Mitch was right. It was Stuart. Thank God. Kathy called out to him and Stuart turned.

He strode towards them. "What are you all doing out here?"

"I think that masked man was trying to gas us in the cafe. Mitch had asked me to keep an eye on Mrs. Horrocks and…"

"He asked you?" Stuart narrowed his eyes and looked at Mitch.

Kathy bristled. She might not like Mitch exactly. But Stuart couldn't think much of her if he thought Kathy wouldn't help a neighbour out in an emergency.

Mitch shrugged. "I ran out of bacon, and I didn't want to leave mum on her own."

Kathy shivered. It wasn't from the cold. She imagined the masked man creeping about the house while she had talked to Mrs. Horrocks.

She felt Stuart's arms wrap around her and crush her into a

D. S. BUTLER

tight hug. Kathy breathed in the comforting scent of leather from Stuart's jacket.

Tim Coleman tried to tend to Mrs. Horrocks as she slapped his hands away.

"For goodness sake. I'm trying to help," Tim said. "I want to make sure you're not hurt."

"I told you there's nothing the matter with me," Mrs. Horrocks said. "Keep your hands to yourself!"

Mrs. Horrocks was a prickly, spiteful old woman. And Mitch was a miserable grump, but why would anyone want to kill them?

Kathy had to believe Mitch and his mother were the ones the masked man wanted to target because if they weren't... It meant he wanted to kill her.

CHAPTER SIXTY-THREE

IT SEEMED LIKE THE EMERGENCY services arrived almost immediately. There were two fire engines, two ambulances and four police cars surrounding the entrance to Mitch's cafe.

Within half an hour all the residents in the flats opposite and all the shops in East Street had been evacuated.

Kathy, Stuart, Mitch, Mrs. Horrocks and Tim had been taken to a temporary incident room, which was a large trailer the police had set up at the very end of East Street, opposite the Catholic Church.

They'd had lots of curious looks from nosy residents as two uniformed officers had escorted them along the road and up the steps to the trailer.

They sat huddled in a circle, sitting on hardback chairs, waiting for someone to come and tell them what was going on. They hadn't even had confirmation that it had been poisonous gas.

Kathy wrapped her arms around herself. She couldn't stop shivering. What the hell was going on? Had she completely over-reacted? Maybe she had panicked after what had happened to Syed. But somebody had put the buckets there.

They'd all been checked out by the paramedics. A cheerful paramedic, who told them his name was Teddy, tried to persuade Mrs. Horrocks to go to hospital. For an awful moment, Kathy was afraid Mrs. Horrocks would hurl her cup of tea in his direction. But luckily, Teddy soon backed off when he realised Mrs. Horrocks was not a typical sweet old lady.

A uniformed PC stayed in the room with them at all times. Every now and then he'd look up and smile at them in a way he probably thought was reassuring, but Kathy didn't find it particularly comforting.

Kathy, Stuart, Mrs. Horrocks and Mitch all sat in silence. Stuart leaned forward resting his elbows on his knees, staring at his hands. Mitch sat back in his chair and linked his hands behind his head, showing off the wet patches at his armpits. His stomach hung over the waistband of his jeans.

The only one who wouldn't sit still was Tim. He paced the small room, huffing and puffing, making sure everyone knew how frustrated he was.

"How much longer are they going to keep us here?" Tim asked for the fourth time. "I have to get to work."

"For crying out loud," Mitch said. "It's not like you're a bloody brain surgeon. I'm sure they'll cope without you for an hour or so."

Tim narrowed his eyes and turned to face Mitch. "People actually rely on me. My job is slightly more important than serving up egg and chips."

Tim turned his back on Mitch and the rest of them and strode up to the PC.

The PC shifted in his chair, looking a little uncomfortable. "They are working as quickly as they can," he said. "There'll be someone with you shortly and they'll be able to tell you exactly what's going on."

Tim rolled his eyes and looked away.

Kathy thought he was being unfair. It wasn't the PC's fault. He probably didn't have any more idea of what was going on than they did.

Someone had handed Kathy a blanket when they were outside. She'd been in such a daze she couldn't remember who. Probably one of the paramedics. She gripped it tightly, glad of the extra warmth. She couldn't stop shivering, but it wasn't anything to do with the cold.

Tim resumed his pacing.

"Why don't you just call them? Tell them you're going to be a bit late. I'm sure they'll understand," Kathy said.

"I haven't got my phone," Tim said. "It was in my bag, and they made me leave it outside the cafe."

Stuart rummaged in his pocket and pulled out his mobile. "Here, you can use mine."

Tim took the phone with a grunt of thanks. He turned away from them and began to dial.

Kathy listened as Tim apologised to someone called Fiona.

They all turned as the door opened, and a young policewoman entered the room. Kathy recognised her and thought again that the woman would look so much better if she would put a few highlights in her hair. If she stuck to her natural colour, she wouldn't look so peaky.

Behind the policewoman, a slightly older man entered. Kathy couldn't remember his name, but she remembered seeing him around after the first gas attack at the newsagent's.

Both of the officers stared at them, coolly evaluating them, before the female officer spoke.

"I'm DC Charlotte Brown, and this is DC Nick Collins. We need to ask you a few questions about what happened this afternoon."

They'd answered questions as soon as the police had arrived, telling them about the buckets and what they were afraid of. But DC Brown and DC Collins wanted to go through things in a lot more detail.

After they'd been talking for half an hour, asking similar questions, each time rephrasing them slightly, Tim began to lose patience.

"Look, I know this is important, and I do want to help, but I have to get to work. So is there any way we can speed this up?"

DC Charlotte Brown gave him a sharp look that made him break eye contact. Kathy mentally cheered her.

"We are doing this as quickly and safely as we can, sir," DC Brown said. "We need to be thorough."

"But it was nothing to do with me," Tim said. "I just happened to be passing. It's them you need to talk to." He waggled a hand in Kathy's direction. "I wasn't the intended victim…" Tim flushed as he realised what he'd said.

Stuart got to his feet, pushing his chair back roughly so it scraped along the floor. "You insensitive bastard!"

Tim took a step back. "I didn't mean it like that."

DC Collins stood up and positioned himself in between Tim and Stuart. "All right settle down. This isn't helping anyone." He turned to Tim. "You can go. But we'll need to speak to you again later."

Tim looked extremely pleased with himself. "I can go?"

DC Brown gave him a tight smile. "Yes."

Tim reached for his light cotton jacket and tossed it over his shoulder. "Well, good." He turned to the group of them and raised his hand. "I'll see you later." Tim opened the trailer door and walked down the steps without looking back.

After the door closed, Kathy asked, "Can you tell us if it was the same gas?"

DC Charlotte Brown settled back in her chair and snapped the lid back on her pen. She tapped it against her bottom lip. "It looks like you disturbed the setup. One of the chemicals was already present in the buckets, but in order to generate enough gas two chemicals have to be mixed together. The second chemical had only been added to one of the buckets."

Kathy swallowed.

DC Collins nodded. "We think that whoever did this was disturbed before he could add the second chemical to the rest of the buckets. In short, you had an extremely lucky escape."

Kathy let the policeman's words sink in, and then exhaled a shaky breath. "Who do you think he was trying to kill?"

"Don't get hysterical, woman," Mitch said. "It's probably just some nut job who picked us at random."

"I am not being hysterical thank you, Mitch," Kathy said through gritted teeth.

"We don't have all the answers yet," DC Brown said. "I know this must be very scary. Is there someone you could stay with for a while?"

"We're not going anywhere," Mitch said. "I'm not being driven out of my own home by some nutcase."

Kathy felt Stuart's hand wrap around hers. "You can stay with me. You'll be okay. I promise."

Kathy felt tears prick the corner of her eyes. She didn't trust herself to speak so she just squeezed Stuart's hand and nodded, hoping he would realise just how grateful she was.

CHAPTER SIXTY-FOUR

STAYING IN THE OFFICE WAS driving Mackinnon crazy.

He'd had to watch Collins and Charlotte dash out after news came in of another gas attack. He couldn't believe he was sitting at a desk while that was going on.

Mackinnon put down the photocopied pages of the black notebook found in the masked man's bag. He rubbed his eyes, which were sore from trying to read the tiny, scribbled text. He'd been trying to make sense of it, to decipher some kind of clue. It was a waste of time. Collins had been right when he said it was full of deranged ramblings.

His only company in the office were the two indexers sitting a couple of desks away and DC Webb who scrunched his face up, looking at his computer screen.

It was so quiet Mackinnon could hear the gentle hum of the air conditioning.

He got up from his desk and walked across to the window, staring out at the grey clouds looming above the city skyline. He'd been thinking about going back to Chloe's tonight and firing up the barbecue. Maybe the weather would be better in

Oxford. There wasn't much point hanging around here if he wasn't wanted. He was supposed to be on rest days anyway.

He returned to his desk and flicked through a few more pages of the dense handwriting. The original notebook had gone to the lab. Mackinnon read through the quotes one more time. Whoever he was, the masked man had a fixation on justice.

Was he some kind of vigilante? That would explain why he had focused on a group of known troublemakers. It didn't explain the most recent attack. Why Mitch Horrocks? He seemed an unlikely candidate for the attention of the masked man. And Mrs. Horrocks? Even more unlikely.

The members of Vinnie Pearson's gang were a bunch of misfits. Could this vigilante be someone whose property was damaged last year during the riots? Had he decided to take justice into his own hands?

Mackinnon had a feeling it was something like that. Something local. But what the hell was the connection to Mitch Horrocks? He shoved the piece of paper he'd been reading away from him and picked up another.

As Mackinnon read through some more of the quotes, he shook his head. He had heard of some of them, but others were really out there, really obscure. He wasn't getting anywhere with this. He re-stacked the photocopied pages into a neat pile on his desk, and then glanced at his watch. He needed to get a move on if he wanted to get back to Oxford at a reasonable time.

He had planned to call in at Fiona's again, to see how they were doing with the new carer, Tim Coleman. Mackinnon felt responsible, after all he put Tim Coleman's name forward. But if he dropped in there, before driving to Oxford, he'd hit rush-hour.

Mackinnon picked up his mobile and scrolled through the contacts to get Fiona's number.

She answered on the third ring.

At first, she sounded great, and pleased to hear from him. He enquired after Anna and asked how she was getting along with Tim. It seemed everything was going fine.

"Tim's running a bit late today," Fiona said. "But he's been really brilliant. I can't thank you enough for recommending him."

"I'm glad he's working out. I…"

There was the sound of smashing glass and a muffled curse.

"Fiona?"

He could hear Fiona's voice, but it sounded distant as if she'd put down the phone and moved away.

"Christ, Tim," Fiona said. "You scared me."

Mackinnon could just about make out the low rumble of a man's voice, but he couldn't decipher the words.

"What's happened?" Fiona's voice sounded high pitched and panicked. "What's that awful smell? Oh, God. It's repulsive."

"Fiona? What's going on? What's wrong?" Mackinnon shouted down the phone, not caring that both the indexers and DC Webb turned to stare at him.

The line went dead.

"What's the matter?" DC Webb asked.

Mackinnon shook his head. "I'm not sure. It might be nothing."

He tried to call Fiona back, but the phone rang and rang. He had a bad feeling about this. Fiona mentioned a smell …

He remembered the smell of the hydrogen sulphide. The putrid, dense, creeping scent. The memory was so strong he almost believed he could smell it now.

Could Tim Coleman be this masked vigilante? Surely not. But then again he'd shown his clear dislike of Mitch Horrocks.

Mackinnon had given Fiona Tim's card. He'd given him

the green light to enter Fiona Evans' house. Had he given a killer unlimited access to Fiona and her children?

Mackinnon got to his feet, feeling sick. He hoped to God he was wrong about this. He scrawled Fiona's address on a post-it note and handed it to DC Webb.

"I'm going to check it out. Make sure she's okay. I can't get through."

DC Webb nodded and took the note. "Do you think something's happened?"

"Tim Coleman just arrived at Fiona Evans' house. She sounded scared… And she mentioned a smell before the line went dead…"

DC Webb reached for the phone on his desk. "I'll make sure the local unit checks it out straight away. They'll be able to get there before you."

Mackinnon pressed the speed dial on his phone for Collins, but he wasn't answering.

He took Collins' car keys from the unlocked top drawer of Collins' desk. He could use a pool car, but that would take time, and Mackinnon was sure Collins wouldn't mind. It was an emergency.

Mackinnon tried to call Fiona again on the way out of the car park. There was still no answer. As the seconds ticked past, he was becoming more and more concerned.

It took nearly forty minutes to get there, but it felt like hours. When he finally arrived, he couldn't find a space to park, so he parked over double yellow lines.

He saw a police patrol car parked two spaces away, and he felt his throat tighten. Please let this be a false alarm. He was already responsible for putting this family through so much.

Mackinnon jogged up the stone steps and rapped on the front door.

After a moment, Fiona opened the door. Her face was white, but she didn't look scared. She looked angry.

She blinked up at Mackinnon. "You got the police to come to my house? Just because I didn't answer the phone?"

Her jaw was tight as she opened the door wider for Mackinnon to come in.

She turned her back on him and stalked into the sitting room. "I hope you can explain to these officers why they are here. Because I can't."

Mackinnon closed the front door behind him and followed her.

The two uniformed police officers sat next to each other on the sofa, cradling mugs of tea. They both looked very relaxed.

On the other side of the room, Tim Coleman sat in an armchair. His hair was wet and he wasn't dressed. He sat there with only a towel wrapped around his waist. Mackinnon wasn't sure why that annoyed him as much as it did.

"Well?" Fiona prompted, sitting down on the armchair next to Tim's and crossing her legs.

"I thought something had happened," Mackinnon said. "Why did you hang up?"

"Er… Perhaps I could answer that," Tim Coleman said and smiled at Fiona. "I was caught up in the incident on East Street this afternoon. The gas at the cafe. It lingers, you see, and I came straight here, smelling pretty awful."

"That doesn't explain why you didn't answer the phone when I tried to ring back," Mackinnon said.

"We didn't answer because Tim got in the shower to try and get rid of that awful smell," Fiona said. "And I had to deal with Luke upstairs."

Mackinnon turned to the two uniformed PCs. "Thanks for your help. I'm sorry to waste your time."

"So long as everything is all right," the taller of the two PCs said. "We'll be on our way."

They both got to their feet and handed their empty mugs to Fiona. "Thanks for the tea."

Fiona walked them to the door. Mackinnon followed. "I need to move my car. I parked on double yellows."

As Mackinnon walked with the officers towards his car, one of the officers said, "Are you all right?"

"Yes. I'm sorry you had a wasted trip. I guess I'm still a little on edge. I had a terrible feeling when she mentioned the smell. It set off alarm bells."

"Well that's understandable." The officer tugged on his beard. "I hope you don't mind me saying, but Mrs. Evans didn't seem too happy about our arrival."

Mackinnon pulled the car keys out of his trousers pocket. "No, she didn't seem best pleased."

The officer with the beard nodded. "Better to be safe than sorry. And we did get a nice cup of tea out of it." He grinned.

After their patrol car had pulled away, Mackinnon parked in their vacated spot outside Fiona's house. He didn't really want to go back inside, but he knew he had to face the music. Perhaps he had been too quick to jump to conclusions, but he'd only wanted to make sure they were safe.

Fiona had left the front door ajar, and Mackinnon let himself back in with a quick rap on the door. He could hear Fiona and Tim laughing in the sitting room.

As Mackinnon entered the sitting room, the smile dropped from Fiona's face, making it clear she still hadn't forgiven him.

"I'll be off then," Mackinnon said.

"What? Is that it? No apology?" Tim scoffed.

Mackinnon rounded on Tim, glad to have a suitable target for his anger. "Me apologise? I think you're the one who needs to apologise for putting Fiona and her children at risk. What were you thinking coming here stinking of that stuff?"

"Well, of course... I didn't mean..." Tim spluttered.

"And put some bloody clothes on," Mackinnon said.

Tim stood up, clutching his towel. "I'll leave you two to it."

As he left the room, Mackinnon turned to Fiona. "I'm sorry, but I was genuinely worried."

Fiona shook her head. Her fists clenched at her sides. "I should have called you back. I should have realised you would be worried. I just got distracted. Luke was distressed, and I had to deal with him because Tim was in the shower."

Fiona walked him to the door. She leaned against the door frame as Mackinnon headed to the car. "I'm sorry. I wasn't really angry, but when I saw those two policemen standing on my step, I panicked. I felt something awful had happened, and it just brought back everything that happened with Bruce."

Mackinnon felt his stomach sink to his shoes. He turned around. "I didn't think."

He moved back to the front door and stood next to Fiona. "I was trying to get here myself, but I thought I'd be too late. I just had this horrible feeling it was the gas… And if it was Tim… And I was the one who gave you his number…" Mackinnon looked away. "I needed to make sure you were all okay."

Fiona smiled. "Let's forget it. No harm done."

As Mackinnon drove back to the station, he had time to think about how he had screwed up. Maybe Brookbank was right. Maybe he did need some time away from the team.

He decided to drive back via East Street. He could leave Collins' car there and finding out what was going on might make him feel better. It might even make him believe they would eventually catch this bastard.

CHAPTER SIXTY-FIVE

EAST STREET HAD BEEN SEALED off either side of the cafe. The blue police tape flickered in the wind. Mackinnon parked Collins' car behind the cordon and approached the two squad cars blocking the road.

Already, a crowd of gawpers had gathered, eager to see what was going on. Mackinnon was surprised the TV crews weren't here already, to gather new material for their next story on 'the masked man.' The heavy sulphurous smell hung in the air and turned Mackinnon's stomach.

He threaded his way through the crowd and showed his warrant card to a harassed uniformed officer, who was doing his best to divert an angry group of commuters. The officer waved Mackinnon through the cordon.

As Mackinnon headed down East Street toward the cafe, uniformed officers escorted residents and employees in the opposite direction, towards the safe area behind the cordon.

Mackinnon spotted Charlotte and Collins straightaway. They stood close to the temporary setup at the end of East Street.

Collins spotted Mackinnon and waved. As Mackinnon walked towards him a clap of thunder echoed over the street. Mackinnon looked up at the angry sky and fastened the button on his suit jacket.

"All right, Jack?" Collins said, walking forward to meet him.

Mackinnon nodded. "Fine, apart from making a complete fool of myself."

Collins grinned. "You should be used to that by now," he teased. "What happened this time?"

"What's going on here," Mackinnon said, rather than answer Collins' question. "Have you got any idea who is doing this yet?"

Collins shoved his hands in his pockets and hunched his shoulders against the wind that whipped around them. "It looks like our masked man was disturbed this time. There were buckets filled with chemicals, but he hadn't had time to add the catalyst to all of the buckets before someone stumbled across them, which means, fortunately, this time there's been no casualties."

"And it was in the cafe this time?"

Collins nodded. "Yes. The hairdresser from the salon two doors along had gone to the flat above the cafe to look after the old lady, while Mitch Horrocks went to the supermarket. She found the buckets."

"Did she see anyone?"

Collins shook his head. "No one. We've got uniform talking to the residents and the people working in the shops in this parade. But no luck so far. No one has seen anything."

Collins stared down at his shoes. "It doesn't feel like we're getting anywhere."

"If he had to leave in a hurry maybe he left behind fingerprints or other evidence."

"Yeah," Collins said. "The team is going through the crime

scene with a fine tooth comb at the moment. It seems like the answers keep drifting farther away. At the beginning, it seemed like there was a pattern. He was targeting Vinnie Pearson's gang. But now he's targeting a little old lady and a hairdresser. How does that fit into the pattern?"

They walked in silence towards St Michaels, stopping by the brick wall surrounding the church. Then Collins continued, "I was thinking if our masked man is some kind of vigilante, you know, taking it upon himself to punish the wrong, maybe in his opinion, Syed Hammad was just as bad as Vinnie's gang. He was selling stolen phones..."

"That's a harsh punishment for handling stolen goods."

Both men sat on the brick wall. Collins swung his legs, hitting his heels on the rough red bricks. Mackinnon's legs were long enough to reach the floor.

"I might have a word with the hairdresser before I go," Mackinnon said.

Collins stood up, with a smile. "I thought you were supposed to be on office duty."

"I'm here now. I'll just have a quick word, can't do any harm."

Collins nodded. He knew Mackinnon well enough not to try and stop him.

CHAPTER SIXTY-SIX

THE HAIRDRESSER, KATHY WALKER, STOOD close to her brother, near to the temporary incident room. Mitch Horrocks had set himself a little further back, as if he were trying to keep his distance. Beside Mitch, a short elderly lady sat on a wooden chair. Mitch's mother, Mackinnon guessed, the woman Mitch was so desperate to stop them talking to, after Syed Hammad's death.

Mackinnon took the opportunity to study the group. By anyone's standards, Kathy Walker looked terrified. She had her arm looped through her brother's and seemed to lean on him for support. In her other hand, she held a cigarette and raised it to her lips before sucking hard. The blanket around her shoulders slipped and Stuart Walker caught it before it dropped to the floor.

Stuart Walker was wearing the same black leather jacket as the first time Mackinnon had seen him. Mackinnon could see Stuart's lips moving as he spoke to his sister, but from this distance Mackinnon couldn't identify the words.

As he drew closer, the brother and sister seemed to sense him, and both of them looked up.

Kathy looked exhausted. "Don't tell me you're going to ask us questions, too."

Mackinnon said, "I hear you are quite the hero, helping Mrs. Horrocks to escape."

"I didn't do much." Kathy shrugged. "I was terrified."

Stuart looped his arm around Kathy's shoulders. "Of course you were. Anyone would be."

Kathy looked close to tears.

"If you don't need us for anything else, I'd like to take Kathy to my place, but I need to get hold of her stuff," Stuart said. "Do you know if I can go inside yet? Her flat is above the salon. I'd like to get some clothes, toothbrush and that kind of thing…"

"I've only just got here," Mackinnon said. "I'm afraid, I don't know if the building is safe yet. If you don't mind waiting a moment, I can find out for you."

Stuart Walker shook his head. "Don't worry. I'll have a word with him." Stuart nodded in the direction of the uniformed PC standing guard at the end of East Street who was beginning to take down the blue-and-white police tape.

"Stuart said he didn't mind going to get my stuff on his own," Kathy said. She shivered. "I don't fancy going back inside yet."

"Of course, I don't mind," Stuart said. "It won't take me long."

As Stuart headed off to the salon, a woman, with two children under the age of five, walked past Kathy and Mackinnon. The woman carried the girl on her hip and held on to the little boy's hand. The little boy kicked at his mother's shins as she tried to pull him along.

"Get off me, bitch," the little boy shouted.

Mackinnon winced. He seemed too young to have such a foul mouth.

The mother responded by yanking the little boy's arm. "Don't mess me about, you little bugger."

The apple didn't fall far from the tree. Mackinnon saw that Kathy was watching the ugly scene unfold, too.

She nodded in the direction of the mother and her two children. "There is no discipline these days. Our mother would never have let us get away with that."

Mackinnon nodded. He could never have imagined talking to his own mother like that. He watched the little boy throw himself on the floor, screaming at the top of his lungs, as his mother desperately tried to make him stand-up by grabbing the collar of his shirt. Finally, losing her temper completely, the woman set down the little girl on the pavement and smacked the boy's backside.

"He that spareth the rod hateth the child," Kathy Walker muttered.

"What did you say?" Mackinnon asked.

Kathy blinked up at him. "Oh, it was just something my mother used to say, spareth the rod, hateth the child."

Mackinnon stared at her.

Kathy smiled. "I suppose it isn't very politically correct these days, but my mother liked to put it into practice. She never spared the rod for me or Stuart."

Mackinnon had heard that saying before. It had been scrawled in black Biro, in the black notebook. He had been looking at it just that afternoon.

He hesitated. He didn't want to jump to conclusions again. It was just a saying. And after everything that had happened with Fiona, he didn't much fancy making a fool of himself again, so soon.

The killer had worn a mask when Mackinnon had tackled him to the ground, but from the build and from the body weight that had pressed down on him, Mackinnon was sure it wasn't a woman.

So if it wasn't Kathy Walker...

"Is something wrong?" Kathy asked, shrinking under Mackinnon's stare.

"That phrase. I've heard it somewhere before."

Kathy shrugged. "It's probably from the Bible or something. Our old mum loved to quote things from the Old Testament."

Mackinnon nodded and turned away. "I'm going to go and see how your brother is getting on inside."

CHAPTER SIXTY-SEVEN

THE BELL ABOVE THE DOOR jingled as Mackinnon entered the salon.

The SOCOs had more or less finished in here. There was only one scene of crime officer left in the salon, George Bright-land. Dressed in a white paper suit, George smiled at Mackinnon and gave him the thumbs-up sign. The other members of the team would be concentrating their efforts on the cafe, looking for trace evidence left behind.

Mackinnon headed out back, to the kitchenette and found the stairs leading to the flat above the salon. He climbed the stairs slowly, treading lightly.

At the top of the stairs, he stepped on a squeaky floorboard and winced. He paused, listening out for Stuart Walker. Muffled sounds of movement came from the room at the end of the hallway.

It wasn't a large flat. The door to the kitchen was open on Mackinnon's right. A bedroom next to that, and another bedroom and bathroom opposite. Which meant the room at the end of the hall should be the sitting room.

Mackinnon walked towards the un-opened door. He raised his hand, touching the smooth paintwork, and pushed gently.

The door opened with a drawn-out creak.

Stuart was in the right-hand corner of the room, hunched over one of the cupboards in the sideboard. He turned slowly.

There was something in the way Stuart looked at Mackinnon, the way his eyes narrowed, that set off alarm bells.

The mask had hidden most of the killer's features when he leaned over Mackinnon, but it hadn't hidden his eyes. The sharp blue irises were the ones he remembered looming over him before he'd passed out.

It was him.

Stuart stood up slowly. The cupboard door remained ajar. Mackinnon saw the white five-litre containers lined up inside. He looked away, pretending not to notice. Mackinnon remembered the lone SOCO downstairs, oblivious to this threat.

All Mackinnon needed to do was get Stuart outside. The place was crawling with police.

"I thought I'd come and see how you were doing," Mackinnon said.

Stuart nodded and leaned down to shut the cupboard door. "That's very kind of you, but I think I'm done here." He tilted his head to the side and smiled.

He walked towards the door to the hallway, and Mackinnon expected him to walk through and prepared to follow him.

But Stuart didn't enter the hallway. He closed the sitting room door, reached inside his leather jacket and pulled out a key. Before Mackinnon had a chance to react, he'd locked the door.

"What are you doing, Stuart?" Mackinnon said, keeping his voice calm and level. "Kathy is waiting for you downstairs."

Stuart smiled again in a friendly way. "I'll explain. I'll explain everything."

He walked across the room, as if he were going to look out of the window. Stuart leaned down and released the catch on the window, before raising it a couple of inches.

Mackinnon had had enough of these games. If Stuart wanted to explain, he could do it at the station.

Mackinnon moved quickly, taking hold of Stuart's left-hand and forcing his arm up behind his back.

Stuart swore and struggled to free himself. Mackinnon kept his grip and shoved Stuart against the wall. "I'm arresting you for –"

Stuart turned to the side, giving himself just enough room to throw the key.

Mackinnon watched in horror as the stainless steel key tumbled out of the window. The keys sailed through the air and hit the pavement below with a faint metallic clink.

As Stuart shut the window, Mackinnon grabbed Stuart's free arm and pulled him away.

Stuart laughed.

Mackinnon kept Stuart pushed up against the wall and fumbled for his mobile phone. "What are you playing at? There are at least twenty police officers on this street. You do realise I can just phone for backup and have that door broken down in seconds."

As Mackinnon started to dial, Stuart took his chance. His fingers closed around the figurine of a dancer on the mantelpiece, and he raised it up before smashing it down on Mackinnon's temple.

The sharp edge of the broken porcelain slashed the skin above Mackinnon's left eye. Mackinnon jerked back and felt the sharp edge slice into his neck.

The gash on his temple oozed blood almost immediately, trickling into Mackinnon's eyes, making it impossible to see.

He lost his grip on Stuart's jacket. His mobile phone tumbled to the floor.

Mackinnon wiped his eyes, trying to clear them from the sticky blood. He blinked rapidly and saw Stuart kneeling down by the cupboard.

"You could ring for backup, but that wasn't exactly how I had planned things," Stuart said.

Mackinnon looked around the floor, but he couldn't see his phone. He had no option but to play for time. "What is your plan?"

"How's Tyrell's girlfriend doing? Has she had the baby yet? I didn't want to hurt her or her mother, but I had to tie them up. I hadn't finished."

"Look, Stuart, Kathy is waiting outside. She'll be worried. Why don't you come with me now and we can talk about all this at the station?"

Stuart laughed. "I don't think so. Not yet. I've got a better idea."

"It will be better for you in the long run if you co-operate now," Mackinnon said. He placed a hand on the wall to steady himself. He felt dizzy.

Mackinnon stripped off his jacket. The arm of his jacket was already saturated with blood. He was feeling queasy. He wasn't really bothered by the sight of blood in general, but he wasn't too keen on seeing his own.

Surely, all this blood hadn't come from the cut above his eye. He raised a hand to his neck and when he lowered his hand it was covered with warm, sticky blood. Black spots swam before his eyes.

He bunched up his jacket and pressed it to the wound to try to stop the bleeding.

"Does it hurt very much?" Stuart asked, lifting one of the white containers. "The gas, I mean, not the cut. I only wondered because you had first-hand experience of it, didn't you?"

"Neither is particularly pleasant," Mackinnon said.

"I always wear a mask, of course," Stuart said. "But I'd like to think it was relatively painless."

"It's not bloody painless. Struggling to breathe is horrific. Of course it is not painless."

Stuart cocked his head to the side. "Perhaps because you only had a small dose. In larger quantities it would act faster, minimising suffering."

Mackinnon hoped he would never have to find out.

"My idea," Stuart said, "is the ultimate statement and you play a part. Now, don't think I had this planned all along. I'm clever but not quite that clever. It was one of my contingency plans. I didn't expect to get away with this forever. But I'd like to go out with a bang."

Mackinnon didn't want to think about what this bang involved.

He leaned back against the wall and slid down it until he was sitting on the floor. Despite pressing the material tightly against the wound, blood was still dripping onto his shirt.

When Stuart leaned down and grasped one of the white containers, the liquid content sloshing inside, Mackinnon moved quickly, standing up and shoving Stuart hard so he fell backwards.

"Now, now, there's no need for that," Stuart said, brushing off his shirt. "I just wanted to show you something." He looked disappointed. "We both want the same thing. I thought you would understand."

"Understand?" Mackinnon was feeling very light-headed. He sank to the ground and lowered his head. "You've been killing people with toxic gas and you think I would understand?"

"I'm not the first to use it. At least it's a humane way to go."

"It is not humane. It's sick," Mackinnon said, remembering how his lungs had felt like they were burning as he struggled to reach Robbie Baxter.

"Just hear me out," Stuart said.

Mackinnon watched him carefully as Stuart moved towards the sideboard, still clutching the jagged edge of broken porcelain. He opened one of the drawers, pulled out a couple of sheets of paper and flicked through them before selecting one and smiling. He put the other sheets back in the drawer and turned to Mackinnon.

He handed the sheet of A4 paper to Mackinnon.

It was another suicide note.

This time it was personalised.

Mackinnon swallowed. His mouth felt dry. The note described Mackinnon's dissatisfaction with the police force and stated he wanted his death to be a wake-up call.

Mackinnon stared at Stuart in disbelief. "Do you really think I'd agree to this?"

"I wouldn't expect you to do it alone," Stuart said. "It could be a double suicide. So much more meaningful that way. They would talk about it for years. People would realise they need to stand up for justice, that it isn't something they can take for granted."

Mackinnon squeezed the bundled up fabric against his neck. He was feeling faint. There wasn't much time left. He had to raise the alarm somehow before he passed out.

Why hadn't he told Collins or Charlotte where he was going or what he was thinking? Or better still, why hadn't he asked one of them to come with him?

He should have listened to Brookbank and stayed in the bloody office.

Stuart licked his lips. He had the light of a fanatic in his eyes as he stared at Mackinnon. "It's the butterfly effect. We make this sacrifice now, only a small change, but it will start ripples. Other people will follow our example. Don't you see? We could –"

"So, what? You're a butterfly now? Is that what you're telling me?"

Stuart's face hardened. "Don't take the piss."

"You're not making sense, Stuart. No one is going to understand why you did this. Why you attacked kids, then went after a little old lady. No one will follow your example."

Stuart laughed. "Those kids were delinquents. They were old enough to know better. They terrorised my sister and other people who live around here. Ask anyone. And as for Mrs. Horrocks, she's a thief. She stole money from my wallet when I visited Mitch. She feeds poison into the ears of anyone who'll listen. She's a vindictive old witch who deserves to die."

"And the newsagent, Syed Hammad? What did he do to deserve a death like that?"

Stuart smiled. "He was the worst one of all. He was pretending to be an upright citizen while he was selling stolen phones from his shop." Stuart leaned close to Mackinnon. His fingers wrapped tightly around the broken porcelain figurine. "Those stolen phones gave me an idea, though. I convinced Vinnie Pearson and his gang of misfits to steal them. That was easy. As you can imagine, Vinnie Pearson didn't take much convincing. Getting rid of Syed was easy too. He didn't put up much of a fight. I added tracking apps to five of the stolen phones and dumped the rest in the canal."

"Then you hunted them down," Mackinnon said.

Stuart nodded. "I gave them a chance. My plan hinged on their greed. If they hadn't stolen the phones, I wouldn't have tracked them."

"What about your sister?" Mackinnon asked. "What will she do without you?"

Doubt flickered over Stuart's face, then he said, "She'll be ok. She doesn't need me anymore." He swallowed. "I didn't know Kathy would be at the cafe. If I'd known, I would never have ... Did you know Kathy wouldn't talk to anyone but me until she was six-years-old?"

Mackinnon stared at the base of the sofa. His phone could have fallen under there. Could he shove the sofa back and make a grab for the phone? He looked back at Stuart still gripping the white sliver of porcelain laced with Mackinnon's blood.

"I didn't know that, but I know she's going to be devastated, Stuart. Don't hurt her like this. Come to the station and you can explain everything."

"I'm not coming to the station," Stuart said, moving over to the dining table. He gripped the white cotton tablecloth with one hand, and with a flourish, lifted it clear of the table.

To Mackinnon's horror, he saw four buckets lined up underneath the table. He heard the rush of blood in his ears.

"Get away from there," Mackinnon said. "I'm warning you."

Stuart hadn't mixed the chemicals yet. There was no smell... It wasn't too late.

Stuart moved forward towards the buckets.

"Stop," Mackinnon shouted. "I told you to keep away from there."

"I can't do that. My life has a purpose. I have to fulfil it."

Mackinnon looked across at the sash window on the far end of the room. He could feel himself slipping away; the edges of his vision were blurred and dark. He didn't have long.

He had pins and needles in his arms. That wasn't a good sign. He looked around for something heavy, something he could throw through the window and attract the attention of the officers in the street. But there was nothing. He wasn't thinking clearly.

His breath grew shallow.

Mackinnon heard a splash as Stuart poured the contents of one of the five-litre containers into one of the red buckets. The reaction was almost immediate. The putrid smell flooded the room. Mackinnon gagged.

He needed to move. It took all Mackinnon's remaining energy to pull himself up on his hands and knees and crawl across to the window.

Stuart didn't attempt to stop him.

Mackinnon grasped the windowsill and pulled himself up, releasing the catch and shoving up the sash window. He leaned outside sucking in cool, sweet air. The freshness momentarily revived him.

He could see other officers milling about at the end of the road and could just about make out the temporary incident room. He called out and waved, frantically trying to attract their attention.

He saw one of the uniformed PCs turn and shade his eyes from the sun as he looked up at Mackinnon. He began to walk forwards, but not quickly enough.

Mackinnon looked around for something to hold on to. He reached across for the black guttering. It didn't look very secure, but there wasn't anything else.

He made a grab for the guttering pipe, and as his fingers closed around it, he felt it move away from the wall.

He didn't have another option.

He heaved himself out of the window. The muscles in his shoulders burned as he struggled to keep a grip on the guttering. His shoes scraped against the brickwork as he scrambled for purchase.

He'd only lowered himself by a foot before the fastening loosened and the whole thing gave way.

Everything seemed to go in slow motion as he plunged towards the tarmac.

The commotion gained the attention of Kathy Walker. He heard her scream.

Mackinnon lay winded on the floor. He didn't know whether it was the fall or the gas, but he couldn't seem to get enough air in his lungs.

Kathy Walker sank to her knees beside him. "Oh, my God. What happened? Where's Stuart? Is he okay?"

Mackinnon raised a hand to grab Kathy's wrist. "Don't go in there… It's Stuart… He's…"

Kathy's eyes widened. "Stuart? Is he hurt?"

"He's…" Mackinnon sucked in another breath. "He's the one behind the gas attacks."

Kathy shook her head and her curls bounced violently. "No." She slapped a hand across her mouth. She tried to get up to move towards the salon, but Mackinnon kept a grip on her arm.

"I have to talk to him," Kathy said. "He'll listen to me. I'll get him to stop."

She tried to pull her arm away, but Mackinnon didn't let go. "It's too late."

Mackinnon struggled to keep his eyes open. He heard the thud of footsteps closing in on them and suddenly they were surrounded.

He heard a voice he didn't recognise say, "He's got a stab wound to the neck. He is losing a lot of blood."

Mackinnon felt firm pressure applied to the side of his neck as he was bundled onto a stretcher.

In the confusion, he let go of Kathy's arm. He heard her wail, "Stuart, please. Junior, come down."

Mackinnon turned his head and saw the second floor window had been closed. Stuart Walker stood behind the panelled glass. He looked down at Kathy and raised a hand. He was only upright for a few seconds before the gas claimed him.

Mackinnon heard Kathy scream again before everything faded to black.

CHAPTER SIXTY-EIGHT

A WEEK LATER, CHARLOTTE WALKED into the Red Herring pub on Gresham Street and spotted Mackinnon and Collins at a table near the bar.

Mackinnon stood up and waved her over. "What are you having?"

Charlotte didn't answer straight away. She reached up on tiptoes and hugged him tightly.

Mackinnon almost knocked over his pint glass. "What's that for?"

"I'm just so glad to see you back in here." Charlotte looked down at the empty pint glasses on the table. "I'm not sure you should have had quite so many drinks, though." She frowned up at him. "You're still looking pale."

Collins grinned, his flushed cheeks dimpling. "It's been a long day. We've earned it."

"This," Mackinnon said, raising his half-finished pint, "is exactly what the doctor ordered. Now, tell me what you're having."

Charlotte said she'd get the next round and told Mackinnon to sit back down. He didn't seem quite as steady on his feet as usual.

It was busy at the bar, but she managed to get her order in quickly, then leaned back against the counter, looking back at Collins and Mackinnon. She remembered seeing Mackinnon lying on the pavement outside the hairdressing salon, his white shirt soaked with blood. He'd been surrounded by paramedics and other officers, shouting at each other and issuing orders, but all Charlotte could remember was the blood.

Charlotte shuddered. Mackinnon was usually so strong and larger than life; it was a shock to see him so defenceless. Bring a knife or another weapon into the equation and he was vulnerable. They all were.

Charlotte turned as the woman behind the bar served up the drinks. After she paid, Charlotte carried the drinks across to the table, weaving her way through the other customers surrounding the bar.

Collins hiccoughed as Charlotte set the drinks down on the table. Then he said, "How did it go at the hospital?"

Charlotte sat down and tucked her purse back in her bag. "Pretty depressing to be honest."

Charlotte had been checking up on Stuart Walker's condition and trying to get information from his sister. "It seems as though Kathy had no idea what was going on. In her eyes, Stuart was the perfect brother. Stuart is still in a coma, and Dr. Sorensen says if he does wake up, he will be brain damaged."

A waitress appeared next to their table and put down two bowls of steaming hot wings in front of Collins and Mackinnon.

Charlotte's mouth watered. The spicy smell reminded her how hungry she was. "Can you bring me another of those?" she asked the waitress.

"What about Estelle Williams?" Mackinnon asked.

Charlotte stole a spicy wing from Mackinnon's bowl.

"Physically she's ok. She had the baby, a little boy. But long term ... I'm not sure. I mean, how do you come to terms with something like that?"

Neither Mackinnon nor Collins had an answer.

Charlotte polished off the chicken wing, then wiped her fingers on the paper napkin.

"So, according to the DCI you are definitely on desk duties for the foreseeable future, Jack," Charlotte said.

Mackinnon raised his glass in a toast. "Here's to desk duties. I'm actually looking forward to it."

"Yeah," Collins coughed over his drink. "And how long do you think that will last?"

Charlotte stole another chicken wing. "About a week."

"Hey!" Mackinnon moved his bowl away. "Eat his." He pointed to Collins' chicken wings. "You can rib me as much as you like but stop stealing my food."

As Mackinnon and Collins argued over the spicy chicken wings, Charlotte felt something she hadn't felt in a while. She was having fun. All the problems of the job and her personal life seemed a million miles away as she drained her drink.

Perhaps she didn't need to move away for that fresh start.

At least not yet.

THANK YOU!

THANKS FOR READING DEADLY JUSTICE. I hope you enjoyed it!

Would you like to know when my next book is available? You can sign up for my new release email at www.dsbutler-books.com/newsletter

You can follow me on Twitter at @dsbutler, or like my Facebook page at http://facebook.com/dsbutler.author.

Reviews are like gold to authors. They spread the word and help readers find books, and I appreciate all reviews whether positive or negative.

If you would like to read a chapter from the next book in the series, please turn the page.

EXTRACT FROM DEADLY RITUAL

A FRANTIC STREAM OF BUBBLES escaped from Alfie's mouth. He was trying his best to keep his mouth shut, but how much longer could he hold his breath?

He struggled desperately, even though he knew it was no use. He fought against the hands that held him, fighting to get fresh air into his burning lungs.

His bony knees knocked against the cold enamel of the bath. He pushed his hands flat against the cold surface, trying to lever himself up. If he could just raise his head a little bit, break the surface of the water, he could take a breath.

But the grip around his throat grew tighter, and the hands above him thrust him back down viciously. His head slammed against the side of the bath.

Alfie's wide staring eyes looked up, and through the trail of bubbles, he could see the tall figures of his aunt and uncle looming above him.

Now there was a high-pitched buzzing in his ears. He couldn't hold his breath much longer.

Just as he started to see little dots dancing in front of his eyes and darkness closing in on him, narrowing his vision, he felt the hands around his throat release their grip.

Alfie's face broke the surface of the water. He gasped for breath, and his legs slid against the slippery surface of the bath as he tried to push himself away from his aunt and uncle.

"I think he's had enough," Alfie's aunt said. "The spirit has gone. I can see it in his eyes."

Alfie's terrified gaze focused on his uncle. The fat man sat on the side of the bath, his grey trousers damp from Alfie's splashes.

He cocked his head to one side. "Has it gone, Alfie?"

Alfie nodded frantically. He grabbed his knees to his skinny chest as coughs racked his body. He wanted to say the devil had gone. He wanted to tell them he would be good now. But he couldn't get the words out.

After what seemed like an eternity, Alfie's uncle stood up and nodded once to Alfie's aunt. Then he turned and walked out of the bathroom.

Alfie rested his forehead on his knees. He wanted to get out of the bath and out of this bathroom as quickly as possible, but his arms and legs were shaking. He was panting for breath.

Alfie's aunt jutted out her chin. "You'll be a good boy now, won't you, Alfie?"

"Yes," Alfie said. His voice was hoarse from coughing. "I promise."

His aunt reached out and grabbed a faded green towel that had seen better days. She held it out to him, and Alfie gripped the side of the bath as he pulled himself up.

The first time it had happened, he'd been shy, not wanting his aunt to see him naked. But after the first time, he knew being seen naked was the least of his worries.

Alfie took the towel from her outstretched hand and pressed the rough cotton to his cheek, smothering a sob.

His hands were still shaking as he clambered over the side of the bath.

"Will this be the last time, Alfie?"

Alfie nodded, looking down at the wet footprints on the bath mat. "Yes, Aunt Erika."

"The spirit has gone? Are you sure?"

She grabbed Alfie. Her hands grasped Alfie's face, one on each cheek, pinching him. She put her head close to his. He could smell the coffee on her breath as her fierce eyes searched his face.

"I hope so, Alfie. I really do," she said.

"I promise," Alfie said, trying to pull his face away from her pinching fingers.

She nodded. "That's good, Alfie. Otherwise..." Her dark eyes locked on his. "Otherwise I'll have no choice but to involve Mr. X."

Alfie felt bile rise in his throat. It wasn't the first time his aunt had mentioned Mr. X.

Deadly Ritual is out now.

ALSO BY D. S. BUTLER

Deadly Obsession

Deadly Motive

Deadly Revenge

Deadly Justice

Deadly Ritual

Deadly Payback

Deadly Game

Lost Child

Her Missing Daughter

Bring Them Home

Where Secrets Lie

If you would like to be informed when the next book is released, sign up for the newsletter:

http://www.dsbutlerbooks.com/newsletter/

Written as Dani Oakley

East End Trouble

East End Diamond

East End Retribution

ACKNOWLEDGMENTS

MANY PEOPLE HELPED TO PROVIDE ideas and background for this book. My thanks and gratitude to DI Dave Carter, Andy Green, Richard Searle and Lexy Cran for generously sharing their time and wealth of experience.

I would also like to thank my friends on Twitter for their entertaining tweets and encouragement.

My thanks, too, to all the people who read the story and gave helpful suggestions and to Chris, who, as always, supported me despite the odds.